Praise for Eden Bradley

'Intelligent, haunting and sexy as hell...for you people
who like story and heart with your erotica, I'd definitely
recommend any of Eden's books' Maya Banks

'People are constantly looking for books similar to
Fifty...well look no further, I have what you need!...Eden
Bradley writes the most sensual books I have ever read'
My Secret Romance

'No one writes erotic love stories like Eden Bradley'
Romance Junkies

'Bradley delivers the goods. There is intense intimacy and
heartwrenching emotions...This is delicious and delightful
from the first page until the conclusion'
Romantic Times

'Everything about *The Dark Garden* worked to
perfection...the most beautifully written BDSM novel
this reviewer has ever read. Ms. Bradley has a masterful
touch to make pain the ultimate reading pleasure'
Love Romances & More

Also by Eden Bradley:

The Dark Garden
Forbidden Fruit
Exotica

Writing as Eve Berlin:

Pleasure's Edge
Desire's Edge
Temptation's Edge

The
Beauty
of Surrender

EDEN BRADLEY

BLACK
LACE

1 3 5 7 9 10 8 6 4 2

First published in the United States of America in 2009 by Delta, an imprint of
The Random House Publishing Group, a division of
Random House, Inc., New York.

Published in the UK in 2013 by Black Lace, an imprint of Ebury Publishing
A Random House Group Company

The Random House Group Limited Reg. No. 954009

Addresses for companies within the Random House Group can be found at:
www.randomhouse.co.uk

A CIP catalogue record for this book is available from the British Library

The Random House Group Limited supports the Forest Stewardship
Council® (FSC®), the leading international forest-certification organisation.
Our books carrying the FSC label are printed on FSC®-certified paper.
FSC is the only forest-certification scheme supported by the
leading environmental organisations, including Greenpeace.
Our paper procurement policy can be found at:
www.randomhouse.co.uk/environment

Printed and bound by Clays Ltd, St Ives plc

ISBN 9780352347206

Acknowledgments

I must acknowledge Tammi Flora, who brainstormed the end of this book with me; Vivienne Westlake, Lilli Feisty, and Lanie Bancroft, for listening to my incessant whining and being my cheerleaders throughout this process. Gemma Halliday, Crystal Jordan, and RG Alexander, always. To my agent, Roberta Brown, for her exuberance, hand-holding, and endless encouragement in dark times. And to S, for being my inspiration, my comfort, and supporting me through an incredibly difficult period in my life. Thank you all!

PART ONE

Serving the Master

Desmond and Ava

Chapter One

AVA PUSHED THROUGH the door of the small café on Columbus Avenue. The rich scent of coffee hit her right away, along with the pungent aroma of garlic that seemed to be everywhere in North Beach, San Francisco's Italian district. She paused, allowing her eyes to adjust to the dim, gray light filtering in through the windows. To take a breath, to allow her heartbeat to calm. It wasn't working. She looked around the café, full of the casual Sunday-afternoon crowd. They hadn't arrived yet. Relief ran warm in her body, mixing with the exquisite tension that had been with her for several days, ever since her conversation with Marina about what she needed.

What she needed. She wasn't used to thinking in those terms, not in any sort of thorough way. She'd spent her whole adult life in a battle between what she desired and what she thought she *should* do. What other people thought she should do. Her family. Michael. Which had left her in a nowhere place she still hadn't figured out how to escape from. Not that BDSM was all about escape for her. She was looking for something deeper.

She'd read about subspace, that trancelike state often reached during bondage or sensation play where a person's mind could let go, get in touch with his or her deeper self. Perfect, blissful release. She knew it was what she yearned for, that it might help her clarify what she wanted, help her work through some of her old issues, but she hadn't quite figured out how to do it. Marina said she thought she had an answer.

She had come to trust Marina, even though they'd known each other only a few months. They'd met at Pinnacle, one of the most exclusive BDSM clubs in San Francisco, and Marina had quickly become a mentor and a friend. Now she was introducing Ava to one of her oldest friends from Pinnacle, someone she'd met there and known for a number of years. Marina believed he was one of the best at what they did: Shibari, the ancient and beautiful ritual of Japanese rope bondage.

Ava paused, looking for an empty table. She gave herself a moment to calm down, pulled air into her lungs, held it, blew it out slowly, as she'd been taught to center herself. But her pulse was still humming, her body trembling.

Today, she would meet him.

Would he be her answer? It was hard not to hope.

She didn't know why this felt so different. She'd been with other dominant men before. But Marina had told her this man was special. And something in Ava's body, in her very blood, answered to the sound of his name.

Desmond Hale.

How could she possibly know, even before meeting him, that with him things would be different?

Wishful thinking.

She hoped it wasn't anything so mundane.

Making her way between the tables, she found one miraculously empty right by the window. Taking her coat off, she sat down and stared out through the glass. It was the usual gray March day in San Francisco. But she wasn't looking at the weather. No, she was looking for Marina. And she was looking for him.

Marina had told her about him, but not nearly enough for this sort of utter certainty. She knew he was forty years old, older than she was by eleven years. Knew he was a software designer, had his own company. And more important, she knew Marina was confident that he was the perfect top to give Ava exactly what she needed: absolute release in the Shibari ropes. Her fondest wish. Her deepest unmet need.

She shifted in her chair, adjusted the hem of her dress, tried to smooth down her unruly mop of blond curls, knowing it was a fruitless task.

What would he look like? How would she know him if he arrived before Marina did?

Her gaze went back to the sidewalk outside just as Marina drew the door open. Ava's heartbeat accelerated as the tall, elegant woman with the gorgeous fall of wavy auburn hair spotted her and made her way to the table.

"Ah, I'm glad you found a place to sit, Ava. No, don't get up." Marina pulled her dark trench coat off, hung it over the back of the chair, seated herself, every motion graceful. "Have you been waiting long?"

"Only a few minutes, Marina."

"You don't have to be formal with me today, you know."

"Yes, Marina."

Marina chuckled. "You want to obey, even when you don't have to, don't you?"

"I can't help it. Especially knowing you're here to turn me over to someone else. I want . . ."

"You want what?"

"I want to be good for him," Ava said quietly, acutely aware of the other patrons around them. She tugged on one curling strand of hair, twisted it around her finger. She always wanted to be good. More than good. It had been ingrained in her since childhood.

"Of course you do." Marina smiled. "Which is exactly why I'm sending you to Desmond. I think you'll please him. And I think he'll be just what you need. He can give you what I can't."

"I'm sorry. I know this is some sort of failing on my part."

"You have nothing to apologize for; we've discussed this already." Marina leaned toward her, lowered her voice a little, but not enough, Ava thought. "You simply need to be played by a man. You were very good for me. You were good in the ropes, but we both know you weren't able to sink deep enough. You need that sexual element to take you where you need to go. And you and I, Ava, are both far too heterosexual for that dynamic to work between us."

"But you play other women all the time."

"Everyone's needs are different. Yours run deep. But Desmond will love that about you." Marina leaned back in her chair, her smoky gray gaze assessing Ava. She smiled. "He'll love everything about you. You're perfect for him, really. I don't know why it didn't occur to me sooner. And he'll be perfect for you. The only other rope master I trust."

They paused while Marina ordered their coffees and one for Desmond from the young waitress who stopped at their table. Marina was a natural dominant; people automatically deferred to her. Ava admired that in her, but it was nothing she wanted for herself. She was far too submissive by nature. She'd never wanted it any other way.

Marina was just the opposite. And she was an expert with the ropes, a master, what was called *nawashi* in Shibari rope bondage. But she was right. There was something missing in the energy between them. What it was exactly, Ava didn't know. How could she? She'd never managed to reach that clear and lovely floating place she imagined deep subspace to be. That place of meditation, freedom. She'd come close several times, but no one yet had been able to take her as deeply as she needed to go. That perfect release lay always just out of her grasp.

Maybe this time, with this man. This master of the ropes. *Nawashi.*

Desmond.

"He's here," Marina said quietly.

Ava immediately rose to her feet, keeping her eyes on the table. She didn't dare look at him. Her pulse was a hot, hammering blur in her veins.

"Good girl," she heard Marina murmur, and felt the answering shiver of pleasure run up her spine.

"Marina." His voice was deep, held the edge of an accent. Scottish, maybe?

"Desmond, it's good to see you. This is the girl I talked with you about, Ava Gregory."

He was quiet a moment, but she could feel the intensity of his gaze, looking her over. She held her breath, hoped he found her pleasing.

What would she do if he refused her?

Her heart tumbled in her chest.

He stepped closer, until she could smell him: dark and musky, like the clean, pure earth.

Then a fingertip lifted her chin and she was forced to raise her eyes to his. Green eyes, like dark, glossy moss. They seemed to see right through her. Shifting her focus, she took in his face, his dark hair swept back from high cheekbones that were a little sharp, a well-defined jaw, a wicked-looking goatee framing his lush mouth. Almost too lush in comparison to the hard male features, making him seem all the more ruggedly beautiful. Intimidating.

She had never expected him to be beautiful.

She had never expected her body to begin this hot, melting sensation from the first glance, the first hint of his scent. But she was going weak all over, her stomach, her heartbeat, fluttering. And she was dimly aware that all of this was happening to her in the middle of a café, in the middle of the day, with other people, everyday life, going on around them.

"Ava." Marina's voice. "This is Desmond Hale, my fellow rope master, my trusted friend."

"Beautiful," he murmured.

He was looking into her eyes, making her tremble. Making her feel as though nothing about her could be kept secret from him. And more than that, she felt power. It radiated from him like some palpable thing.

Marina, a formidable dominant herself, wore an air of authority. Ava had recognized it, responded to it, immediately. But even with Marina she hadn't felt this sense of being completely overpowered. And when he brushed one finger along her cheekbone, she had to press her thighs together to ease the ache there.

Oh, yes. This man could be exactly what she needed. Craved. And more.

"She's even lovelier than you led me to expect, Marina." Yes, definitely a Scottish accent, making him seem all the more exotic. "And so tiny. Like a doll. Yes, exactly like a porcelain doll. Beautiful pale skin."

"Desmond, why don't you sit down? I've ordered coffee for you. Ava?"

Ava nodded, sinking back into her chair as Desmond took his seat across from her. She could feel his unwavering gaze on her. Searching. Intense.

"Ava, we're not in role now, do you understand?" Desmond said to her quietly. "We need to talk, to come to an agreement about what we need and can expect from each other."

"Yes, Sir, I understand." She'd been through this sort of negotiation with other dominants she'd played with before. It was standard practice among people in the lifestyle. But she felt so completely awkward now. What was wrong with her?

He watched her closely for a moment, leaning toward her in his chair, and she caught his scent on the air again.

"You're very submissive, aren't you?"

She nodded her head. "It's always been natural for me. There's never been any confusion for me about that."

"Marina's told me a little about you, but I want to hear from you. Talk to me, Ava. Tell me about yourself. About how you came into the lifestyle. What you've experienced, what you understand about what we do."

"I've been exploring these things my whole adult life. Power exchange. Bondage."

Was she really saying these things out loud, surrounded by people who would probably be shocked to know what they were discussing? But it didn't matter as much as it should have, somehow.

"And how old are you?"

"Twenty-nine, Sir."

"Go on."

"I was . . . one of those kids who had strange thoughts, even as young as eight or nine. I had fantasies about being kidnapped and tied up. But it was never frightening to me. Does that make sense?"

"Absolutely. I dreamed of kidnapping pretty girls and tying them up at that age." He laughed, making her smile. Making her bones go warm and loose.

"Well . . . I did a lot of reading. Fiction, of course, but also some of the instruction books, over the years. I went to my first club five years ago." Yes, just leave out that one other detail; no reason to tell this man about her experiences with Michael, how he had made her question herself in such a harsh light. "It took me a while to . . . be brave enough."

"Where was that?"

"In Seattle. That's where I'm from."

"You have family there?"

"Yes. My parents are still there, my sister, Andrea. I don't talk to them much. Is that . . . important?"

She wasn't sure what he wanted from her, where this was going.

"Every aspect of your life is relevant. Any of life's experiences can affect how we feel about ourselves, about our sexuality, and in particular how a submissive responds during a scene. So, yes. It's important that I know as much as possible about you. But we'll talk more about your family another time."

Ava nodded. It made sense.

"Tell me what your experience in the Seattle club was like. How did you respond?"

"It was confusing at first, a little overwhelming, as I suppose it would be for anyone, but good. It was what I wanted; I knew that right away. People say some things are better left as fantasy, but not for me."

"Exactly."

He smiled again then, a slow, spreading grin taking over that lush mouth, and pleasure washed over her simply knowing he was happy with her answers.

The waitress came, set their cups on the table. Desmond took his with one packet of sugar, she noted.

Marina was watching them quietly, but Ava was focused on Desmond. She could barely look away long enough to add cream to her coffee with shaking hands.

"But . . . I've never gone far enough. I've never gone deep enough. I feel as though I hit the edge of subspace, my mind begins to let go, and then I'm pulled back into reality, a thousand thoughts racing through my brain, almost as if . . . my mind is defending me from seeing what's really in there. In those deep places. I struggle with it. I try to give in but . . . I don't know why it won't quite work for me. I mean, maybe I understand some of it, but . . . should I go into detail right now?"

"We can talk more about it as we go. Just tell me a bit about your experiences with bondage."

"Well . . ." She sipped her coffee, even though it was really still too hot, scalding her tongue a little. "I've played with some people who were very good, with cuffs and chains, harnesses. Even some rope. But until Marina it was never the formal Shibari, which is what appeals most to me. To be decorated that way. For the binding itself to *mean* something. And I need someone who can stay with me. I mean, I think I need to be bound and made to stay there for hours. I don't understand these people who go to the clubs, tie someone up, then immediately let them go and it's over. I don't get the point of that. I'm sorry. Am I . . . am I saying too much?"

She glanced at Marina, who nodded in encouragement.

"These are exactly the things I prefer," Desmond said. "For the ropes to be more than the simple act of binding someone. For the ropes to be beautiful, to be organized into a symbiotic visual and physical form. And I'm a stamina player; I prefer to go for several hours, an entire evening." He paused, lifted his cup, drank. He lowered his voice, his gaze steady on hers. "But we'll have to see what you can really take, Ava."

She shivered as he said those words. What could she really take? She could barely wait to find out.

"I want to try, Sir. I want to try it all. I need to," she told him. It was the truth. And she suddenly felt that she couldn't hide anything from this man. She didn't want to.

"Let's discuss our arrangement, then. You should know how I operate. I don't play well with too many limitations. If you are the kind of submissive who insists on no sexual contact, then I am not the right choice for you. Will this be an issue?"

Her heart was thundering in her chest at a thousand miles an hour. Her sex went damp, aching.

"No. That's not a problem, Sir."

No, definitely not a problem. She had to bite back a moan.

He leaned in then, took her hand in his, skimming his fingertips over her wrist beneath the edge of her cotton sweater. Her pulse was racing wildly under his touch, her skin on fire.

"I believe we have an understanding, then."

She nodded. "Yes, Sir."

"You can call me Desmond. I prefer it, actually."

"Yes, Sir. Desmond."

Beautiful name. Beautiful man. And that accent was like warm whiskey in her veins.

"Tell me what else you're looking for, Ava."

She had to stop to organize the million images and ideas

whirling through her head. How to explain? But it was such a re-lief to have someone ask her about these things she'd thought about, mentally dissected, her entire life, it seemed. "I'm looking for that headspace. I want to . . . go empty all over. And the pain play has never done that for me, although I've tried. It's all about being bound for me. Being . . . peaceful. And there's one more thing . . ."

"Yes?"

"I love to play in public, at the clubs. I'm an exhibitionist, I suppose. But I love to be vaguely aware of people watching. It makes me feel . . . beautiful."

"Ah, Ava," he said quietly, "you just may be the perfect girl for me."

Too good, to hear those words from him. But she had some-thing more to tell him. "But . . . I also feel that I have a tendency to use the exhibitionism as a distraction from my ultimate goal. So maybe sometimes it's good for me, and sometimes not."

Desmond nodded. "You're very thoughtful. I like that."

Sliding his fingers down, he took her hand, lifted it, and pressed his lips to her palm. She let out a small gasp, pleasure flooding her senses like an electric current: that hot, that shocking.

Oh, yes, perfect.

Ava shivered, a long, slow heat seeping up her spine, spreading, spreading. She was on fire. Burning. For him.

When Marina had suggested that a male dominant might be able to take her deeper into that lovely space she craved, a man who could bring the sexual element into bondage play, Ava knew she was right. And she trusted Marina to choose a good partner for her. But she had no idea she would meet a man who made her feel like this.

Desmond Hale was intense, a dominant through and through. There was something about his presence, the way he carried him-self with confidence, as though he understood perfectly well that no one would dare to defy him.

She wanted nothing more than to serve this man from the first moment she'd heard his voice, even before she'd raised her head and seen him.

And now, knowing that what he wanted from her was exactly what she wanted—needed—to give, she could hardly stand to wait.

"Sir . . . Desmond. May I ask a question?"

"Of course."

"When can we get started?"

He laughed, and she wasn't sure at first if she'd made a mistake. But he squeezed her hand, ran his fingers over her wrist again so lightly she could barely feel it. It was enough to reassure her. To make every nerve in her body come alive.

He let her hand go, turned to Marina. "Tell me what went on exactly when you played her."

He picked up his cup once more, took a long sip, and Ava watched, fascinated, as he swallowed, the long line of his throat working.

"She was good," Marina said. "Very submissive, as you've noticed. She follows instructions perfectly. And she loves the ropes; I could see that right away. She slipped into the edge of subspace easily, but she never went deep, no matter how long I kept her bound, the intricacy of the knots, just as she's told you. I never tried suspension; we played only three times. She never went deep enough for me to try that with her. There is definitely some sort of block."

He turned to face Ava again, his gaze assessing her once more. "We'll break through that," he said, his voice certain, commanding. His accent was stronger than ever. "Whatever it is. Whatever it takes."

She nodded, her throat going tight. A small, lovely shiver of anticipation ran through her, imagining what he might do with her. Not that it mattered; she would do anything he asked of her, she knew that already. And she knew he would ask her to push her boundaries just enough, and no further than she could truly handle.

"I think you will break through with her," Marina said. "If anyone can, it's you, Desmond. And she seems to like you well enough." She grinned at Ava, who blushed, her cheeks heating.

"Ava?" He was watching her, that green gaze intent on hers, gleaming in the dusky filtered sunlight coming through the windows of the café. "Tell me, is this what you want? For us to work together? For me to play you? Train you in the ways of Shibari?"

She had to swallow past the hard lump in her throat, a lump made of exquisite anticipation, nerves, pure desire, to get the words out. "Yes. Please, Desmond."

"Very well. I will send you a questionnaire through e-mail. You've done these things before, I assume?"

"Yes, I have."

"Fill it out, return it to me. And with it, you may ask any questions of me. I want us to be open with each other. This is the only way it will work."

She nodded, her head too filled with the possibilities for her brain to function properly.

"I'll look it over, and we'll talk again about whether or not you'd still like to do this."

"Oh, I'm sure she will, Desmond." Marina turned to Ava, her gray eyes sparkling. "She's practically vibrating with need already."

Ava's cheeks heated once more. It was true. She'd never been so full of yearning in her life.

He laughed, a low, rumbling sound that Ava swore she could feel reverberating through her body.

Oh, yes, anything for him.

"Go home now. And wait to hear from me."

"Now?"

"Impatient, Ava? But don't worry, you'll be in my hands soon enough. In my ropes. Unless you change your mind, of course."

"I won't, Sir. Desmond."

He smiled, lifted her hand, brushed his lips over her knuckles: the lightest touch, yet it burned through her.

"I'm afraid I must be off; I have an appointment. I'll speak with you soon, sweet Ava."

Marina stood, and she and Desmond hugged briefly while Ava sat in her chair, hardly daring to stand on her shaking legs. The damp ache had started to pulse between her thighs, and she crossed them.

Excruciating.

Lovely.

How was she going to manage to wait to hear from him? To see him again?

He walked off, and she could only stare after him, her head spinning.

"Ava?"

"Yes? What? I'm sorry, Marina."

Marina laughed, taking her chair once more. "No need to be sorry. I think you two have made a connection, yes?"

"Yes." She put a hand to her hair, smoothed it away from her face. "God, yes."

"I thought you might. Go home now, as he said. Think about the conversation today, about what you want from him, what he might ask of you."

"I won't be able to think of anything else!"

"No, I don't think you will." Marina's cool gray gaze was steady on hers. "But are you truly ready for this, Ava? Because I think this could be a life-changing experience. I think with Desmond you may be able to open up in ways you never have before. You might finally get what you've wanted, and that can be terrifying sometimes."

"Yes. I'm ready."

She was. Ready for anything, because it would be with him.

Desmond.

She'd never met anyone like him in her life. Never met anyone who made her feel this way: so full of desire she thought she might burst. Filled with the need to please, to do anything to make him happy. She realized then that she'd always held a part of herself back, had never allowed herself to tap into the full extent of her desires. But with him, anything else was impossible.

Impossible to feel this way after having talked with him for twenty minutes! Impossible to know, on some very deep level, that this man was going to change her life, just as Marina said.

Her pulse was racing, her heart hammering. With desire. With anticipation. With the old dread pounded into her head by Michael, telling her that what she wanted was wrong. Different. Bad. Even as he gave it to her in some twisted, hurtful way.

But she was not going to think of him now. No, she'd worked past all that, hadn't she? Realized the urgency of her desires had simply made him afraid because he didn't really understand them, and that's where it had all gone wrong.

Stop thinking about the past. It's ancient history.

All she wanted to think about was right now. Because she was about to get everything she'd ever dreamed of. And Marina was right. No matter how badly she wanted it, it scared the hell out of her.

Chapter Two

AVA JAMMED THE KEY into her front door, nearly stumbling into her apartment. She wasn't quite sure how she'd made it home, all the way across town to her place in the Sunset district, near the beach.

Heading straight to her bedroom, she dropped her purse on top of her low antique dresser, startling her cat, Wicked, who jumped off the bed and darted down the hallway, a blur of black fur. She shed her clothes as quickly as possible until she stood, naked, in front of the ornate oval-framed mirror over the dresser. She stopped to look at her reflection. Her hair was its usual wild mass of pale blond curls falling around her shoulders. But her round, blue eyes were glossy, enormous. Her skin was flushed: her cheeks, her breasts. And her nipples were two hard, pink points, begging to be touched.

Yes . . .

She yanked open the top drawer of the dresser, dug around until she found a pair of nipple clamps, two small alligator clamps attached by a length of chain. She paused to caress her breast, her fingers grazing the nipple, and she moaned softly. Touching it again, she twisted it between her fingers, tugging on the tender flesh, and a flash of damp heat answered from between her thighs. She teased both nipples, pinching, twisting, until they were hard and pulsing. And then she took one between her fingers, pulling it out, elongating it, and fastened a clamp there.

A shock of pain and pleasure went through her, and her sex swelled, went soaking wet.

Oh, yes . . .

The small, metal teeth were cool against her skin but heated quickly. Taking her other nipple between her fingers, she pulled on it, pressed the other clamp closed, and hissed at the sensation rocking her body. It wasn't the pain itself so much as the sense of restraint on her flesh, the image of subservience.

Her gaze went once more to the mirror. She loved to see herself like this: flushed with need. Her breasts, her sex, engorged. Sliding her hand between her thighs, she found her wet, aching slit.

What would Desmond think if he saw her like this?

She pictured his rugged face, his large hands. They would be on her soon, but not soon enough.

Her camera sat on the dresser next to her discarded purse, an old Nikon she'd had since she'd learned to develop her own photographs in high school. She should take a picture of herself for him, record her flushed skin, her glazed blue eyes. But no, nothing unless he asked for it, and then she would do exactly as he asked.

Yes . . .

She slipped her fingers between her swollen folds, finding the hard nub of her clitoris.

Desmond.

The telephone rang, and she jumped.

Pulling her cell phone from her purse, she flipped it open.

"Yes? Hello?"

"Ava."

Desmond.

She was shaking all over.

"S-sir?"

"I have some instructions for you."

Oh, yes. His voice in her ear, commanding her. And her body already shivering with need, the clamps tight on her aching nipples.

"Yes, Sir. I'm sorry. Desmond."

"This is something very basic. But necessary."

"Anything."

Oh, yes. Anything for him.

"Until I see you again, you are not to touch yourself. Is that understood? I don't want you to climax, in any way."

God! As though he could read her mind. She could barely breathe.

"Ava? Are you there?"

"Yes, I'm here."

"Do you understand what I'm telling you?"

"Yes, I understand."

And she did, all too well. She understood, and she would not disobey him. No matter how hot she was right now, no matter how her body trembled with the need to come.

"Very good. I'll contact you again soon. Check your e-mail for that questionnaire. Get it back to me as quickly as possible, but don't rush your answers."

"Yes, of course."

"And, Ava?"

"Yes?"

His voice lowered. "I need to tell you . . . I can hear your panting breath. I can almost smell your desire over the phone. I know exactly what you're feeling at this moment. But you are to hold back. For me."

Yes, for him!

"Yes, Desmond. I will, I promise."

"Good girl. Wait to hear from me."

He hung up.

She wanted to cry!

But she would do it, do whatever he asked.

She put her cell phone down, but not before she caught the faint ocean scent of her own juices on her hand.

Oh, God . . .

Looking at her reflection once more, she took in her eyes: glowing, luminous. And the clamps sharp on her nipples, the metal chain swinging gently between her breasts with every breath, taunting her. She shook her head at herself, pressed on one of the clamps, hissed in pain as she took it off and blood rushed back into the taut flesh. Taking a deep breath, she removed the other, tossed them back into the dresser drawer.

She was vibrating with hunger, desperate. But she would do exactly as Desmond had told her. Even if it made her crazy. Had anyone ever lost their mind from unsated desire? She was about to find out.

DESMOND PULLED ONTO Doyle Drive, passing the densely tree-lined road through the old Presidio military base, heading for the Golden Gate Bridge. The windows in his black Lexus were open, letting in the scent of ancient eucalyptus trees and salt air.

Have to get home. Just get home and . . .

What? How was getting home going to be any better? At least he'd had the distraction of work today, a long meeting with a client in the financial district. At home he'd be alone with his thoughts.

Every thought he'd had was about Ava Gregory since the moment he'd met her, seen her perfect doll-like features, that creamy porcelain skin, the flawless curve of breasts beneath her sweater. They were almost too large for her tiny figure, her breasts. Pornographic, with a face so sweet. And that little pink mouth of hers . . .

He groaned, shifted in his seat against the erection that was becoming painful again.

Had to have her. Touch her.

Yes. And he would. Unless the girl changed her mind. He didn't know what the hell he'd do if she did.

She wouldn't.

Was he as certain of that as he wanted to be?

When was the last time he'd doubted himself this way? Doubted anything in his life?

He'd spent his entire adult existence being certain about everything. He'd chosen his life very carefully. He chose his bedmates every bit as carefully.

He had no choice when it came to Ava.

But it would be good. Better than good. If he could just get through this damn introductory period that he was too noble to bypass. He'd been the one to set up the rules this way: get to know the girl, the formal questionnaire, the long conversations by e-mail, by telephone, in person, before he ever touched her. Fucking torture, thinking about waiting this time. But he would not break his own rules. They were there for a reason. It was his responsibility to handle a submissive correctly. Safe, sane, and consensual, as always. And part of that saneness, that consent, was everyone involved being well informed.

Foolish to even imagine going back there, into the city, going to her house, getting her to let him tie her up . . .

But that was exactly what he was thinking.

Control!

Yes, control was the key. Always had been. Always would be.

He downshifted as he pulled onto the Golden Gate Bridge, slowing as he rolled through the toll gate, then speeding up a little as he moved onto the long expanse.

The San Francisco Bay stretched out on his right, the lights of the city gleaming against the velvet dark of the water beneath him. To the north was the paler glow of Marin County, the small seaside town of Sausalito, which was his home.

Home. Have to get home. Be alone.

He'd ordered Ava not to touch herself, but he had no such strictures.

He hit the gas a little harder, the sleek car shooting smoothly over the half-empty bridge. He reached the other side, swung off the highway, and took the road curving down into Sausalito. Even through the wispy fog he could see the moonlit water, the boats bobbing in their docks. A million-dollar view, one he never tired of. But he didn't care tonight.

Taking the road a little faster than he should, he gunned the engine, the car holding fast around the turns. Making a left onto his narrow street, he shifted again to climb the steep hill. Finally he reached his driveway, pulled in. He switched the engine off, not even bothering to put the car in the garage.

He got out, swung the iron gate aside, stormed up the narrow front path, pushed through the front door. He was nearly breathless.

Tossing his keys down on the console table in the entry hall, he strode to the window overlooking the bay. That million-dollar view again, but tonight it didn't matter. All that mattered was that he could see San Francisco laid out before him like some miniaturized map of itself, and somewhere down there was Ava. The girl with the flawless skin, that beautiful mouth, the enormous innocent blue eyes.

His groin tightened, throbbed.

There was nothing innocent about her; he knew that. No, the girl had plenty of experience already. That was what was so striking. Shocking, almost. That air of innocence, the way she looked, and that wicked bit of knowledge about her.

How delicious that he would have his hands on her soon, would touch her bare skin, push his fingers into that tiny body . . .

He pulled his stiff and aching cock from his trousers, ran his fingertips over the head, groaned aloud.

Yes, just to touch her. To bind her. Make her his.

He curved his fingers around his hard shaft, began to stroke, pleasure spearing into his body. Deep. Intense. And the girl's face always in his mind, just behind his eyes.

So beautiful. How much more beautiful in the ropes?

Using his free hand to lean up against the cold glass, he stroked harder, faster, his cock so swollen, so sensitive, it almost hurt. But the pleasure was swallowing him up; he couldn't stop.

Ava . . .

He could see her in his mind's eye, bound in the black ropes, his favorite. So dark and evil-looking against her pale flesh.

His hips thrust forward, into his tight fist.

Would she feel this tight inside?

Had to find out. Fuck. Had to fuck the girl. Had to, had to . . .

Ava . . .

He pumped faster, so damn hard it really did hurt now. And he came into his hand, his vision blurring, the glimmering bay diffusing in front of him.

Christ. That girl. That face. His legs were shaking.

He leaned his shoulder into the glass, half collapsing against the window. His hand was covered in come, the scent hard in the still, cool air.

To come into her . . .

He had to get some God damned control where this girl was concerned if he was going to play her. And he was going to. But tonight he just needed to work some of this tension out of his system. Yes, that would be all that was necessary. He'd get it together before he saw her. Even if he had to spend the next week jacking off. Every day. Five times a day. It may well take that. But he'd do it, get it together. By the time he saw the girl, he'd be in perfect command of himself. Of her. This was what he did, why he was an expert. The control itself was a big part of what he was in it for. What he wanted, craved.

He groaned.

That was exactly the problem. He wanted it too much with this girl. What he wanted most was fucking with his head for the first time in his life.

DESMOND WOKE TO the sound of the telephone. He opened one eye and peered at the clock. Eight a.m. He was usually an early riser, but last night he'd been up until at least two in the morning, getting himself off over and over again. In the shower. In his bed. His body couldn't seem to get enough. He couldn't get her out of his mind.

Damn it. He had to answer the phone; it could be a client.

"Hale here."

"Desmond, it's Marina."

"Oh. Hi."

"Ah, a little grumpy this morning?"

He shoved a few pillows behind his head and leaned into them. "You are the only person on this earth who can get away with saying something like that to me."

She laughed. "That's because you don't dare to contradict me any more than my playthings would."

"Don't push me, Marina. Someday I could have you in my ropes, you know."

"Hardly. I'd just as easily tie you up."

"It's a standoff, then."

"As usual. So, tell me, why the difficult morning?"

"I was up too late."

"Work?"

"No."

"You're being very closemouthed, Desmond. You know damn well I called to talk about Ava, to see what you think about her."

"I offered to work with her; you were there."

"Yes. And?"

"And what?"

"Oh, come on, Desmond. I *was* there. I saw the way you looked at the girl."

"How exactly did I look at her?"

There was a brief pause. "Like you were going to eat her alive."

"Maybe I was." He had to smile at that.

"So, you're pleased with her?"

"So far. Yes."

Marina laughed. "You really are keeping your thoughts about this one to yourself. Alright, I'll let you do that. For now."

"No one 'lets' me do anything, Marina," he said, his voice low, mock-threatening.

"I'll be sure to remember that. Meanwhile, let me know how it goes, will you?"

"I'm sure you'll be talking with her, too."

"Of course. I sent her to you. It's my responsibility to follow up."

"Of course."

"You don't sound pleased about that."

"What? No, it's fine. I understand perfectly well that this is how we operate."

Marina was quiet a moment. "You'll have to tell me what's going on in your head sooner or later."

"I'm not exactly the sharing type, Marina."

"Maybe not. Neither am I. But still . . ."

"Alright, look, we'll talk more later."

"Yes, we will."

He usually enjoyed these little battles of will between them, but this morning he was getting irritated.

"I need to get ready for work, Marina."

"I'm being dismissed, am I? You're in too lousy a mood to talk anyway. I'll call you in a day or two and check in."

They hung up. He ran a hand over his hair, pushing it back from his face. He *was* in a lousy mood. And he didn't understand why. Four orgasms last night shouldn't make him wake up on the wrong side of the bed. Thinking about Ava certainly shouldn't. Everything about her was good, great. Exciting. Thrilling as hell.

And maybe that was the problem. Maybe what was really bothering him was the dark suspicion that this girl was the one who could actually make him lose control for once in his life. For the first time since . . .

No, he didn't need to think about that now, that awful night with Lara, and everything further in his past that experience had brought up. It had been ten years; why was he thinking of it now? He'd put that all behind him, had chosen a different path, made certain that loss of control would never happen again.

Don't think about it.

No, all he wanted to think about was Ava. To figure out what his response to her was about and how to get himself reined in.

Yes, definitely a little out of control where this girl was concerned.

Impossible. Unacceptable.

And quite possibly true.

God damn it.

Chapter Three

Ava sat with her laptop at her tiny painted kitchen table, a cup of coffee next to her keyboard. Wicked sat in the chair across from her, carefully using his paws to wash his face, his fur dark and gleaming. The cat was a silent companion, which she preferred. He was a little distant, occasionally demanding attention but mostly keeping to himself. He watched her, she thought, in somewhat the same way Desmond did: carefully, intently, with glossy green eyes she couldn't fathom.

She had Desmond's questionnaire in front of her, had been working on it since he'd called right after they'd met two days ago.

She'd done a few of these things before. The questions were usually the same: Did she like to be tied up? Spanked? Humiliated?

Yes, maybe, and no.

But some of the questions were more interesting this time, and she had to really think her answers through.

When had she first thought about bondage in sexual terms?

That was easy: almost from the beginning, as a young girl. Those early fantasies had caused that tingle between her thighs even before she was able to understand what it meant. But they'd already talked a bit about that over coffee. She searched deeper.

She didn't know where the rope fetish had come from. She remembered playing cowboys and Indians with the neighborhood kids, or pirates, that distinctly sexual thrill when she'd been the one tied to a tree. But that was just a childhood game. Or was it?

She closed her eyes and caught the fragment of memory at the edge of her mind: being tied to the tree in her neighbor's yard, one of the boys running the ropes around and around her legs, in between her thighs, pressing against her summer shorts . . . that exquisite pressure, and the friction as he pulled the rope a little tighter.

Yes . . .

Her body was heating up, that lovely sensation returning as though she were ten years old again. She could almost feel the bark, rough and scratchy against her back, through the thin cotton of her tank top.

She forced her eyes open, typed it all onto the questionnaire, tried to focus on her task, to ignore her wet, needy sex.

Next question.

What did she hope to learn from the ropes?

Ah, this one was much harder. She wasn't quite sure how to answer. All she knew was that Desmond was going to teach her. About Shibari. About finding that space in her head she yearned for. And much more. She could feel it.

Desmond. So hard to concentrate with his image in her mind, with her body burning for him, burning for the ropes. She was submissive enough to really want to do this for him, answer these questions, but he was distracting her from her task every bit as much as he drove her need to do it and do it well.

Her head was spinning.

She sipped her coffee, tried to concentrate.

What did she hope to learn? She wanted to find a way to shut off the outside world, to focus inward. She wanted to learn to truly give herself over to the process. Even if the idea scared the hell out of her.

She shook her head, picked up her coffee mug, stared out the window. The fog hung heavy in the air, low and close to the apartment buildings across from hers. If it hadn't been for the fog, she'd be able to see the rising moon hanging over the ocean a dozen blocks away.

It was easier to think about the fog, the moon, than it was to think about what she was so afraid of, and why. But the seed had been planted and she couldn't shake it off.

Michael.

She tried not to think about him too much anymore. She'd moved on with her life, she really had. But at times like this, when she was doubting herself, afraid to go after what she desired, she couldn't help but remember the things he'd said to her, the way he'd made her feel. Dirty. Abnormal. Oh, yes, he'd used those words when she'd confided to him that she wanted to be tied up. But he'd done it, hadn't he? Only the way he'd gotten off on it hadn't been about sex. It had been about having power over her, and not in a good way.

She'd known even then that wasn't how it was meant to be. And it hadn't stopped her; she'd stayed with him for a year. But she knew her experiences with him had held her back on some level. Still did.

The problem was, she'd loved him. And that was what had made her so vulnerable to his judgment of her. That and the judgment she'd lived with her entire life from her family. It had all melded together: being judged by the people she loved. Or tried to love.

Michael had hurt her. And still she'd stayed. Until the hurt had become too big and she'd finally had the sense to leave him.

Picking up her coffee mug, she got up to refill it from the pot on the old green-tiled counter.

She loved her tiny kitchen, her small apartment in the old

stucco building. She felt safe there. Cozy, surrounded by her grand-mother's antiques, the bits and pieces she'd collected herself, combing flea markets and estate sales. She even loved the uneven wood floors, that scent of old wood and musty plaster so common in the older structures in San Francisco. The history of it held some sort of odd familiarity for her, as though these old buildings were solid, unchanging, regardless of the life going on around them.

Why was she being so philosophical today? And with her body still burning from her memory of being tied to the tree, with the relentless image of Desmond's face in her mind.

She shook her head, sat down, and looked once more at the questionnaire. Maybe this was part of it, getting her to really *think*. To access those old buried memories, the moments everyone stored in their brains, all of those things that affected the subcon-scious mind in subtle ways. She knew a good dominant used the whole mind-fuck thing as much as they did anything physical. She understood that was part of how they broke through a bottom's reserves. Or maybe she was simply mind-fucking herself, trying to analyze this?

Her cell phone rang on the table next to her. She looked at the caller ID.

Desmond.

Her pulse accelerated, her blood pumping so hard she felt dizzy. Exhilarating to see his number, to know it was him on the other end of the phone. Terrifying.

She took a breath before answering. "Hello?"

"Ava, you're there."

"Yes."

"I haven't received the questionnaire I sent you yet."

A small, lovely threat in his low, even tone.

"I'm filling it out right now. I called in sick to work today so I could focus on it."

"Ah, very good. Since you have it in front of you, we can dis-cuss it."

A hard lurch in her chest, in her sex. Swelling. Pulsing.

"Ava, are you there?"

"Yes . . . yes, I'm here."

"I'm going to ask you some questions. I want you to think carefully about your answers."

"Yes, Desmond. I will. I have been."

"Tell me which sexual acts are acceptable to you while you're bound or sceneing?"

"Oh."

He jumped right into it, didn't he? Her head was spinning, her body yearning. On fire.

"Why don't I give you a list, Ava? That will be easier. All you have to do is answer me: yes, no, or maybe." He paused. "What about breast stimulation?"

She nearly groaned aloud but managed to murmur, "Yes."

"Clitoral stimulation?"

Oh, God, how was she ever going to get through this?

"Yes."

"Vaginal penetration?"

"Yes."

"Anal penetration?"

Her body began to shake, desire flooding her. She was soaking wet, squirming in her chair. She could hardly speak.

"Yes, Desmond." It came out on a whisper.

"And all of this with my hands, with toys?"

"Yes, with anything!"

Anything, as long as it was Desmond doing it to her.

He was quiet then. But she could hear his gentle breathing over the phone. How could he ask her these things and remain so calm?

"Let's talk about something else now." Another long pause. "Tell me about your hobbies. What sorts of things you enjoy other than being tied up."

"This is . . . part of the process?"

"Everything is a part of the process."

Her gaze wandered to the pair of framed photographs on the kitchen wall of Wicked lying in a shaft of sunlight. "I like to take pictures. I wouldn't call myself a real photographer, though."

"Why not?"

"Oh, it's just something I do in my spare time."

"How long have you been doing it?"

"Since I was a kid. I especially love black-and-white photography. I love the whole idea of using shadow and contrast . . . I'm sorry, this must be boring you to death."

"On the contrary. I want to know about you. And I like that you're passionate about something."

"I do love it. I used to dream . . ."

"About what, Ava?" he asked quietly, as though he didn't want to interrupt her thoughts.

"I used to imagine I could be a professional photographer."

"A commercial photographer?"

"No. More as . . . art. It's silly, I know."

"Is it? I don't see why."

"You can't really live as a photographer."

"There are people who do. Why don't you feel you can take your desires seriously?"

Why was a knot forming in her stomach simply trying to think of how she would answer his question?

"In my family, you earn your living as a professional. Have a real job."

"And being a photographer isn't a real job?"

"No. Well, for some people. Not for me." Her hand tightened around the phone.

"And what is your real job, Ava?"

He didn't sound at all sarcastic. He was simply asking.

"I work in the mortgage-and-lending branch of a large bank."

"And is that a real job?"

"I'm just a contract worker."

"Do you like it?"

"I hate it. It's not what I want to do."

"You want to take photographs." It wasn't a question.

"Yes. But that's . . . I can't do that."

"Because of your family?"

"Yes. No."

"I'm sorry, Ava. I don't mean to judge you. You don't need any more of that, from the sound of it."

"No, it's fine. I just . . . you're right. My family does judge me. Endlessly. I can't seem to do anything right where they're concerned. Especially with my mother. I keep hoping I'll grow to some point in my life where it no longer matters. But it still does, whether I like to admit it or not. Is that foolish of me?"

"It's not about whether or not you're being foolish. It's about how you feel. How you think."

"You make me think about things."

"That's good, then. You should think about what you want in life."

"Yes, I suppose so. But if I think too much about what I want that I don't have . . . I'm sorry. I don't mean to get so philosophical."

"That's exactly what I want you to do."

"Oh."

He was quiet again. She didn't know what to say. Finally he said, "I want to see you, Ava."

"When?"

"Now."

"Now?"

He was quiet once more. She didn't understand.

"Ava, I always use a particular protocol, a method I adhere to. The first meeting, the questionnaire, a number of e-mails, telephone conversations, before I ever play a girl."

"Yes?" Where was he going with this?

He paused once more, a long, silent span. Then, "But I want to see you. I don't want to wait any longer."

"Oh . . ." The breath went right out of her at the raw need in his voice. Was it possible he wanted her as much as she wanted him?

Desmond wanted her. Wanted her as he hadn't wanted any-thing—or anyone—in a very long time. He pulled in a long breath, gripping the telephone in his damp palm. He leaned into the edge of his desk, ran his fingertips over the smooth, dark walnut.

What the hell was he doing with this girl? But he was going to do it. He could barely stand not to have her in front of him right now. Not to *have* her.

Restless, he stood, ran a hand through his hair, gazed out his of-fice window, over the bay view, the setting sun glinting gold on the water, the last of the day's sailboats skimming the darkening gray-blue swells. He drew in another breath, tried to draw in the sense of peace he usually found watching the water, the endless sky.

"You understand that I operate under the credo of safe, sane, and consensual. I'm sure you know Marina does. I'm sure she ex-plained that to you, that everything must be negotiated. Must be by your consent."

"Yes, of course."

He could hear her breathless confusion. It only made him harder.

"Are you willing to see me? Now? Tonight? Before all of these formalities have been completed?"

"I am willing to do exactly as you wish."

Such pure honesty; it hit him like a blow to the chest.

Christ, he had to pull himself together, do his job.

"Come to my house tonight, then. In Sausalito. I'll e-mail you the address, directions." He paused, ran a hand over his hair. "Are you certain about this, Ava? You must be absolutely certain. You must be clear about what you are getting yourself into."

Yes, Mr. Responsible.

"I'm completely certain, I swear it. I understand . . . I under-stand the possibilities, at least. I understand that my experiences with you will be . . . different. But this is where I want to go. Need to go, I think. With you."

"Promise me you will always be this honest with me, Ava," he said fiercely.

What was going on with him? What was it about this girl? He had to find out. He was about to. He could hardly stand to wait even a few hours.

"I can promise you that, Desmond. Without any hesitation."

He could hear her voice trembling as she said it, but he believed her.

"Be here at eight o'clock."

"Eight, yes. I'll be there."

"Tonight, then, Ava."

Hanging up the phone, he shoved both hands in his pockets and paced his office in the lower level of his hillside house. He ran his small software company from home; his office took up the entire basement floor and was outfitted with every necessary piece of equipment, as well as a few luxuries: the best computers, state-of-the-art video conferencing equipment. He didn't spare any expense when it came to running his company. Luckily, he'd had enough success that he didn't have to. He had an assistant, Lucy, who worked from her home in San Jose, and they met when they needed to. And his old friend Caleb sometimes took contract work from him when Desmond got overloaded. But he preferred to do most of the work himself, liked to be completely hands-on with the clients. His control issues, Lucy often told him, and she was right. But it served him well in business. And in other areas of his life. Lucy had no idea to what wicked uses he put those control issues.

He stopped and stared out the window once more, as he'd been doing all too often lately. Staring across the bay at the San Francisco skyline, wondering where in that bustling city she was, exactly.

Ava.

He must be losing his mind, telling her to come over tonight. This was not how he did things. And he never deviated from the procedure he'd established years ago.

Until now.

But she was an adult. One who had played these games before. She knew enough to understand what might happen between them, had given her consent.

In that breathless voice of hers, so purely female . . .

He was hard again. Or still, maybe. He couldn't seem to calm down.

He pressed a hand to his aching cock. Soon enough. Soon enough he would have her in his home, in his hands. Under his command.

That was all he could think of. All he wanted from her. To command her. Bind her. *Have* her.

But was that really all there was to it?

Had to be. He didn't take his relationships any further, and for good reason. And he'd just met the girl. It was some mad infatuation. Maybe tying her up, fucking her, would work it out of his system.

Ah, Christ, fucking her . . .

He groaned. His cock pulsed. In a few impatient strides he was in the bathroom off the office. He stood in front of the mirror, pulled his cock out, and began to pump into his fist right away. Glancing up, he found his own fevered gaze in the mirror.

A few more thrusts into his fisted hand and he was coming wildly, spurting all over the edge of the sink, for God's sake. His heart was beating like a drum: that tight, that insistent.

Tonight.

Not soon enough.

Still trying to catch his breath, he grabbed a hand towel and cleaned up the mess he'd made. He just needed to see her, touch her, and everything would be fine.

Liar.

No, he'd be fine. Just fine. He'd grow bored with her soon enough. He always did. This girl would be no different.

So why, then, was everything different with her already?

He didn't want to know the answer to that question. Couldn't even consider it.

She was just a girl. Just another girl, like so many others.

Liar.

Whatever. If he had to lie to himself, he would. Whatever he had to do to be with her. Touch her. Fuck her.

And then he would get over it. Done.

Liar.

God damn it.

Chapter Four

At two minutes of eight that evening, Ava stood at the door to Desmond's house. It was one of those three-story modern brown-shingled homes that were so common in the Sausalito hillsides, almost hidden beneath the dense canopy of oak trees. She could smell them, the damp green of the lush growth. So different from her city neighborhood, where the occasional spindly tree grew in a tiny plot on the sidewalk, where the air was filled with the scent of the ocean, the concrete sidewalks, the musty old buildings, and exhaust from the buses.

She pulled in one more long breath, faced the tall double front doors, painted red, like the gates to some important place. Imposing. Or maybe that was just her nerves, strung tight, making her neck ache. That old voice whispering in the back of her mind that there was something wrong with her for wanting this . . .

Stop!

She'd sworn to ignore those old tapes that ran in her head a long time ago, and it hadn't been a problem in the last couple of years. Not since those first few years after she'd left Michael. Why was she thinking of these things now?

Something about how vulnerable Desmond made her feel.

But that was also part of the thrill. Why she felt she could go that much deeper with him.

Calm down.

She pulled at the hem of her pink leather dress, cleared her throat. Her body was already humming with expectation, her head already sinking into that lovely weightless place where her mind opened up, readying her for what was to come: subspace.

Her pulse beating a sharp rhythm in her veins, she lifted the brass door knocker, let it fall. The hard thud had her heart pounding.

Calm.

Impossible, standing at Desmond's front door. Waiting for him to open it. To lead her inside, into his lair.

To bind her.

She nearly groaned.

The door swung wide, a shaft of light spilling onto the doorstep, momentarily blinding her. She blinked, but all she could make out was his tall silhouette.

"Ava." His low voice like a caress. Like velvet. Exactly as she knew his hands would feel on her skin. "Come in."

His hand on her then, just touching her shoulder, slipping her coat off. But thrilling, even that simple, innocent touch.

When she looked up into his fiery green eyes, there was nothing innocent there. Oh, no, he was all dark, wicked pleasure. Anticipation. Heat.

He led her inside, and she had to consciously force her gaze off him, to take in her surroundings.

The place was spectacular, in a quietly stated way. Large, heavy pieces of modern brown leather furniture, totally masculine. Artwork on the walls, most of it Asian: wood carvings, masks, a woven wall hanging in muted, earthy shades, but all of it sparsely placed. Elegant, beautiful, the slightest bit exotic. Just as Desmond was himself, with his faint Scottish accent, his sharp features, and those piercing eyes that took in everything about her in a single glance.

"Sit down, Ava."

He gestured to one of the sofas and she took a seat on the edge, twined her fingers together on her lap. She found it hard to look at him. She looked instead out the gloriously wide windows.

"Your view is incredible, Desmond."

He glanced over his shoulder at the window, then quickly back at her.

"Yes, the view is beautiful from here; it's why I bought the house. I love the open feeling. I love to look at the water. The boats, the gulls flying. I even love the view on a winter's day, cloudy and gray, with the sea dark and violent with wind."

His answer was so unexpected, she didn't know how to respond. He stood and watched her, that calm, assessing gaze of his. His eyes were the most brilliant shade of green.

"Are you uncomfortable here with me, Ava?" he asked softly. Tenderly, almost.

"I'm . . . I'll admit I'm a little scared of you."

He laughed, a low rumble in his chest. "Perhaps you should be."

She had to smile. "Your words aren't exactly encouraging, Sir."

"Aren't they?" He stepped closer until he stood before her, seeming to tower over her. "Isn't that what you're here for, Ava? To give yourself over, despite your fears? Despite those things which hold you back?"

God, she could smell his scent. And he was so tall. So thoroughly dominant. The tension in her body was quickly turning to liquid desire. Warm, intoxicating.

"Yes. I suppose it is."

"What else are you looking for?" he said, his voice soft. She couldn't figure out his mood, what he was trying to learn about her that he didn't already know from their previous conversations.

"I want . . . to become lost in the ritual of it. In the placement of the ropes. In the act of being bound. But I don't want to feel as though I'm at a distance from it. I'm not sure I'm making sense."

"You are. Go on."

"I'm looking for release. But we all are, aren't we? Bottoms? Sexual submissives?" She shook her head. "It's more than that, though. That part is easy enough. I want . . . more. I want . . . perfection. And to *be* perfect, which are two different things." She sighed, pushed her hair away from her face. "Maybe I don't know exactly what I want."

He eased onto the sofa next to her, and she swore she could feel the heat of his body only inches from her own.

"Tell me about the need for perfection."

"Is it that unusual?"

"No. But I want to know what it means for you."

She pulled in a breath. How much to tell him? But she wanted to tell him everything. She was coming to understand that maybe why this would all work with him in a way it never had with anyone else was because he made her feel so wide open. Made her want to be.

"I've always wanted to be perfect. I've always been told I had to be."

"By whom?"

"My family. Mostly my mother. That message was always loud and clear. As clear as her disappointment in me. And I know that's not healthy, to internalize that negative message. But in this scenario, in the lifestyle, I feel I've been able to channel that need in a more positive direction."

Desmond nodded, and she felt some relief that he seemed to understand.

"There's more, though, isn't there?"

God, she really did not want to tell him about Michael, didn't even want to have any reminder of him in the same room with Desmond. But she couldn't keep it from him.

"I was . . . in a relationship when I was twenty. Michael was a few years older than I was. He was in the Coast Guard, very macho. Very commanding, which I responded to."

"Yes, of course you did. What happened with him?"

"I told him what I wanted. To be tied up. To be under his control. But I didn't know nearly enough. And neither did he, I realized later. I didn't understand that the verbal humiliation wasn't part of it. I know some people are into that, but in this case it was simply . . . abusive. He told me how depraved I was for wanting these things even as he tied me up, slapped my face. And I never wanted the pain play. But he had no boundaries, and I didn't know then that I could."

"I'm sorry, Ava."

Desmond's eyes were dark; she could see sympathy there, and a simmering rage. And she felt oddly protected.

"Well," she went on, "it was the same message as the one from my mother: I wasn't good enough, there was something wrong with me. And finally he was telling me how bored he was by it all. That I was boring. But even then I couldn't figure it out. How could I be any more boring than all those girls who are into vanilla sex?" She was getting angry all over again. "I left him after a year. Not soon enough. Because I still struggle with these things."

"But you did leave. That shows some strength, don't you think?"

"Yes. Maybe. But do you think this need I have to please has been twisted in some way? Or maybe it always was."

"It can be whatever you make of it. You don't have to let other people's judgment shape you or your desires. And your desires are very much the same as my own. To seek perfection in the ropes, within the power dynamic. And it is achievable. It's entirely subjective. And I will tell you, I felt from the first moment that you could be perfect with me."

"Desmond . . ." She glanced away, flushed, flustered. Glowing with pleasure.

"Ava . . . I must also tell you, as I said on the phone, I am interrupting my own protocol, having you here so soon. I need to be up front about that. But we've talked, and I feel certain we are looking for the same things. To use Shibari as a means to an end, an end we both crave. And I believe we are on the same page about how to get there, about what you need, about what I require. Do we have an understanding?"

"Yes, Desmond."

He was quiet again. She wondered what was going on in his head when he went silent like this, watching her so carefully. Her heart beat wildly, a hard flutter in her chest. And her body was heating up, her breasts full and aching, simply imagining what was about to happen.

"Do you have any questions?"

"I . . ." There were a million things she wanted to know about him, personal details, but none of it mattered right now. And she loved that sense of mystery about a Dom the first few times she played with someone new. She trusted him. She wanted him. She didn't need to know anything else just yet. "No, Desmond."

"We'll begin now, then," he said, his voice that quiet command that went through her like a sensual pulse.

She nodded. He stood, took her hand to help her up. Oh, she loved these small gentlemanly details. That and his lyrical accent, his rugged face, his large, beautiful hands . . .

But he was ushering her through the dimly lit house and she had to pay attention. Through a large dining room full of wide windows overlooking the darkly glimmering bay, an enormous modern table and leather-covered chairs the only furniture but beautiful in its simplicity, with a spray of tiny green orchids in a tall pewter vase in the center of the table. Then down a hallway, the walls of which were covered in small framed black-and-white photographs, architectural pieces, but she couldn't concentrate enough to really look at them. They passed two open doors, and she glimpsed a bathroom and what appeared to be a guest room, but it was too dark for her to see inside. At the end of the hallway was an ominously closed door.

He paused just outside of it, turned to her. Again he stood silently. Then he raised a hand, lifted her chin, peered into her eyes.

So much intensity in his gaze. Too much, almost, and his fingertips warm on her chin. Her insides knotted up. She was more afraid than ever. And more anxious for him to touch her. To lay his ropes on her body. Desire was like a warm, undulating wave shimmering over her skin.

"Ava . . ." Was there a small tremor in his voice? It had to be her imagination. "This is your last chance to change your mind."

She shook her head. "I am exactly where I want to be."

He smiled, moved in, and brushed his lips over hers, just the lightest feather touch, but heat swarmed her system like water, rippled through her, settling between her thighs.

He opened the door and led her through.

An enormous bed with carved wooden posts soaring toward the high ceiling. More windows open to the incredible bay view, letting the night right in: the dark sky, the glittering stars, making her feel all the more vulnerable, even though she was certain no one could see inside. The room was dimly lit by amber glass sconces on the walls. Music played quietly, something soft, meditative. And against one wall was a large wooden frame, like the ones she'd seen at the fetish clubs. But this one was beautiful, carved, with benches and bars padded in brown leather and shining brass hooks placed all over it. Next to it stood a tall rack with coils of colored ropes hanging from it: white, black, red, blue. Her breath stuttered in her chest.

He came to stand behind her so she couldn't see him. She could only feel his presence, the faint heat of his body. And his scent, warm and enigmatic, filling her senses.

"Do you know what this is, Ava?"

She nodded her head. "I think so. It looks like the bondage frames I've seen at some of the clubs."

"Yes, that's right. I can do complex web work here, full harnessing, suspension. Anything." A short beat. "And I will."

Oh, she was going to sink to her knees right now, right here!

"Ava, take your clothes off. All of them."

She paused, opened her mouth, but found she had nothing to say. Everything he was asking of her was well within the boundaries she was used to, but for some reason she felt startled.

She wasn't going to argue. She didn't want to. But she was trembling all over with excitement, and with a little fear still. She wasn't afraid of him exactly. It was how he made her feel.

But she was doing it, slipping out of her dress, her bra, her high heels, and finally her damp, white lace panties, which he took from her. He held the small scrap of fabric in his fingers, stroking the lace with his thumb.

"I love this, that you would wear something so sweet-looking. That's one of the first things I noticed about you," he told her as he set her clothing down on the dark suede coverlet on the end of the bed. "That aura of innocence."

She could hardly believe he was talking to her so calmly while she stood naked in front of him!

"And this," he said, his voice quiet, almost reverent. "This incredible skin." He drew one finger between her breasts, and her nipples went hard immediately. She shivered all over. Moving in closer, he spread his fingers wide, his entire palm covering the skin between her breasts.

"I can feel your heart beating, Ava. I don't mind telling you mine is beating just as hard, just as fast."

He took her hand, placed it on his firm, muscled chest, and she could feel his thudding heartbeat beneath his black cotton shirt.

God.

She was melting all over, into his heat, into her own.

"This is why we're here together right now," he said.

He took a step back and she saw him pull in a deep breath. She was unable to speak, her mind beginning that lovely slip and slide, filled with nothing but his rugged beauty, his command, her own sense of submission. And overcome, she clasped her hands behind her back, bowed her head.

"Ah, good girl."

Hot flash of pleasure at those words, at his tone.

"Stay just as you are while I get set up," he told her.

She waited. Breathless. Dizzy with need, anticipation.

Then that familiar whisper of rope smoothing over rope, and in a moment he was in front of her again, taking her hands from her back, leading her forward.

"We begin now, Ava."

Her body was loose all over, pliant, as he placed her in the center of the wooden frame. Her mind was absolutely emptying out. *Desmond.*

It was only him. Desmond, the ropes, the sensations assaulting her body even before the first rope touched her.

And when it did, she shook, hard, her muscles tensing, then releasing, her sex filling, going wet. And Desmond working so silently as he pulled that first loop around her waist.

He leaned in and asked her, "Do you know anything of Taoist philosophy?"

"No, Desmond," she whispered.

"I'll tell you, then, although I'm going to have you read more about it later." He wound the loop across her back, around the front of her body, crossed the rope over itself; she could feel the motion against her skin like cool silk. But firmer. Lovely. "The main concept, as it seems to me, anyway, is to learn to cease the inherent human struggle against the inevitable. To let go. When I first read of this, it immediately translated into what we do in this lifestyle. Do you see where I'm going with this, Ava?"

"I . . . I think so. Yes. You mean to give myself over to you. To the process. To yield."

"Yes, exactly," he went on, his voice quiet, soothing. "Because the freedom you're seeking lies within that act of submission. Of total submission. I don't mean it in the sense of complete slave mentality; that sort of thing doesn't interest me. When you are not in the ropes I want to be able to have an intelligent conversation with you. I want you to be a thinking, functioning individual being, not some mindless piece of furniture. But now . . . when you are under my hand, you must learn not to struggle against what is happening, what you yourself have asked for, what you desire. And what I desire, if that makes it easier for you. This is what you and I will work on together. And we will utilize some tools to get you there. We're going to start with some meditative breathing. If you've done yoga before, you may be familiar with this kind of practice. But I want you to put all of that out of your mind. Focus only on my voice. On what the ropes make you feel."

Oh, she could do that easily enough. Nothing else existed for her already.

"Breathe in, Ava," he said. "In through your mouth, into your diaphragm, then push the air down into your stomach. Good. Now let it out slowly. And as you do, focus. My voice. Your breath. The ropes."

She felt the silken pull of the rope against her skin as he wound another length of it over her shoulders, beginning what she knew would be a body harness of some sort. And she let herself sink into the ropes, into the brushing of his fingertips, his knuckles, against her skin as he worked.

If only he would really touch me . . .

But she was getting ahead of herself.

Focus. Breathe.

Yes, just let herself sink in, give it all over . . .

"Another deep breath, Ava. Take your time, slowly . . . yes, that's it. And again. My voice. Your breath. The ropes."

Desmond could not believe how easily this girl went down, into that space. He watched as her eyes glazed, then closed. She was still following his instructions: breathing in, out. He would almost think she was asleep, except that her nipples were two hard, dusky points. Swollen. Unbelievably luscious.

He drew the rope over her pale flesh, fighting to maintain his focus.

Control.

It was all he could do not to shake all over with need for her.

Soon enough.

Yes, once he had her bound, once he had done all he could to take her down into subspace, once he did his job with her . . .

His cock went hard as rock, pushing against the fabric of his trousers.

Control!

Christ, but she was too gorgeous. And the black rope looked every bit as good against her fair skin as he'd imagined. Hell, it was better than he'd imagined, in every way. The way she looked naked . . . almost more than he could stand, she was so damn beautiful, those large breasts on that tiny frame. Yes, doll porn.

His cock gave a sharp jerk, and he reached out and brushed the underside of one perfect breast with the back of his fingers.

She sighed, a small breath of sweet air escaping her lips, and she squirmed.

"Still, Ava."

He had to still himself. Steel himself.

Get it together.

She pulled in a deep breath, and he did the same. He moved the rope over her body, and soon he found his rhythm, with the music, with her breath, with his own. Around her torso, between her beautiful breasts. Her flesh was like satin. Babyskin.

No, don't think too much about it.

He was there now, into the languorous pacing of the ropes, really taking his time, drawing it out. And the body harness was beginning to take shape, the ropes crossing over themselves in a herringbone pattern, leaving only her breasts bare. He stayed there for a long while, their breathing in tune, his hand on the deliciously silken skin at the back of her neck, his cock rock-hard. But he maintained his focus on the process, on her, as she slipped further and further into subspace, her body going slack all over as she leaned her weight into him.

It must have been nearly an hour later when he slipped the rope between her thighs, the back of his hand brushing against her sex. Christ, she was wet. Soaked. She moaned, her hips arching. Suppressing a groan, he slid the rope behind her, moving around her body as he worked.

"Ava, still with me?"

"Yes, Desmond," she murmured, her eyes still closed. He could see the delicate blue veins beneath the skin of her lids, which touched him in some odd way he didn't want to analyze.

"Very good. Continue. My voice. Your breath. The ropes."

She nodded almost imperceptibly. Oh, yes, she was there, in that floating space. Now to find a way to take her deeper, to take her all the way.

He pulled another length of rope from his wall rack and moved behind her once more, pulled her arms back, and began to bind them, working carefully, checking the tension of the rope for evenness as he went. Even a small error could cause a lack of circulation, or a visual disturbance in the perfect symmetry, which was as important to Shibari as the ropes themselves, the act of being bound.

He could feel her shivering, just a small tremor running through her, over and over. The heat coming off her was incredible. He wove the rope over and between her biceps, her forearms, until they were bound together, from upper arms to wrists, pulling her shoulders back tightly, making her breasts thrust forward. She held perfectly still.

"Beautiful," he murmured. "You are so beautiful, Ava. Impossible for me not to tell you that."

"Ah, Desmond . . ."

She let her head drop back, and he could smell the fresh scent of her hair. He reached up then, buried his fingers in the silky, twining strands, pulling her head back. And she went with him, her body bowing, arching, her response filling him with that sense of absolute power over her. And even more, with the awe-inspiring sense of her submission to him.

She was giving in. But he could feel some underlying tension in her even now. She was holding something back. But Marina had told him to expect it.

With one hand still in her hair, he moved the other down the front of her body, in between her breasts. He hesitated one brief moment before sliding his palm across the ropes, filling it with that plump flesh.

"Oh . . ." Her soft sigh, her panting breath, and he was hard as iron now, if he hadn't been before. Nearly bursting.

He slid his hand to the other breast, over her smooth skin, and finally he brushed one tip with his fingers.

"Oh, Desmond . . ."

She was writhing now. He should make her hold still, but her gently undulating body was too beautiful to make her stop. Instead, he took her nipple between his fingers and tugged.

She grunted, her hips arching, and he did it again, tugged, pinched, twisted. She was panting hard, all rhythm gone. But he could see over her shoulder that her eyes were still shut tight in dream mode.

He let her hair go so he could use both his hands, sliding them over her breasts, then torturing her nipples again. He loved the idea of simply throwing her down and fucking her, just plowing right into her body, and he could do it. But he wanted to wait. The anticipation, seeing her like this, was too good. And he always loved these long sessions, the exquisite torture of the waiting, the desire itself a meditative force.

He kept his hands on her nipples, twisting, flicking, stroking softly. He sank into the experience, her labored breath, her lovely little gasps when he squeezed hard, the pulsing of his cock. Only the fatigued muscles in his legs finally reminded him that he'd been playing her for several hours already. That and the almost unbearable ache in his cock.

He shifted, drew her up against him, one palm flat and firm against her rope-covered torso, her sinuous back against his chest, his stomach. His erection pressed against the top of her bare, rounded buttocks. And he moved his hand down over the ropes until he reached the apex of her thighs.

"Ava . . ." His voice was ragged in his own ears.

"Yes . . . yes, Desmond."

"Are you wet, Ava?"

"Oh, yes."

"Do you want me to touch you? To put my hand between your legs? To make you come?"

"Please, Desmond," she whispered between gasping breaths.

"Then tell me, Ava. Tell me you're mine. Mine to do with as I please." He was trying hard to ignore the edge of desperation in his voice.

"Yes! I'm yours, Desmond. Yours . . ."

His body went still, as though time had stopped.

Yours.

What was it about those words from her that made his head spin? He felt as though something inside him was unraveling, coming apart.

His. He had never wanted anything so damn much in his life. He didn't understand what was happening to him, between them. But it was too good to stop.

All he knew was that he wanted to make this girl his.

Ava.

Something weird was happening in his head. Something that

went beyond any sense of ownership, of being in control. And the truth was, the way he wanted her, *needed* her, meant he wasn't entirely in command.

What did it all mean? He didn't know. Right now, all that mattered was that she was here, she was his. He'd deal with the leftover mind-fuck later. He was pretty damn certain she'd be worth it.

Chapter Five

DESMOND'S HEAD was spinning, his pulse thrumming with a reckless, staccato beat.

Ava.

So beautiful.

Have to have her.

He slid his fingers down and right into the wet folds of her pussy. So swollen, so slick. He was going to lose his mind. He plunged his fingers into that wet, silky heat. And she went off like a shot, her sex clenching around his hand as he pumped into her. She was groaning, crying out.

His cock pulsed; he needed to come. But this was all about her.

Ava.

Christ.

She was still coming, quivering against him, moaning softly. Then shivering, leaning into him as he held her up.

"Very good, Ava."

Oh, yes, very good. Almost too good. He could barely stand himself, his painfully throbbing cock. And that other thing happening in his head . . .

Moving her over to the bed, he carefully laid her down on her stomach. He saw that her eyes were still closed, her hair falling all over her face, her shoulders, in a wild blond tangle. He knelt beside her, trying to ignore his aching cock. He concentrated on the lovely curve of her back beneath the ropes, on her buttocks, her perfectly formed legs.

"Ava." Her eyes fluttered open, a blaze of bright blue. Glossy, her pupils enormous. Even now he was struck by that air of innocence about her. "I'm going to have you do some more breathing now."

"Yes . . ."

He brushed her hair aside and laid his hand over the back of her neck, pressed down just enough so that she could feel him holding her still.

"Breathe in, into your stomach. Yes, and hold it for a moment. Good. Let it out slowly. And again."

He took her through the breathing, talking to her softly, falling easily into a pattern with her, needing to relax, to focus, as much as he needed her to. In moments her body went loose beneath his hand.

His cock was pulsing as hard as ever.

But he noticed it now only as if it were something at the edge of his vision. He was in top mode, that space where his responsibilities to his bottom meant more than his own needs. And this was where he'd needed to take her, the climax meant to bring down her defenses so he could take her even deeper.

"Very good, Ava. I'm going to stop directing you now. But you are to keep breathing as I've told you, to feel my breath, to keep in sync with me. And let your mind go loose, as loose as your body is right now. To find that place."

He stayed with her for maybe twenty minutes, his hand never leaving the silky flesh at the back of her neck. Her body was still, but he could *feel* the energy humming away inside her, in the air between them. It was sexual, yes. But there was something more, something even in the texture of her skin beneath his palm . . .

When he checked her hands for circulation they were a bit paler than he liked. Time to bring her out of it.

His own body buzzing with that sensual, muted energy, hers and his own, he leaned over her, whispered, "I'm removing the ropes, Ava. Stay still."

He untied the knot, carefully uncoiled the ropes from her arms, went to hang them on the wall rack. When he came back to the bed she was breathing evenly, but he felt the shift in her awareness even before he lifted her, sitting her upright on the end of the bed.

Her eyes were open, that spectacular blue, glowing as though her body were illuminated from within. He could feel the heat of her, coming off her in waves. And he was still rock-hard, needing her. Needing to fuck her. But not tonight.

Torture.

But this was his job: doing what was best for her.

He helped her to her feet. Almost too much to hold her up, his arm encircling her naked waist, with her bare breasts luscious and full only inches away. If he pressed her close, right up against him, he could have his hands on her breasts again in moments, in between her sweet thighs, in that slick heat . . .

She swayed, and he held her a little tighter.

"Are you steady, Ava? Can you stand?"

"Yes. I'm fine."

He untied knots, slipping the rope over her skin, enjoying the sensation of the soft nylon running across his palms, as he always did. And she stood so still, really like some sort of doll, with her big blue eyes, her pink pouting mouth. Her face was nearly expressionless. Except that her eyes were gleaming, alive, dynamic.

When he was finished he sat her down on the edge of the bed, seated himself next to her, wrapping a throw blanket around her narrow shoulders.

"What are you feeling, Ava?"

Why was he so desperate to know? In a way that went beyond his responsibilities as a top.

"I'm feeling . . . nothing, really. Just floating on the endorphins a little, still."

"Nothing else?"

"No, I don't think so."

He was quiet a moment. This, he thought, was the problem.

"Has it ever occurred to you that part of the issue is that you don't allow yourself to feel everything the ropes have to give you? That something is holding you back from really feeling what's happening to you?"

"I . . . I don't know."

"I want you to think about it when you go home, before we see each other again."

She nodded.

"Are you cold?"

"No, Desmond."

"Thirsty?"

"No, thank you, Desmond."

He watched her face. It was too still. Yes, something was going on with this girl. He wanted to know what it was. He wanted to help her move beyond it. The mystery of it intrigued him.

Hell, she intrigued him.

Don't fool yourself. It's far more than that.

Fuck. He had to calm down.

"Ava, do you want to see me again?" he asked, more harshly than he meant to.

"Yes."

"I'll ask you once more when you've had a chance to come down."

"Of course."

Maybe she'd normalize with the armor of her clothing on.

"Let's get you dressed."

She let him help her slip back into her white lace panties, her dress. He had her carry her shoes and follow him to the living room, where he made her drink a glass of water, had her curl up in one corner of the sofa, the blanket over her lap. She was really coming out of it now, out of subspace, out of that odd numbness.

"Ava, we'll talk more after you've had a day or two to absorb what's happened here, talk seriously. Right now, let's just talk to each other."

"About what?"

"About anything. Who we are. What we do. Where we come from. Tell me how you met Marina."

She brushed her blond curls from her face, the motion a bit listless still, her voice soft. "I went to one of her lecture nights at Pinnacle. She was doing a workshop on bondage, and I went up to her after, told her I was looking for someone to work with, someone who knew what they were doing. Really knew. She worked with me several times . . ."

Ava paused, bit her lip. And watching her make the small dent into that lush, pink flesh made him want to put his fingers there, to feel her lips, to kiss her. His fingers clenched at his sides.

Ava went on. "Then Marina told me about you. She told me you both belong to the club, that it's how you know each other."

"Yes. And that's where I plan to take you, eventually."

"When I heard her that night, talking about Shibari, the formality of it, I thought maybe she could . . . but it didn't work with us; you already know that."

She stopped, glanced away.

"What is it?" He put a hand on her shoulder, felt her shiver.

"Tonight . . . it didn't . . . I didn't . . ."

"You went deeper than I expected you to, but you are still holding back. But this was our first time together. We'll try again, unless you change your mind."

"I won't!" She stopped again. "I'm sorry, Desmond. I won't change my mind, unless you have."

"No." He reached out, gave in and touched a finger to her flushed cheek. "In fact, I'm more eager than ever to figure you out."

She smiled, the first real expression he'd seen on her face since he'd brought her out of the ropes. He leaned in, took her hand in his, stroked her knuckles with his fingertips. Yes, that babyskin. Beautiful.

"Desmond? May I ask you something?"

"Yes, certainly."

"Why do you want to do this with me? Is it simply a challenge? It feels . . . important for me to understand."

"Yes, it's a challenge, which most Doms appreciate. But there is something . . . special about you. You're like a puzzle, and I want to find the missing pieces. I don't mean that in any sort of offensive way. I was intrigued the moment Marina told me about you, and more so after meeting you."

More so now. So much more.

"Marina . . . will you tell me about when you met her?"

She was relaxed again as she curled deeper into the sofa cushions. He was glad to see it.

"We're old friends. We met years ago, nearly ten years. She was so young. Beautiful, as she is now. She was just beginning her exploration of Shibari. I used her as a model for demonstrations and quickly discovered she was a top. She didn't know it herself until then."

"Ah, you were lovers."

Was that a note of disappointment he heard in her voice?

"No, we never were. It would have been a horrendous power struggle. We became friends instead. Although we were less close the years she was with Nathan."

"Nathan?"

"Her lover. Her submissive. They had a very intense relationship. He died of cancer four years ago. Marina stayed away from the clubs for a good year after that. She came back eventually, but she hasn't played a man since."

"How awful."

"Yes."

He caught her gaze, found her eyes swimming with tears. She didn't seem at all self-conscious about it.

Why, if she could cry in front of him, couldn't she let go within the ropes? It was more than simply feeling vulnerable. After what she'd told him this evening he felt he had some grasp on it, but how to help her break through?

Have to see the girl again.

Oh, yes.

He wrapped his fingers around her hand, squeezed it.

"Let's talk about next time, and what I'll require you to do in between."

She nodded her head, shifted on the sofa, her breasts pushing against the corset-like dress. He was still half hard for her. Had been since she'd arrived, except for when he'd bound her, when he'd been as solid as a steel pipe. It didn't matter what they were talking about. They could talk about the weather.

"I'll send you a list of books," he told her, "on Shibari, on Taoism. You're to get them, read them." She nodded. "And you are still not to touch yourself, not to bring yourself to orgasm."

"Yes. Of course."

"I'll see you again next week. Complete the questionnaire in the interim. And one last thing, Ava."

"Yes?"

"I have to work in the South Bay for the next few days, but beginning on Thursday, I will call you every evening, at eight o'clock. Be home, answer the phone."

"Yes, Desmond."

She smiled, and he saw how being instructed pleased her. Ah, yes, she was nearly perfect, this girl.

"Are you ready to go home now? Do you feel alright?"

"Yes, I'm fine. I'm just a little tired."

He called a cab, chatted with her about Pinnacle while they

waited, put her into the taxi when it arrived, paid the driver in advance for the long drive back into San Francisco.

As the car drove off into the night, he stood at the curb, watching the taillights fading into the dark and the fog that had rolled in off the bay, damp and heavy in the air.

He felt off-balance, almost as though he was topping out, something that hadn't happened to him in a long time. Years. And only after very long, intense play sessions. But it was that same sensation of vague confusion, of mental exhaustion. Rawness.

He ran a hand over his hair. He must not have been sleeping enough lately. Working too hard on that San Jose project with Caleb. Maybe he should just hand that one over to him entirely. Yes, that must be it. Too much work, too little sleep. It was as simple as that.

Then why was he standing out on the street long after the cab carrying Ava back into the city had disappeared in the cold night air, his body humming with unsated need, his mind filled with images of her eyes so prettily filled with tears, her beautiful doll mouth, the scent of her hair?

Watch it. Don't get involved.

He never did, did he?

He turned and went back inside, slamming the door a little too hard behind him. Slamming his mind shut on Ava Gregory, and everything she was making him think, making him feel.

Yes, just shut her out, shut your mind down.

Easier said than done.

Fuck.

Chapter Six

THE LAST FEW DAYS had gone by in a blur. Everything but her evening in Desmond's home on Tuesday night, in his ropes, was vague. She'd felt at a distance from everything, at work, at home. Alone in her apartment, Ava didn't know what to do with herself. She'd bought the books Desmond had told her to get on her lunch break on Wednesday, had started to read them. But she couldn't seem to get through more than a few pages at a time before her attention wandered. And always back to Desmond.

She fell asleep at night with his spare, elegant house in her mind, his face, the surprisingly gentle touch of his hands.

Except when he'd been pumping his fingers inside her . . .

She groaned, got up from the kitchen table, and poured herself a glass of wine. Half a glass; she didn't want to be out of it when Desmond called.

Seven forty-five.

Her stomach twisted, in lust, in nervous anticipation.

She sipped at the heavy cabernet, sipped again, twisted a curling strand of hair around her finger.

Reaching down, she stroked Wicked's dark head, the cat in his usual seat at the table, before sitting once more, pushing her plate of uneaten dinner away. She had no appetite tonight, not for food.

She'd done exactly as he'd asked: the reading, thinking about why she couldn't get past the block that kept her from reaching those deeper levels of subspace. She hadn't come up with any answers—nothing she didn't know already, anyway. She understood that Michael had a lot to do with why it was hard for her to move beyond a certain level of trust with anyone. But it had been so long. She didn't understand why she hadn't been able to put it completely behind her, why the terrible things Michael had drummed into her head were still there, echoing in her mind, even though she knew he was just being awful, echoing that same message she'd gotten her whole life from her mother.

Her mother had always required perfection from herself, and from her daughters, seeing them as some sort of extension of herself. Her sister, Andrea, had always been the perfect photocopy of their mother. The good girl. The one who made everyone happy and did everything right. And Ava had always disappointed. She'd fought the pull between the need to please her mother and the need to be her own person since she was a teenager, even as she strove for the perfection she'd never been able to attain. Why did it still feel like a losing battle? Why couldn't she stop struggling?

She would never be perfect. Some days, it was harder to accept that than others.

She lifted her glass, sipped again, the silken liquid sliding easily down her throat, warming her.

Don't want to think about this now.

No, all she wanted to think about was Desmond, that she would talk to him soon. What would he say to her? Would he issue a new command? Ask her if she'd masturbated?

She hadn't, although it had been difficult as hell. The sexual chemistry with Desmond was intense and was made all the more so by his absolute confidence. His absolute sense of command. She didn't think she could refuse him anything.

And maybe that was part of what scared her about him, that she knew already she would do anything for him. Even opening that part of herself she'd kept closed off for so long. She'd already started, by confiding in him about her issues with Michael, her mother. She didn't know herself what lay beneath that. Something uglier, maybe? She realized with sudden clarity that she'd always been afraid to find out. But the truth was that she had no idea how far Desmond could push her, how far she would go for him.

Excruciating. Delicious.

Her body began to heat, and not with the wine. Her sex was going damp just thinking about him. It had been like this since she'd first met him. But it was so much worse now that she'd experienced for herself his clever hands, the brief touch of his mouth.

God . . .

She glanced at the clock. Seven fifty-five.

Five minutes.

Her pulse accelerated, and she swore she could feel it reverberate in her veins, in her chest.

She got up, scraped her plate, took it to the sink, ran the hot water over it.

She loved these dishes; they were vintage Depression ware. Green Princess. Rather precious, but she adored them, the clear green like sea glass, the ornate pattern etched into the surface. She'd collected an entire set over the years, searching out flea markets, estate sales.

She dried the dish carefully with a soft terry cloth, turned, and pulled the cabinet open.

The telephone rang, like a shot through her nerves. She dropped the plate, the glass shattering on the old black-and-white tile floor.

Startled, Wicked darted from the room.

"Shit!"

She looked at the shards of glass scattered over the floor, at her cell phone sitting next to her wine on the table.

Desmond.

Running a hand through her hair, she took a breath and picked up the phone. "Hello?"

"Ava."

"Desmond?"

"Were you expecting someone else?"

"What? No. Of course not. No."

"Are you alright, Ava?"

No, she wasn't alright. Her heart was hammering away in her chest, as though it were trying to pound its way through, to escape the confines of her body.

"Yes. I'm fine, thank you." She paused, stepped carefully over the broken glass with her bare feet, moved into the living room. "How has your week been?"

"Long. I don't like working away from home, but it was too long a drive to come home each night, so I stayed over. Terrible hotel. Tell me what you've been doing. Have you been reading?"

"Yes, Desmond."

"And?"

That utterly commanding tone, which scared her a little and excited her just as much. She loved it.

"I found *The Tao of Pooh* the easiest to understand. I'm afraid I'm not very sophisticated when it comes to spiritual study."

"No, that's fine. That's why I gave you that title to read. It's a very approachable introduction to the Tao. I thought you might find it the most relatable."

"I did."

"Tell me what you've learned, what you've discovered."

She had to stop and think how to articulate the series of small epiphanies her reading had brought her.

"It's as though . . . there are things which should seem perfectly obvious, like not bothering to struggle against the inevitable, as you said. It seems so logical once it's pointed out. But I know that I do this. Not only in my resistance with the ropes but in my everyday life. It really made me think . . . that I have to decide what's really important. To choose my battles. And why I should never choose to battle with myself."

"Yes, that's exactly what I hoped you would get from it."

"And yet I find myself continuing to do it, to struggle against myself, my own needs. My desires. Because of latent guilt, I suppose. Out of . . . fear. For whatever reasons. Which makes it frustrating."

"The Tao talks about those things we should aspire to. None of us are perfect. None of us get that idea on a deep level all the time. It's not possible. We're human."

"Even you?"

He was quiet a moment. Had she really said that to him?

"I'm sorry," she told him. "I didn't mean . . ."

"No, it's fine. I suppose I should seem superhuman to you. That's part of the lovely mind-fuck, that a dominant is godlike." He laughed then, and she relaxed a bit. "Don't apologize. I love your honesty with me. Tell me what else you've done since I saw you."

"I've . . . followed all your instructions."

"I meant what else has happened in your life, aside from the things we do together."

"Oh. Well. I took Monday off, so I've been working late the last few nights."

"Tell me about your work, Ava. Mortgage banking, right? What is it like for you?"

"It's the most boring job in the world, but it pays fairly well, and it's the sort of thing my family wants me to do. But I'm a contract worker; they hate that."

"Ah, you don't like commitment," he said, humor in his voice.

"Maybe. I hadn't thought about it that way. But yes, you're right. I don't like to be too tied down."

"Except that you do."

She laughed. "Yes."

"Tell me about your family, about growing up."

"Really? This is what you want to hear about?"

"Yes. It's exactly what I want to know."

She could hardly believe he was talking to her like this, this normal conversation. Except that it wasn't quite normal, really. She had the sense that he was looking deeper. And she was ignoring the warmth seeping into her system, a heat that had little to do with sex. Except that everything about Desmond had to do with sex.

She twisted a strand of hair around her fingers, pacing her small living room as she spoke.

"Alright. Well, my family is pretty average, I guess. I grew up in Seattle. Just outside of it, actually, on Mercer Island."

"I've been there; it's beautiful. Sausalito reminds me of that area, in some ways. The trees everywhere, all that green. The damp weather."

"It's true what people say about Seattle, it really is gray most of the time. It made my childhood seem . . . lonely. Or maybe that was just because of my family."

"What do you mean?" he asked.

"They're very conservative in their thinking. My parents, my sister, Andrea. My mother has this idea that she's a hard-core feminist, and my sister is a carbon copy of her. Andrea lives her life exactly as my parents want her to, want me to, except I never did, even as a kid. She's two years younger than I am, only twenty-seven, but she's done it all already. She went to college, got started in real estate, moved up in the company. Got married. Had a baby a few months ago and went right back to work as though nothing had happened. I don't know how she does it. I don't know how anyone can be happy like that."

"So, you're a rebel. The family black sheep."

"God, if they only knew . . ."

He laughed, making her relax, allowing her to let some of the tension go she hadn't realized she was holding in her shoulders. She moved to the sofa and sat, pulling a pillow onto her lap.

"I'm sorry. This has all got to be incredibly boring for you, hearing about my family."

"On the contrary, I find it fascinating. I want to know about you, Ava. Tell me why you say your mother has an 'idea' about being a feminist."

"That's probably an unfair judgment for me to make; I shouldn't have said it."

"No, you're just being open with me. I like that. So, tell me what you meant."

"Oh, she just . . . claims to be this modern woman who thinks you can do it all, have it all. But that's such . . . bullshit. I mean, sure, she worked through my childhood, but she was never really there. We were fed and clean and educated, but I never really had a mother. At least, that's how I felt. And my sister is doing the same thing, spending twelve hours a day at work rather than with her kid. It's not right."

"So, you don't think women can have it all?"

"I don't know. Maybe. What do I know about it, anyway? I don't have kids, I don't even hold down a full-time job."

"You're very hard on yourself."

"Am I?"

But she knew it was true.

He was quiet again.

"Will you tell me what you're thinking about the things I've just told you, Desmond? I feel sort of . . . foolish."

"No, there's nothing foolish in what you've told me. I'm simply absorbing information. I'm not qualifying anything you're saying. But all of these experiences make up who you are, contribute to how you'll respond to certain things. Knowing you is my job."

It was her turn to be quiet for a moment.

"You take your job, as you call it, very seriously," she said to him.

"It is serious. It's a responsibility. I'm not one of those Doms who just plays a girl and lets whatever happen, without thinking about it. Without contemplating the results of my actions." His accent was thick again. It seemed to get heavier when he felt strongly about whatever he was talking about.

"I appreciate that, I really do. But I wonder . . . what makes a person like that? What makes you—anyone—feel that intense sense of responsibility, seek it out?"

"I think we're simply born with these tendencies, and in this world of overstimulation, the tendencies are brought out, until we can't resist our own natures."

"Forgive me for saying so, Sir, but that's too easy."

"Desmond."

"Alright, Desmond. Is that what you do with all your submissives?"

"With some." They were both quiet. Then, "Maybe there is more to it," he said quietly.

"Yes?"

"Yes. But maybe it's not something I like to think about."

"But . . . is it . . . is what you do, then, a healthy expression of whatever it is you shy away from thinking about, talking about? I don't mean to pry, and you certainly don't have to tell me. I'm just trying to figure this all out. And you don't seem to mind . . . well, you seem to be allowing me to get to know you, as well."

"Yes, I want you to get to know me; that's my intention." Another long silence. She could hear him breathing on the other end of the line. "I like to think it's healthy: the Shibari, the power play. It has been a positive outlet for me."

"So, there's something . . . something has happened to you."

"That's the nature of life, isn't it? Everyone goes through something, lives through it, comes out the other side."

"Yes. I suppose so." She paused, twining a curl around her finger, tugging on it until she felt the pull in her scalp. "I'm sorry, it's really none of my business. I shouldn't have asked."

"No, that's alright. It's fine. I started this conversation."

"But it's not my job to analyze you."

"Maybe . . . maybe it is." Another long pause. "Ava. I need to tell you, things are different with you. I don't know yet what that means exactly. And I'm not entirely comfortable with it. Some of it is the blocks you have when we played. That numbness, that lack of feeling."

"Desmond . . ." Panic gripped her. "Do you mean you don't want to see me again?"

"No, of course not. But I need to let you know that. I need to be honest with you. Honesty is part of a strong, effective power exchange. And it has to come from both sides in order for it to work. That's one of the most basic concepts involved, and the one thing that can make the exchange falter, or even fail."

"Yes, that makes sense."

She heard him draw in a deep breath, blow it out. His voice was so low she could barely hear him. "Ava, I will admit that I have seldom been as attracted to a woman as I am to you. Possibly never. And that challenges my sense of control. But I swear to you, I am able to maintain it. It won't affect my judgment with you. It does not make you unsafe with me."

The edge of desire in his voice, the raw power of what he was telling her, went through her like an electric charge, lighting her nerve endings with need. Lust, sharp and pure. Her breasts tightened, her sex swelling between her tightly clasped thighs.

God, if he could do this with only his voice, a few plainly spoken words, what else might he do to her?

"Sir . . ."

"Desmond."

"Desmond." The name sounded strange on her lips. Strange but lovely. Seductive. "The feeling is mutual."

"We are on the same page, then."

"Yes," she said, breathless. Her body, her head, was buzzing.

"I want you to come to me again. At the club this time. I want to see how you respond in front of an audience. You did say you had a streak of exhibitionism."

"Yes! Please."

He laughed. "We are going to have a very interesting journey together, Ava."

Journeys. They always had a beginning, and an end. She didn't like to think about that part.

"Yes, I think we will."

"Read your books. I'll pick you up tomorrow and take you to Pinnacle. Nine o'clock. Dress all in white for me. Clothing, lingerie, everything."

"Yes, Desmond."

"Good girl."

A wave of pleasure rippled through her. She wanted to be good for him, more than anything. Perfect. Or as close to it as possible.

"Good night, sweet Ava. Rest and be ready for me tomorrow."

"I will. I'll be ready."

Ready and wet and pliant for him. Oh, yes . . .

They hung up the phone.

Desmond could not believe how easily he'd sidestepped getting into talking about his own past with her. He could not believe how much he'd wanted to tell her. His dark secrets, those things he didn't talk about, think about. Not even Marina knew the whole story. She knew nothing about Nessie.

Small shot of pain even thinking of her name.

Marina knew only what had happened with Lara. How she'd left him. How that had embittered him.

As though he hadn't been bitter before.

But no, when he'd met Lara he'd opened himself to her, put his past behind him. And look what that had wrought. No, he was better off like this, living his life as he had for the last ten years.

Until now. Until this girl had reached inside him somehow.

He went to the window, his stomach knotting, but he wasn't really seeing the view, the sparkle of lights against the night sky.

Not too deeply. He'd make sure of that. He wasn't going to go through that shit ever again. He knew himself. Knew what he was capable of. And what he no longer was.

Things with Ava would be just fine. He had to have her, really *have* her, and she'd be out of his system. But the timing had to be right in order for him to serve her needs in the way he owed her, owed any bottom he played with.

He moved away from the window, went to the dining room and opened the doors on the sideboard, pulled a bottle of Scotch out of the bar inside. Glenfiddich single malt, forty years old. One of his small indulgences, aside from the gadgets in his office. He poured two fingers, threw it back in one swallow. A shame to waste rare Scotch in this way, but he needed it.

It warmed him quickly, and he poured some more, not really paying attention to how much.

He should go downstairs, into his office, get some work done. He lifted the glass to his lips, inhaled the sharp, sweet scent, thought better of it, and took it into the kitchen, poured it down the sink.

What the hell was going on with him?

He ran a hand over his hair, blew out a slow breath.

Work it out, damn it.

Yes. Work. He headed down the stairs, into his office. His re-treat, if he was being honest with himself. He'd been honest enough on the phone with Ava already tonight. He'd had enough honesty. Right now, he would bury himself in work and simply forget.

Chapter Seven

HE WAS UNDER the water. Above him the sun was shining through in undulating, glassy shafts. But beneath him everything was murky. Muddy.

He kicked, swam through the water, so light and pure, the sunlight casting gold into the blue, his body carried along effortlessly.

One more kick upward and he was almost at the surface, but somehow it grew farther and farther away.

Small hitch of panic in his gut.

Control.

But he needed air. He couldn't calm down. The panic rose and began to choke him, panic and the lack of air. His lungs were going to burst! And the surface was gone now; everything as murky as the bottom of the lake had been, and he didn't know if he was going up or down, if he was moving at all.

He stopped swimming, his lungs too empty to keep going. And he saw her.

Nessie's face, as sweet as it had ever been, that small bit of baby fat on her twelve-year-old features still. Her long, dark hair like a mermaid's, like a halo around her head.

Nessie!

He wanted to yell for her to swim for the surface. Needed to. But he couldn't speak, couldn't move, couldn't *breathe*.

It was too late. She floated a few feet away, but even through the hazy water he could see there was no life in her pale, staring eyes.

God damn it!

Not again. I will not let it happen again.

He kicked once more, hard, but he couldn't reach her, couldn't reach the surface. And the water was closing in on him, almost as though it were something solid. Drowning him. And he was helpless against it.

Helpless.

God damn it!

He kicked, his leg tangling in the blankets, and came up gasping. His bedroom was dark around him, the pale light of the moon coming through the fog outside his windows, washing the room in silver and smoke. His heart was thundering, his pulse wild.

Only a dream. That damn dream again.

He ran both hands over his head, fisting his fingers in his hair and pulling tight.

It's fine. Everything is fine.

But it wasn't. When was the last time he'd had that dream? Had to have been a year or more.

He knew what had sparked it: his conversation with Ava earlier tonight. He'd come too close to talking about it. He'd allowed himself to think about it.

Not it. Her. Nessie. His baby sister.

His chest was still so damn tight he was having almost as much difficulty breathing as he'd had in the dream.

He got up, went to stand naked at the window, touched his hand to the cold glass, needing it to center him.

Was opening up to Ava a mistake? He always held certain things back when he was getting to know the women he played with. He was well aware of that. Sure, he shared about his work, his hobbies, his desires, certainly. But nothing about his past. Nothing about his pain. Why the hell this urge to tell her . . . everything?

He'd just met the girl.

It didn't feel like that.

If he hadn't already said he'd see Ava tomorrow he'd take a few days to get his footing again. But no, that was bullshit. He couldn't wait to see her.

He looked at the glowing numbers of the clock on his night-stand. Five in the morning.

There would be no more sleep for him tonight. He was too worked up. Ava. Nessie.

He went to his dresser, pulled out a pair of cotton pajama pants and a long-sleeved T-shirt, slipped the soft fabric over his body. He'd do some work, make use of the time.

He would not think about this anymore. Plenty of time to deal with it later, when he saw her.

A small clenching sensation in his chest, not entirely unpleasant.

Is this what infatuation felt like? It had been so long, he couldn't seem to remember. But it was better to think of Ava than to think of Nessie. To remember the dream, to remember what had happened all those years ago.

No, don't go there. Don't even think of telling her about it.

He'd read somewhere that infatuation was chemically similar in the human brain to going mad. He was beginning to believe that. And it was totally unacceptable to a man like him.

If only he knew what the hell to do about it.

AVA WAS FOREVER watching the clock when it came to Desmond. Five minutes of nine.

She'd done exactly as he'd asked. She'd dressed in a short, white leather dress, white patent-leather stiletto heels that were impossibly high, white lace panties and bra. No jewelry other than a pair of tiny silver hoop earrings. Jewelry only got in the way of the ropes.

The ropes.

Her pulse sped up.

The ropes and Desmond Hale to tie her up.

Oh, yes . . .

The doorbell rang, and her fluttering heartbeat shifted into high gear. She could swear she heard her blood thrumming in her ears. Taking a breath, she went to answer the door.

He really was beautiful. Masculine. Imposing. Regal.

He was dressed all in black, as the Doms often were, and he looked damn good in it: the finely made slacks hanging low on his waist, the black button-down shirt making his shoulders look broader on his narrow frame. And that evil-looking goatee that made him look like the devil himself. She loved it.

He reached for her immediately, taking her hand in his.

"Are you going to invite me inside, Ava?"

"What? Yes, of course. Please come in."

Such nice manners from them both, when they intended to do such depraved things later. She loved that, too.

Desmond stepped through the door, seeming to dwarf her small apartment. She'd never noticed before how tiny the place was. It must be his height. Or perhaps the enormity of his presence.

Out of the corner of her eye she saw Wicked scurry down the hallway to her bedroom.

"You have a cat?"

"His name is Wicked. He's good company."

"I'm fond of cats."

"Are you?"

"Does that surprise you?"

"Everything about you surprises me."

He smiled but didn't respond.

"And you collect antiques?" He moved to the oversized dresser she had against one wall in the living room, ran a hand over the carving on the front of it. "You have some very nice pieces. I'll have to really look sometime. But we should be off to Pinnacle now."

A small thrill ran through her at the insinuation that he would see her again, be in her apartment. That he approved of her choice in furniture. Such small things, yet she couldn't help but love them, revel in his approval of her.

"I'll get my coat."

She opened the hall closet and pulled her trench coat out, was surprised once more when he helped her into it.

"You're different from some of the Doms I've been with, Desmond."

"Am I?" He led her out the door, waited while she locked it, then they walked down the narrow staircase.

"Yes. You're more commanding than anyone else I've been with. But at the same time, you're so . . . careful with me."

"That's part of my duty, Ava. If these other men have failed to understand that, then they aren't true dominants in my book. And they aren't true gentlemen."

"Marina told me that about you, but it's different actually experiencing it."

His car was parked right in front of her building, as though he had some strange power even over the street. It was a sleek, dark Lexus, which fit him perfectly.

He opened her door for her, helped her slide onto the seat before closing the door and coming around the car to get in on the driver's side.

He buckled his seat belt, started the engine. "What else has Marina told you about me?"

Was this some sort of test? He was just letting the engine run, looking at the dark street rather than at her.

"Oh, well, not very much. Just that you were *nawashi,* a Shibari master, to surpass even her. That she'd learned a lot from you over the years. That she trusted you completely. That I could, as well."

He nodded, seemingly satisfied with her answer. He pulled out, gunned the engine to make it up the hill.

They were both quiet on the drive to the other side of the city. The club was at the foot of the Potrero Hill district, tucked away between warehouses. Not the safest part of that neighborhood; she'd never walk around alone there at night. But it was best for a fetish club to have some distance from residential areas. And she wasn't alone. She glanced over at Desmond, at his strong, angular profile silhouetted by the silvery wash of light from the street-lamps. A small stab of excitement went through her: anticipation, lust.

Desmond parked in the lot behind the structure that housed Pinnacle. It was an old brick building, three stories, with shuttered windows on the top floor. The enormous front doors were gated in black iron. There was no sign, nothing to indicate what went on inside, but Ava shivered as they approached the entrance. She'd been in Pinnacle before, knew exactly what happened within the old brick walls. But she'd never been there with Desmond. Never felt this lovely sense of titillation mixed with fear.

She recognized the doorman but remained silent while Desmond greeted him, keeping her head bowed, clasping her hands in front of her. Oh, yes, she was sinking down already, into her role as a submissive. Into that dark and calming place that was also somehow energizing, making her light up inside. And when Desmond took her hand to lead her into the club, that light turned into pure heat, suffusing her system.

They stepped inside, and Desmond took her coat, handed it to a female attendant dressed in black and red leather, a steel collar around her slender neck. When he slid a hand around Ava's waist, that heat moved lower, between her thighs, all slick, liquid fire.

"Are you ready, Ava?"

"Oh, yes." Her voice was a low moan.

They moved through a curtained doorway and into the main room of the club. She had to blink, trying to adjust to the dim lights in red and amber. Taking a breath, she pulled in the scents of old brick and plaster, and something dark and earthy: excitement, sex, along with the lingering fragrance of someone's perfume.

But she didn't have time to think about it. Desmond was taking her across the room, past the Saint Andrew's crosses, enormous wooden X's with mostly naked bodies cuffed and chained to them, the row of leather-covered spanking benches. Past the low leather sofas scattered around the perimeter of the room, where people gathered to talk, to relax, to watch. But it was all going by in a blur. All she could think of was Desmond's hand burning into her skin even through the leather of her dress, his solid presence beside her. What he was about to do to her.

He led her to the back of the room and to a spiral wrought-iron staircase, held her tightly to his side as they walked up, making her feel *owned* already. Then they were in the bondage room on the second floor, a more open and quieter space than the open playroom on the first floor. A more meditative space.

Some sort of trance music played softly in the background as the rope masters worked silently on the racks and large bondage frames she'd seen before, like huge wood-framed boxes with no walls, just the hooks and eyebolts set into them every few inches so that the ropes could be run through them in different ways.

She was really shaking now, the sense of expectancy building moment by moment. Desmond's presence was both reassuring and oddly frightening. What was she so afraid of with him? She couldn't figure it out. Still, she didn't want to be anywhere but here with him.

He chose a piece of equipment, set his black bag of rope on the floor.

"Ava, down on your knees now while I set up."

A simple command, but it went through her like a jolt of electricity. She sank to her knees. She couldn't have done otherwise, her legs were so weak. And as soon as her knees hit the floor, she folded her hands in her lap, bowed her head, and let herself fall into that quiet place in her mind, her head buzzing.

Lovely.

Even better when she heard Desmond murmur "Perfect" as he stroked a hand over her hair.

Heat flashed between her thighs, and she had to bite back a groan. This was what she strived for. This was exactly what she wanted. *Needed.*

Trembling, she watched him from beneath her lowered eyelids, not really able to see too much higher than his waist. But she could see he was laying out the rope, some of it black, some of it red. And in her head the switches were flipping at an alarming rate, her mind emptying of rational thought.

Don't fight it.

No, this was what she wanted. And she knew in some certain and inescapable way that Desmond could take her further than she'd ever been.

She had no idea how long she was there before she felt his hand taking hers, helping her rise to her feet. He pulled her in close; she could feel the heat of his tall, lean body against hers. Too good.

"I'm going to undress you now, Ava."

And he did just that, unzipping her dress and pulling it from her with unexpectedly gentle hands while she stood, shivering with need.

"Hold perfectly still," he said, his voice an authoritative whisper against her cheek.

He ran his hands lightly over her lace-covered breasts, and it was all she could do not to surge into his touch. Then he slipped her bra off, bringing his hands back to her breasts. His touch was so gentle she thought she'd lose her mind as he brushed his fingertips over her aching flesh.

Please, touch me.

But she couldn't say the words out loud, couldn't have spoken at all. She was soaking wet already, needing his hands on her, needing some sort of brutality from him for reasons she couldn't explain to herself. But he kept up that soft stroking.

She really was going to lose her mind.

When he gathered her breasts in his hands, sweeping his thumbs over her hard nipples, she moaned, her breath leaving her in a sharp, panting gasp.

"Ah, that's good, Ava. Beautiful. Off with these, now."

He moved his hands away, and she was empty, wanting, as he slid her damp lace panties over her legs, leaving her in nothing but her heels.

"Such pretty legs in your sexy high-heeled shoes," he said, running his hands over her thigh. "But they'll only get in the way."

He bent and helped her step from her shoes, steadying her with a firm hand. And she was aching all over, her mind a blur of need and sensation.

Really going to lose it the moment he puts the ropes on me.

Oh, yes. But she wanted it so badly she could hardly wait.

He led her to the bondage frame, stood behind her, and held her with one arm tight around her waist. His fingertips absolutely burned into her bare flesh.

His face was against hers, his cheek resting on her own. "I'm going to bind you, Ava. And you're going to do the breathing we've talked about. I want you to be in the moment. To slide into subspace, but you must keep part of yourself here with me, tuned in to what's happening. Do you understand?"

"Yes . . . I understand."

"I'll be right here with you. Guiding you." He paused, ran a hand over her hair. "Give it all over to me, Ava. Can you do that?"

"Yes."

"Can you, tonight?"

"Yes, Desmond. Yes!"

God, she wanted nothing more than to let it all go, to turn herself over to him. Into his hands.

His hands.

"You can do it, Ava. You *will* do it, for me." He stroked her cheek, making her tremble. "And I want to do this for you," he told her, his voice a rough whisper.

So sweet. So tender. Why did it make her want to cry?

"Come on, now, take a breath."

Desmond laid a hand on her chest, just above the rise of her breasts. His palm was warm. And as much as his every touch, even his voice, caused surges of desire to shimmer through her in long, lovely waves, his hand on her body was reassuring, calming.

She followed his voice as he instructed her to breathe, and soon her body was emptying of all weight, filling up with light, and she floated with him, her limbs going loose.

"Time to tie you up, Ava."

Oh, yes . . .

He left her for a moment, came back quickly, his hands on her, the rope slipping across her skin. And it was all a blur of sensation as the ropes lashed softly over her flesh, his low voice whispering encouragement as he bound her torso in a full harness. She wanted to see it, what she looked like with the crisscross patterns the ropes made against her flesh: across her shoulders and back, over and under her breasts, across her belly, and finally threaded between her thighs, where two lengths of the soft rope ran over her aching sex. But it was so good just to feel it, that sense of being bound. Safe. She sank deeper, her mind really going blank of everything but the feel of the ropes, his voice, the increasing sensation of being restrained as he tightened the coils around her body.

Time was lost as the ropes were pulled tighter, holding her up. When he drew her arms behind her and bound them in a tight coil that ran from her wrists to her elbows, she felt a stirring sense of completion, of truly giving herself over to him. And the familiar switch flipped in her head, opening her up inside until she was raw and aching. Entirely vulnerable. And so full of wanting she could hardly stand it.

She wanted to cry again. She wanted him to touch her. She wanted to belong to him.

Oh, yes, to be his . . .

"Beautiful," Desmond said quietly. "So damn beautiful, Ava."

She could feel his body close to hers, the cotton of his shirt against the tips of her breasts as he moved in closer.

"Where are you, Ava?"

"I'm here."

"Are you? Are you right here with me?"

He took her chin in his hand, forcing her gaze to his. His eyes were dark, burning. She shivered at the intensity there, at the way it broke through even the haze of subspace.

God, to have him touch her! To be in the ropes for him. And she wasn't even certain what the tears beginning to brim in her eyes were about, except that she wanted this so much. That it was really happening, finally. And she was grateful and afraid and still willing to go there with him.

"Do you see the people, my beautiful Ava? Do you see how they watch you? Admire you? Want you."

She blinked, saw the group standing around them. A dozen pairs of eyes on her. Her body surged with lust. With pride. She felt utterly beautiful. Desired.

"Yes, Desmond," she whispered. "I see them." She brought her gaze back to his, held it. "But mostly I see you."

"Ah, Ava. You are so damn perfect."

A wash of pleasure, of keen desire, simply knowing she pleased him. He leaned in and pressed his lips to hers, and her body tried to bow toward his, but the ropes held her fast, making her burn even more.

Yes, kiss me. Touch me.

He opened her lips with his, slipped his tongue inside, hot and sweet, and she moaned into his kiss.

He pressed deeper, his hands going around her waist, immobilizing her even further. Her head was spinning. And she was exactly as he'd wanted her, lost in the meditative trance of subspace yet right there with him: his hands, his mouth, his earthy scent. And the sweet knowledge that she was, at that moment, *his*.

Desmond's hand slid lower, between the lengths of rope wrapped around her body, between her thighs. His fingers parted the ropes pressing against her sex. And she was aching, needy, his fingers sliding into that wet, waiting heat, making her gasp.

"Ah!"

"Yes, you need it, don't you, Ava? I need it, too. I need you. To touch you. To make you come. To have you. And I will. But first, come for me. Come for your admirers. Look at them. They're adoring you, as I am."

Another brief glance through her fluttering lashes at those watching her.

Yes, for him. For them.

Then his hand was working between her thighs, his fingers plunging inside her, his thumb pressing onto her swollen clitoris. Sensation filled her, flooded her, desire building, making her go tight all over. Tight within the ropes, her clit, her nipples, throbbing and hard.

"I'm going deeper, Ava."

And he did, his fingers pushing into her sex, thrusting. Desire was a tide, hot and powerful. Her hips arched into his hand, wanting more. And he gave her more, plunging into her soaking-wet sex, faster and harder.

"Oh, please . . ."

"Please what?"

"Please let me come, Desmond."

"Come then, Ava. Come on."

Her body clenched as pleasure washed over her, surged, shafting deep inside her. She felt her sex grabbing around his thrusting fingers, desire pulsing, harder and harder, until she didn't think she could take it any longer.

"Desmond!"

It went on and on, her body shaking as the force of her climax pounded through her, drowning her.

"I have you, baby. I have you."

His arms tightened around her as she sagged into the ropes, all strength gone. Her body was still pulsing, small, orgasmic waves flowing, receding.

"That was perfect, my beautiful Ava," Desmond whispered into her hair.

Perfect. Yes, that was all she wanted: to be perfect, for him. His words still buzzing in her ears, she felt her body go limp as she let herself fall into his embrace.

Chapter Eight

HOURS PASSED, or so it seemed, with Desmond whispering to her, taking her through the breathing, checking the ropes. Holding her, bound so tightly she couldn't move, in his arms as the room, the people, faded into nonexistence. Her mind had been everywhere, floating through past and present. And she had sunk deeper and deeper, her body, her mind, releasing a little at a time, until finally she had felt that lovely sensation of letting it all go and simply *being*. She had no idea it would feel so good.

Her mind finally reconnected with the earth as though she was waking from a dream, with the sensation of Desmond holding her body firmly against his as he began to release her from the ropes.

It was a slow and sensual process, as everything had been with him, and then she was in his arms. He took her to one of the small sofas, laid her across his lap. She leaned into him, her head on his shoulder, loving the solid strength of him, his hands in her hair, on her cheeks. There was something quietly lovely about the way he was touching her, talking to her in hushed tones. She didn't know what he was saying to her. It didn't matter. What mattered was being there with him like this, the connection she felt between them.

Was she only imagining it? She couldn't figure it out now. She was too limp, too loose. And still buzzing with desire.

She squirmed in his lap, the hard ridge of his erection pushing against the soft flesh of her buttocks. Oh, she wanted him.

He stroked her cheek, his hand falling lower to caress her breast. Her nipples went hard as she pressed into his hand, moaning softly.

His voice was low, rough with desire. "I need you, Ava. Need to be inside you."

"Yes, please . . ."

He lifted her, carrying her in his arms to a small curtained alcove, one of several that surrounded the playrooms at the club. He laid her down on the high, iron four-poster bed, and she held perfectly still as she watched him strip his shirt off. His shoulders were broad, his skin pale but beautifully so. And his nipples were dark against the light sprinkling of hair across his chest. She wanted to reach out, touch them, take them one by one into her mouth. But she couldn't move.

His slacks came next, and in moments he stood naked over her, his cock erect, beautiful.

He was watching her, his gaze intent on hers, as he spread her thighs. He sheathed himself in a condom pulled from a small shelf next to the bed, and as the latex rolled down the length of his shaft she could see how rock-hard he was. Then he moved between her legs, slipped his hands under her buttocks, and in one smooth thrust he was inside her.

She cried out, her body taking him in, trembling with pleasure. And his green gaze never left hers.

When he began to move, his hands hard on her flesh, possessing her, she could barely breathe. Pleasure, intense, sharp, knifing into her body with every hard thrust of his hips, his cock driving into her.

"Desmond!"

"Yes . . ."

He was panting now, and she could see it all in his eyes. They were blazing, seeming to reach inside her. To *see* her in some new way.

"I need you, Desmond . . ."

What was she trying to tell him? She didn't quite know herself. All she knew was that sense of desperation for him to know her yearning.

"I have you, Ava." He plunged deeper, his cock moving inside her as his hand went into her hair, gripping hard.

"Yes. Have me . . . yes . . ."

One arm slid around her waist as he held her tighter. "You're mine, Ava. Mine."

Those dark green eyes, gleaming in the dim light. Beautiful. And his rigid, plunging cock, his hands on her, making her body burn.

Desire was peaking again, her sex pulsing, hot, tightening around his solid shaft. He drove deeper, and now she could hear his panting breath, could feel it warm and sweet on her face. And still his gaze never left hers, his face an expression of exquisite need, the same need she felt herself.

"You are mine, Ava," he said again, thrusting savagely, filling her, owning her.

Her ears were roaring with a pure, white heat, and when her climax hit her, it was like a wall coming down on her: heavy, over-powering. And she was drowning again, in pleasure, in the green fire of Desmond's eyes, in his groans of pleasure as he came in-side her.

"Ava!"

His hips ground into hers, hurting her. But all she wanted was to be as close to him as possible, her body still shuddering, clenching.

She could feel his cock still pulsing inside her, a steady beat of pleasure, when he wrapped his arms around her and pulled her in tight, burying his face in her hair.

Her heart was beating wildly, driven by some emotion she didn't understand. How could she feel so much with this man she'd just met? She hardly knew him.

But that was a lie. They knew each other in some deep and inexplicable way. Impossible. But true. Where he had taken her tonight, what he had given her, had shown her that.

Desmond was opening her up already. And it was beautiful and terrifying.

Her eyes welled, and she bit her lip.

Don't do it.

But she couldn't help it, the tears spilled, slid down her cheeks.

"Ava?" Desmond lifted her head, brushed her hair from her face.

"I'm sorry," she told him. She was desperate to stop crying.

He sat up, taking her with him, holding her close. "Are you alright? Did I hurt you?"

"No. I'm fine. I just . . . I don't know."

"You're crashing."

"Yes."

He was right; that's all it was. That feeling of being lost and scared, too vulnerable, that many submissives experienced after they played. Most often it was hard pain play that caused it. But for her it was being given exactly what she'd wanted, what she'd asked for. It was overwhelming, nearly unbelievable. And she was so full of gratitude and longing and some strange sort of guilt she could barely comprehend.

Stop it!

But she couldn't. The tears kept coming. Desmond held her tighter.

"It'll be alright, Ava. Come on, now. You're okay. I'm right here. I'm here with you."

Yes, he was there with her. But for how long?

She buried her face in his shoulder, willed the tears to stop. She took a breath, held it, steeling herself, and finally the tears did stop. But her heart was still flailing in her chest. She was still in a panic.

Don't get too close. Don't do it.

But it was too damn late. She'd let him in, and he'd gone deep. Deeper than he'd been inside her body. To that soft and tender place she thought she'd locked safely away a long time ago.

"Ava, stay with me."

"What? I'm here."

"No, you're not. You're closing yourself off. I can feel it."

He pulled back, looking into her eyes once more. And she couldn't escape him, not with him looking at her, right inside her.

"Ava . . . God damn it, girl."

"Desmond?" A sob escaped her. "Are you . . . you're not happy with me?"

"No, that's not it. Christ, no. You're too damn perfect. Fuck."

"I'm not. I'm not."

She didn't know what to think. But he bent his head, kissing her before she could try to make sense of what was happening. And his mouth was soft and tender on hers, giving her exactly what she needed once more. But *this* . . . this was something she hadn't even known she needed. Until now.

Desmond buried his hands in her hair. So damn soft, just like the rest of her. And her sweet mouth on his. He couldn't get enough of her: her taste, her scent, her flesh beneath his hands.

Just kiss her. Don't think.

No, he'd been thinking far too much all night, about the way she affected him. *Had* to think or he'd lose all control.

This girl . . .

But she was kissing him back, her soft tongue like silk in his mouth, and her quiet sighs and moans were making him hard again already.

Had to have her, one more time. Had to know her body.

Her mind.

Yes, talk to her. But later. Now she was all soft female flesh in his hands, melting under him, and he couldn't wait. Didn't make one damn bit of difference that he'd come only minutes before. Nothing mattered but her.

Ava.

He was in trouble with this girl.

Fuck it. He didn't care.

He pulled back and watched her face. Her blue eyes were sleepy but alive and gleaming with fire beneath the half-closed lids. Her mouth was pink, swollen from kissing. Fucking beautiful.

His chest ached.

Just have her. Do it. Have to . . .

He laid her body down, held her with one hand splayed on her stomach while he pulled another condom from the shelf. Then he rolled it over his swelling cock, keeping his gaze on her face.

She was watching him, biting her lip. He could see her breasts rise and fall as her breathing sped up. Ah, she was as eager as he was. When he slipped his hand between her thighs and found her soaking wet, he smiled. Yes, she was ready, wanting as much as he was. And her blue doll eyes were big and round, fringed in dark lashes. That innocent face. And some expression there . . . he didn't know what it was exactly. Intensity. Emotion. Almost too much.

But he had to have her.

"Ava, turn over."

He helped her shift until she was on her knees, her head bowed, resting on her outstretched arms. She was too beautiful like this. Submissive. And when he slipped his cock inside her, she was his. He felt it, that giving over, her body softening all over. Yielding to him completely.

He began to move, one hand tight on her hip, the other on her back, pressing her down. Pleasure was like some living entity, snaking its way up his cock, into his belly, his limbs. He pressed harder into her loose and willing body, every pale curve like some sort of art to him. Her quiet, whimpering cries were making him crazy, driving him on.

He bent over her, wrapping his arm around her tiny waist, pulling her tightly into his body. His heart was a hammer in his chest, breaking him apart.

Why couldn't he get close enough?

All he could do was push his cock into her, into that wet, silken flesh.

"Ava . . ." he whispered, not knowing what it was he wanted to say. Perhaps just her name.

Crazy.

She made him crazy.

She was pushing back against him now, taking him in, her pussy like heated velvet around his cock. So damn good. And her breath was coming in short, sharp little pants.

He moved a hand down between her lovely thighs, pressing his fingers against her hard clit. And in moments she was crying out, shaking, her pussy clenching around him.

"Christ, Ava . . ."

Then he was coming, hot and furious, pumping into her small body.

When it was over he pulled his cock from her, rolled onto his side, taking her with him. He was shivering. So was she. And his mind was in chaos, his heart beating like thunder.

What was it about this girl?

This was more than sex. More than the power exchange. She was really getting to him.

No.

But it was happening, whether he wanted it to or not. Even

now, with his mind a blur and his body exhausted, he couldn't escape that fact.

Ava had reached inside him somehow, gotten in deep. And there wasn't a damn thing he could do about it.

SEVEN DAYS. Seven long days in which Ava thought she'd lose her mind. Why didn't he call?

She paced her small kitchen, a cup of hot chocolate in her hands. It had been one of her favorite sources of comfort since she was a little girl, but it wasn't helping tonight. She stared out the window, watched as a bus stopped at the corner, spilled people out onto the sidewalk. Watched them scatter, everyone going in a different direction, leaving the sidewalk empty once more.

Desmond had left a message the morning after their night together at Pinnacle, saying he'd be gone most of the week on business. She hadn't heard from him since. Not a call, not a quick e-mail.

The days were hard enough, but at least she'd had work to distract her. But now, alone in her apartment, the sun going down and the sky turning a gloomy gray-tinted blue that grew darker and deeper, she could barely stand it. Could barely stand to be in her own head.

She hadn't stopped thinking about that night. The bondage. The sex. *Him*. The way he'd opened her up inside, given that to her like some sort of amazing gift. The way he'd been so incredibly tender with her when she'd crashed. The way he made her body buzz with desire simply by standing next to her, talking to her. Touching her.

But it was more than desire, lust. It was a craving to be near him, to serve him. She was truly submissive enough to want that with him, always. But there was something deeper, more powerful, driving her need for him.

How was it possible to feel so much for a man she'd known only a few weeks? And how much of what she felt stemmed from the fact that Desmond gave her more of what she'd always needed than any other dominant ever had? Her feelings seemed to go much further than mere physical need. Had she imagined their connection? Those moments of pure intensity when he gazed into her eyes?

Maybe her mother was right. She was impulsive. Illogical.

She couldn't figure it out. And now he'd disappeared. He couldn't possibly want to be with her the way she wanted, yearned, to be with him, or he'd never be able to stay away this long. She felt . . . cut off. Lost.

She'd felt the same way with Michael so often. He had met her need for submission, but his command had been overly harsh, leaving her with a sense of emptiness.

Desmond filled her up. Until he'd gone away, leaving her alone to figure out what the hell was going on between them. And all of that with Michael had been so long ago. Why was she even thinking of him? Why couldn't she seem to separate her feelings for Desmond, for what they had done together, from what had happened with Michael? And somehow her mother's voice kept getting in there, telling her she wasn't good enough.

She'd thought Desmond had taken her away from all of that. But maybe he was nothing more than a catalyst for those things she had to learn for herself, finally.

She wanted to. And even processing these thoughts was probably a move in the right direction. If only she could calm down enough to really think it through. If only he would call her!

She sipped at her cocoa, but it was too sweet on her tongue. She poured the rest into the sink, rinsed the mug, shoved her hair from her face, burying her fingers in the dense curls until it hurt.

She felt too alone with this. She wanted to talk to someone about it. She wanted to talk to him.

Screw it. She was going to call him. D/s protocol be damned. Grabbing her cell phone from the counter, she yanked the charger cord out, began to scroll for his number. When the phone rang, the familiar chiming notes startled her and she fumbled, nearly dropping the phone.

Desmond's name on the caller ID on the small screen.

Her heart fluttered, tumbled in her chest.

She took a breath, held it, blew it out, before answering.

"Hello?"

"Ava. You're there."

"Yes."

God, she couldn't speak, couldn't think. She was absolutely flooded with relief. And a little resentment, which surprised her.

"I need to talk to you."

"Okay."

"Ava? You sound . . . distant."

"You're the one who's been gone, Desmond."

Was that really her own voice, so bitter?

"Are you angry with me, Ava?" he asked quietly. "Tell me what's going on with you."

"Desmond . . ."

How could she tell him all she was feeling when she could barely figure it out herself? But yes, she was angry. She could deal with that part, at least.

"Desmond," she tried again, "I don't understand what's happening here. The other night was so . . . amazing. Am I the only one who thought so?"

"It was amazing. Incredible."

"Then why haven't I heard from you? I know, you said you had business to attend to, but not even a phone call in the evening? An e-mail?"

"I'm calling you now."

"It's been a week, Desmond."

"I know. I . . . I made sure you were okay before I took you home that night. That you'd recovered from your crash."

"I haven't recovered from it yet," she said, understanding only then it was true.

"Christ, Ava. I'm sorry. Are you alright? I should have been there. Fuck."

Real alarm in his voice. Real concern. She melted a little, as much as she wanted to stay angry with him. It seemed so much easier than this need to feel his arms around her. This need to cry.

"Ava, I'm sorry. I am. This was . . . irresponsible of me. As a dominant, I should have—"

"Are you kidding? This is what it's all about for you? Being responsible?"

"It's my job, my duty."

"Yes. But is that really all it is to you? Because if it is, I need to know now, before we go any further. If you even want to. If that was why you were calling me."

Tears filled her eyes, but she wouldn't let them fall.

"I don't know why I called. I don't know why I haven't. Damn it, Ava."

"You don't know why you called me." She shook her head, her fingers gripping the phone in her hand until it hurt. "God, Desmond. I can't . . . I can't do this. I have to go."

She flipped her cell phone shut, her body going numb.

How had she been so foolish as to think the man had any real feelings for her? It was Michael all over again: her thinking she was in love, and him loving only being in command of her.

God, is that what she'd been thinking all week?

Impossible. It was too soon, too fast.

But it was the truth.

Don't think about it.

Yes, what was the point now? She wouldn't see him again.

She knew it was for the best. After Michael, she'd promised

never to set herself up for that kind of hurt ever again. And she'd done that, protected her heart, all these years. She wasn't going to let that all go now.

Yet the tears welled, slipped down her cheeks, surprising her. She reached up, felt her damp cheek with her fingertips.

Maybe she was every bit as foolish as Michael had said. As her mother always said.

But she had to stop feeling sorry for herself. She'd done the right thing, hadn't she? She wouldn't see him again, talk to him. She would be strong. She *was* strong. Stronger than ever after that last night with Desmond, ironically enough.

Why, then, did she feel so awful?

The damn tears were still coming. She wiped them away roughly.

She went to the refrigerator and pulled out a bottle of chardonnay, poured herself a glass, went to stand at the window once more. Wicked jumped up onto the sill, bumped Ava's hand to be petted, and she stroked his soft fur absently.

The city was dark now, the streetlamps illuminating the sidewalks in amber. It looked more empty to her out there than ever. Cold. Lonely. She sipped the wine, and it was smooth and cool on her throat, but it warmed her inside after a few moments. She sipped again.

She drank the glass down fast, then a second more slowly, and was pouring another when a knock on the door made her jump. The glass slipped in her hand, crashing into the sink. Wicked took off, darting into the hallway.

She knew it was him before she even opened the door. And when she did he seemed to loom there, all dark, hard, male beauty, and something like rage in his eyes.

She realized instantly that her cheeks were still wet with tears.

She could not do this. She couldn't face his rage, whatever it was about. Her hanging up on him. She was too hurt.

She shook her head, found her voice.

"Desmond, I can't talk to you. Please go away."

"Ava."

Command in his voice, but she would not yield to it.

"No. Just go."

And as hard as it was to turn him away, she shut the door. And let the tears fall.

Chapter Nine

DESMOND POUNDED on the door.

"Ava, let me in!"

She leaned her back into the door, shaking her head mutely.

"Ava." His voice was softer now. "You have to let me in. I have to apologize to you."

"You . . . you're here to apologize?"

"Don't make me do it through the damn door."

She turned and opened it. He was still there, but whatever she'd seen in his eyes had calmed. And as he stood, watching her, his face went soft, his brows drawing together.

"Christ, Ava, I'm sorry."

Then he swept her into his arms, and she forgot for a moment to be mad, just letting him hold her, his arms tight around her, soothing her.

"God, Desmond."

"I know. I'm an ass."

"Yes, you are."

He laughed a little at that, and her body went warm and loose all over.

"Can we begin again, Ava? I've been thinking. And all of this . . . this lovely ritual that I've spent years losing myself in is the perfect distraction from anything . . . more important."

"Only because you let it be."

"Yes." He pulled back, his gaze on hers, his eyes a dark, glittering green. "But haven't you done the same? I think that's what your block is about."

"I know what it's about." She was angry again, suddenly. "It's about things that happened a long time ago. And I thought I'd let it go, but apparently not. This is . . . the bondage, the domination, is what I've sought to release me from all of that."

"But you haven't been completely released, even after what I saw happen with you the other night," he said, his voice low. "That's still to come for you. If you want to go there with me still."

His face was all hard lines once more, his jaw absolutely rigid, but she could see emotion flickering in his eyes. Had some idea what it cost him to come to her like this. To say he was sorry. To ask if she would allow him to see her.

"You're right. There was a big shift for me the other night, but there's still something missing, something unresolved. I haven't quite reached that point yet. And I want to. With you."

He smiled then, his features relaxing. And she felt it, felt at that moment they were on exactly the same page.

His hands were in her hair, and although she still felt that sense of absolute command in his touch, there was more there. Tenderness. Emotion. And when he pulled her in and kissed her his mouth was soft and sweet, just kissing her lips over and over.

When he opened her mouth with his tongue and slipped inside, she moaned quietly, unable to contain it. There was so much happening to her all at once. Her body, her mind, was reeling with sensation.

Desmond pulled away and whispered against her mouth, "I want you, Ava." His accent was heavy, his voice low, rough. "I want you now, without all the ritual, the ropes, even. Tell me what you want."

"I want you. Without the negotiations and the ropes and the formality. I just want *you*. But I need it to be hard. I still need you to take me over."

"Ah, girl . . . have I already told you how perfect you are?"

Then he was stripping her jeans off, her panties, leaving her in nothing but her soft cotton T-shirt, and pushing her into the living room, bending her over the back of her old overstuffed sofa. He came up close behind her, his still-dressed body all hard muscle against her back. Wrapping an arm around her, his fingers brushed over her wet sex. She moaned, arched into his hand. And he slid his fingers inside her.

"Christ, you're soaked. I need to be inside you."

He slipped his fingers out of her, and she held still, waiting on shaking legs, listening to the soft slip of his zipper, the tearing of a foil packet.

"Spread your legs wider, Ava. Yes, that's it."

His hand on the back of her neck, then, forcing her down, and his other hand pulling her hips toward him. She spread for him, her sex hot and aching, desire pulsing through her like one small shock after another.

"Please, Desmond. I need you."

She felt the tip of his latex-sheathed cock at her entrance, then he plunged inside. Pleasure drove into her, sharp and keen, making her clench around his rigid length. His hand was between her thighs again, his fingers teasing at her clit, rubbing, pinching, as he began to slide his cock in and out of her.

She backed into him, needing to feel the strength of him, loving even that he hadn't undressed, that he shared this basic, primal need. And he drove harder and harder, her body going weak under his.

"Tell me, Ava," he demanded, panting, "is this what you need?"

"Yes . . . to be under your hands."

He pinched her clit, hard, and pain and pleasure merged as she moaned.

"Please, Desmond . . ."

"Please what?"

"Please . . . I need more."

He thrust into her, burying deep.

"Yes . . . more . . ."

He pulled his cock out, his fingers stroking over her wet sex for a few moments before she felt the head of his cock there again. Then that lovely plunge as he thrust back into her.

"You are mine, Ava."

"Yes, yours, Desmond."

His wet fingers stroked between the cheeks of her ass, then lower, pressing at her anus. He rubbed there, his finger circling as his cock moved inside her. She backed into his hand, wanting, needing, to be filled in every way.

"Do you want it, Ava?"

"Yes!"

Then she felt the tip of his finger slip into that tight hole. Just the tip, but the sensation was exquisite, the feeling of being completely taken over carrying new currents of pleasure into her body.

"Oh . . ."

He moved his finger in and out, the merest motion, yet desire was a scalding heat, coming at her from every direction.

"Come for me, Ava," he told her.

He reached up and pushed her hair aside, and she felt his warm breath on the back of her neck for one lovely moment before he planted his mouth there. His tongue flickered over her skin, then he latched on, sucking her flesh. He pushed his finger deeper into her ass, his cock still moving inside her sex, and it was all too much: his cock, his commanding hands, his lovely, wet mouth on her skin. And the scent of him enveloping her as his body heated behind her.

Her climax came in sharp, stabbing surges, shafting into her body, his cock driving the sensation. Behind her eyes a million stars exploded, her mind losing itself in the glimmering light, then in the darkness, as she sank into the sensation, into him.

"Christ, Ava. You are fucking beautiful, my girl. I love to hear you come. To feel you come. I want you to come again."

"Yes . . . anything . . ."

He pulled his hard cock from her, his finger still in her ass, and his other hand went around her body and in between her legs. She was soaking wet, her juices running down her thighs. He moved his hand between the lips of her sex, inside her, and she shuddered, her body giving one long squeeze, nearly coming again already. And he pressed his finger ever deeper into her ass.

"Does this hurt you, Ava?"

"No. It's good . . . so good."

He added a second finger, and it slid right in.

"I think you're ready for me. You're so damn wet."

"Yes."

He slipped his fingers out of her ass.

"We need lube. Do you have any?"

"Yes."

"Go get it."

She nodded, made her way on shaking legs to her bedroom, pulled a bottle of lube from her nightstand, returned quickly to Desmond, who stood naked now and beautiful in the lamplight. His latex-sheathed erection was like some sort of homage to his desire, and hers.

He reached for her, taking the bottle from her hand, paused to kiss her mouth before turning her over the back of the sofa once more.

"Spread for me. Yes, just like that."

Then his fingers at the entrance to her ass, spreading the cool lube on, his fingers dipping inside, pushing the cool gel into her body. Then he pulled his hand away and it was the head of his cock there. She shivered.

"Breathe in, Ava. Relax."

She did as she was told, and he slipped the tip inside. Pleasure ran hot and deep in her body. She was shaking.

"Again, Ava. Long, deep breath. Good girl."

Another wave of pleasure at his words.

Good girl.

Oh, yes, she wanted to be good for him. She wanted to do everything for him.

"I'm really going in now. Relax."

He slid his cock in farther, and there was a small burning sensation. But she willed her body to go still, took him in deeper. And it was all good: his cock moving gently in her ass, his hand playing with her clit. Pleasure built, multiplied, until she couldn't tell which direction it came from. It didn't matter. All that mattered was what he made her feel: desire. Desired. As though she was his.

His.

"You feel so damn good, Ava. So good . . ." His voice was a panting breath in her ears, his male scent all around her, his body hard and strong. And in moments she was coming once more in long, shimmering waves, just falling into sensation until she could barely breathe. Her body clenched, trembled. She called his name over and over as she shook with the power of it.

She went limp against him as he cried out, came, pumping into her body, his arms tight around her.

Keeping her safe.

Making her his.

Her mind was numb, but through the fog she knew it was true: She belonged to him. And she would never be the same again.

～

HE STAYED WITH HER all through the weekend. She could hardly believe it was happening. But when she'd woken in the early mornings, dawn sifting soft and gray through the curtains, he was there beside her, his sleeping body sleek and graceful, full of contained power.

It was Sunday now, the late afternoon turning to dusk. They were in bed again, or still, she couldn't be sure. They'd gotten up to eat, to shower, a few times. But somehow they always ended up naked and twined together, his big body thrusting into hers, coming together in a frenzy of heat and need. And the power play was more subtle, less structured, just him holding her down in that way he had that made it clear he was in command, a few quiet words letting her know she belonged to him.

Lovely.

It was all so good she didn't want to question it. But the questions were there, at the edge of her mind. The sex was amazing, and she felt so close to him, but still . . . there was something missing. Because although they'd opened up to each other physically, he still held something back from her. They'd talked about her dreams of being a photographer, her family, his travels, his work, everything but his past. And she felt instinctively that he was hiding something from her, something deeply personal. Something crucial.

She sat up, pushing the pillows behind her, and watched him. His eyes were closed, his breathing shallow, even. In the dim light she visually traced the hard lines of his jaw, his cheekbones, over his impossibly lush mouth. So beautiful. She reached out and touched one fingertip to the rough hair of his goatee, then his lips, and his eyes fluttered open. He smiled.

"What are you doing there, my girl?" His accent was heavy, his voice low and rough with sleep.

"I'm thinking."

"Are you, now? What about?" He grabbed her hand, pulled it to his lips, and laid a soft kiss across her knuckles.

"You're trying to distract me, Desmond."

"Am I?"

"Yes, and as usual you're doing a very good job of it."

"As usual?" He paused, his dark brows drawing together.

"Desmond . . ." She needed to say something; she just didn't know how to go about it. "This weekend has been wonderful. And I feel . . . I feel so close to you. Is that . . . I don't know if you want to hear that."

His gaze shifted to their joined hands as he wrapped his fingers around hers.

"I do think we've become closer. You've opened yourself to me completely. But this was our goal, wasn't it?"

She pulled her hand away. "God, Desmond. You're such a man. It's not all about goals. It's about . . . how I feel. How *we* feel. Don't make me feel like a complete idiot here."

"Ava. You're not an idiot." His green gaze was on hers again. "I'm trying to understand you."

"Tell me I am not the only one here who's feeling something," she said softly, her heart pounding.

He was quiet for an endless span of moments. "No," he said finally. "You're not the only one."

Her heart wanted to soar, but she couldn't let it happen. "Then tell me what you're hiding from me. Tell me what it is you hold back from me."

"Ava . . ." He ran a hand through his dark hair. "There are some things I keep to myself. Things I don't discuss with anyone."

"Then we can't go any further, Desmond. I can't do it. I've opened too much to you, made myself too vulnerable, not to get the same back from you."

Panic knotted her stomach as she said it, but she couldn't stand to be with him and feel this terrible sense that they would never truly connect on the deepest levels. She felt too much for him already to be denied that.

He shook his head. "Fuck, Ava. I don't know if I can."

Tears flooded her eyes, and she wiped them with the back of her hand. Pain shot through her stomach. "Okay. Okay."

She got up, walked across the room, pulled her silk robe from the hook on her closet door, and wrapped it around herself. She couldn't be naked with him now. Couldn't be that vulnerable with him.

"Ava."

He was next to her, taking her into his arms. She tried to pull away, but he held fast.

"Desmond. Please."

"Ava . . . I'll do it. I'll tell you. But I have to . . . I have to do it in my own way. I need you to come with me, back to my place." His eyes were dark, wild.

"What?"

"Just say you'll do it. Say you'll come with me."

She watched his face, his features drawn, his eyes shadowed with emotion, making her chest ache. She couldn't refuse him anything.

"Alright. I'll come."

Chapter Ten

IT HAD BEEN an endless drive through the city and across the bridge into Sausalito, but finally Desmond turned onto his street, pulled his car into the driveway. His stomach was a solid ball of dread. Dread at having to tell her about those things in his past he'd kept safely locked away. Dread at the thought of her walking away if he didn't. And maybe walking away if he did, if she knew the truth about him.

He was screwed either way. But he had to do this. He understood that he owed her that much. He understood what he'd lost before by being so damn stubborn about keeping his secrets. Time to change that, maybe.

Life was about lessons; he knew that. And he supposed this was a time when he was meant to learn something. About himself. About Ava. About being with her. That didn't mean it was going to be easy.

She'd been absolutely silent on the drive, her body tense, as if waiting for a blow. He felt that same strain himself.

He parked, helped her from the car, led her into the house, and shut the door behind them, flicking on the light in the entryway.

"What now, Desmond?"

He looked at her, those enormous blue eyes as sweet as ever but shadowed with concern. That babymouth lush and sad. He couldn't bear to see her like this.

She was so damn beautiful.

Just do it.

"Come with me, Ava."

He took her hand and led her through the house to his bedroom. He needed to get her in there. Needed to strip her down before he could talk to her.

His stomach was tied in a hard knot. He did not want to do this.

Have to.

He stopped at the foot of his big bed, and Ava was watching him carefully. He stroked a hand over her cheek, down her jawline. "I need to tie you up," he whispered to her.

Her head fell back a little and her eyes fluttered shut for a moment, an expression of pure yielding. In the pale moonlight he could just make out the translucent skin of her lids, her long lashes, wanted to touch the fragile flesh there.

"Ava, do you know how hard this is for me?"

"Yes. I think I do."

"Then you'll forgive me for how I must do it. I understand that I need more from you than a reflection of my own power. I'm not happy to admit to myself, or to you, that too much of the power exchange all these years has been about ego for me. About facilitating my own escape and need for control. And I am not objectifying you now, I swear it. But this is the only way I feel . . . safe enough."

She nodded, and he dropped his hand, stroked the soft skin of her neck, before he began to undress her.

She was quiet, standing there, letting him strip her. Yes, just like a doll, so still, so utterly pretty with her wild blond curls, her flawless skin. Soon he had her naked, and he went to the rack and

pulled several lengths of plain white rope from it, brought it all
back to the bed. The air was still, night closing in beyond the windows. He didn't mind that it was almost dark; he wanted the
anonymity of it. The darkness and the silence enveloped them as
he began the ritual of the ropes, weaving them into a simple pattern over the lovely curves of her body: over her shoulders, between her breasts, around her slender torso. He took a second,
shorter, length of rope and bound her wrists in front of her.

It was enough. He needed the symbol of the binding more than
anything. Wasn't that what it was truly about, anyway? And she
was so beautiful in her surrender, simply waiting, the ropes making her appear helpless. But he had come to know the strength of
her. The fire. And he loved how it contrasted with that inherent air
of innocence. With the way she gave herself over to him. He loved
the way she looked, that sweet face. The way she moved with such
grace. He loved . . .

What the hell was he thinking?

His hands clenched, the nails biting into his palms.

"Desmond?" she whispered.

"Shh." He forced his fingers to uncurl, his mind to focus.

Too much now. Just tell her what she wants to know.

He took her in his arms then, and laid her back on the bed
against the pillows. She was warm and pliant beneath his hands.
He didn't want to let her go. He could bury himself in her soft
flesh and she wouldn't protest. But he stepped back.

"I'm going to tell you, Ava. I'm going to tell you what I've not
spoken about to anyone in years. And when I'm done you might
understand why I have to do it this way. I lost my last relationship
because I held my secrets so close. That was ten years ago. And
now I'm going to tell you. But once you've heard it, you may decide to get up and leave." He saw her start to shake her head. "No,
don't say anything until I'm done."

He took a long breath in, let it out slowly, and began to pace.

"I had a sister." A sharp pain in his chest, making him draw another breath. "I don't talk about her. But she's the reason why I feel this sense of responsibility. This hyperawareness of being responsible for . . . everyone. Everything. But in particular those under my command. This is why I seek it, why I operate the way I do. It doesn't help, the knowing." He stopped, not daring to do more than glance at Ava's bound body, so pale against the dark bedcover. "Her name was Nessie, and she was three years younger than me. She was . . . she was a pretty girl. Smart. Funny. She was . . . my responsibility. And it was my fault that she died, Ava. I'll be honest with you about that."

"Desmond . . ."

"No, it's true. She drowned, right in front of me, and I let it happen. We were at the lake, my family. We went every summer." He ran a hand through his hair, clamped it hard at the back of his neck. "She was only twelve. I thought she was playing around. But she went down and she didn't come back up. By the time I figured it out, went in after her, it was too late. Too damn late."

Nearly impossible to get the words out; they burned at the back of his throat.

"Oh, Desmond. I'm so sorry."

There were tears in her voice. He couldn't stand to hear her like this.

"No, don't be sorry for me. I should have done something. I should have fucking saved her." Pain in his gut as it all came back, slammed into him like a wall. He bent his head, gripped his neck harder. "Fuck."

"Desmond, let me out of the ropes," Ava said quietly.

"Not yet."

"Desmond, please."

"It doesn't matter, you know, how many people tell me it's not my fault. I know damn well and good it is. Fault lies every bit as much in failing to do what's right as in doing something with wrong intention."

"That's not true!"

"Oh, it is."

"Let me out of the ropes," Ava said again, her voice low.

"Fuck. Ava." He blew out a long breath, looked at her, saw her gaze steady on his face. Saw the strength there.

He had to do it. He couldn't keep her bound against her will. That wasn't how this worked. And the words were out already. The hideous truth.

He went to her, and she was passive beneath his hands as he untied her wrists, then pulled the harness apart. The moment the last rope dropped away from her body her arms wound around his neck, the sweet scent of her enveloping him.

"Desmond!" Ava pressed her face into his chest, felt his heart thundering beneath her cheek, which was wet with tears. "I'm sorry. So sorry that you've believed this about yourself all these years." She pulled back to look at him. He looked absolutely stunned. Her heart hurt for him, a heavy weight in her chest. "I understand how you must feel. I'm trying to, at least. But it wasn't your fault. You can't be responsible for everything."

"Can't I? I've tried to be."

She reached up, stroked a lock of hair from his face. He seemed surprised.

"I'm glad you told me. I needed to know what drives you. I needed to be let inside."

"And I needed to tell you. But does it really explain anything? Because it doesn't to me."

"It explains why your sense of absolute control goes so far. Too far, Desmond."

She saw his jaw clench.

"It can't ever go too far."

"You're wrong. It goes too far when it gets in the way of you having a life."

"I have a life. I have everything I need."

How was it he wouldn't let her break through, even now?

"Desmond." She took his face in her hands, her gaze hard on

his. "Don't do it. Don't shut yourself away from me again. It's too late. I know." She felt desperate that he see the truth of it. New tears stung her eyes, blurring her vision. She was afraid. Angry. "Desmond . . ."

"Fuck, don't cry, Ava." He pulled her roughly into his arms. "God damn it, girl."

Then he was kissing her, hard kisses that seemed to reach down inside her. And she knew she loved him, that he loved her, whether either of them were ready to admit it or not. She was almost too afraid to allow it to happen.

Almost, but not quite.

A thousand old thoughts and memories wanted to flash through her mind, through the sheer terror of being in love, of taking that risk with her heart: her mother's censorious voice, Michael's hurtful words. But she pushed it all away, let herself melt into Desmond's arms, into his kisses.

In moments his clothes were off, and she felt the now-familiar crush of his warm, solid flesh against hers. He pressed her down onto the bed, his hands more tender than ever before, and yet she still felt his command as he covered her body with his. His weight was sweet on her, his thighs strong as he used them to part hers. And she was melting beneath his touch, her chest aching with need and unspoken love.

As he drove into her, solid flesh into pure, wet heat, she wrapped herself around him. "Desmond," she gasped.

"Ava . . ."

"Be with me."

"I'm right here."

His hands tightened on her flesh, his fingers digging in as he plunged into her, over and over, pleasure like liquid fire burning pure and sweet in her veins.

And they came together, crying out, a tangle of heat and desire, and the fear of losing it all winding through her, magnifying every sensation.

She had never wanted anything more than to be with this man. *Desmond.*

When it was over they lay together, damp skin and panting breath. And she was as afraid as she'd ever been in her life.

But he was there with her.

It would have to be enough for now.

IT WAS EARLY STILL when Desmond woke her with a flurry of soft kisses over her cheeks.

"I have to go, Ava. I have a business meeting. But I want you to stay here. Can you do that? Wait for me here? I know you have a job. Can you call in? I'll be only a few hours."

"Yes. I can stay."

"Sleep, then. Help yourself to anything in the house you might need."

She nodded, and he smiled at her, so ruggedly beautiful in the gray morning light. She reached out, touched his cheek. "Desmond . . ."

"Yes?"

"Kiss me."

He leaned in and pressed his lips to hers, smelling of soap and tasting of toothpaste. A long, sinuous shiver ran through her.

He pulled away. "I have to go. I'll be back as soon as I can."

Then he was gone, and she drifted back to sleep in his big bed, her face curled into his pillow, taking in the scent of him.

When she woke again the fog still lingered outside the windows, but she knew she'd slept at least another hour. She felt rested. Wonderful.

The air was a bit chilly when she got out of bed, her feet hitting the cool wood floor. She found Desmond's discarded shirt on a chair, pulled it over her head. His scent surrounded her, and she breathed deeply, wanting to take some of him into her lungs, to hold him there.

She would have to let him know she loved him. But not yet. For now it was some sort of delicious secret.

She looked around the room: his bedroom. She'd been there before but never had the chance to explore. The dark wood of the big bed was beautifully carved, the posts at least eight feet high. The rest of the furnishings were similar in style: all dark, masculine pieces, mostly imports, which seemed to fit him somehow. The fabrics were all earth tones, to match the chocolate-brown suede on the bed, utterly masculine. And then there was the enormous bondage frame, tall and imposing, flanked by the racks of colored ropes. She walked over to it, swept her hands along the silken wood. A small shiver of need ran through her simply from looking at the ropes. But her need for him went far beyond that now.

Moving across the room, she went into the bathroom. Here it was all sleek stone finishes and more soothing neutral colors: sandstone, gray, taupe. The mirror, framed in heavy bronze, showed her reflection. Her cheeks were flushed, her eyes glossy, her hair a wild mass of curls. She leaned in closer, smiled to herself, loving how her mouth looked swollen from Desmond's hard kisses. Felt her sex go wet simply thinking about his mouth on hers.

She loved seeing his things here: his wooden-handled hairbrush, his soap in its stone dish. She picked the bar up, smelled it. It was dark and earthy, like him. Putting it back, she opened a drawer built into the sink vanity, found a tube of toothpaste, lifted it to her face, and breathed it in. Ah, yes, that minty fragrance, that and the soap, were so wonderfully familiar to her, his morning scent.

Desmond.

She missed him. His touch. His presence.

He would be back soon.

She put the toothpaste down and turned on the shower, stripped the cotton shirt off, and stepped under the water, letting the heat beat down on her skin. More of his soap in the shower, and she washed herself in it, letting the suds linger on her body. It was like having him all over her skin. She found his shaving cream, sprayed it into her hands. Ah, yes, that was *him*, that and the soap together. It made her feel closer to him, almost as though he was there with her.

A sharp pang of craving.

Desmond.

She should be ready for him when he came home.

She rinsed, shut off the water, and stepped out, drying herself with a towel. The sensation of the thick, soft terry cloth on her skin was almost too much for her. She needed it to be him, his touch on her flesh. Needed to feel him close.

Why couldn't she think of anything else?

Because she was in love with him.

Lovely.

Excruciating.

She smiled at her reflection one last time before making her way back into the bedroom. And found Desmond standing there. He opened his arms, and she went into them, naked, the wool of his trousers scratching her skin a little. But it was *him,* Desmond, his arms solid around her as he drew her to the bed.

Oh, yes, she loved him. But there would be plenty of time to tell him later. Now all that mattered was being with him, the feel of his body against hers, then in hers.

Everything was nearly perfect.

HE WAS FALLING. Into the darkness, deeper and deeper. The water rushed past him, like a thundering storm, like a waterfall, except that it was his body surging downward, down to where there was no air, no light.

Nessie was down there.

He tried to swim, his arms and legs moving against the current, which was thick as mud.

Had to get to her.

Nessie.

The mud solidified, and he moved ever more slowly, creeping now. His heart was a hammer in his chest, hard and hurting. He couldn't breathe.

He had to find her.

Nessie.

Solid now, it was like trying to move through a concrete wall. And his lungs were burning.

He had to save her!

Nessie!

Ava!

When had it become her? But it didn't matter. What mattered was that he couldn't do it, damn it. Again. He couldn't save her. He couldn't breathe. And suddenly the water opened up, sucking him down into the dark, into that lost, empty place. And he couldn't fight it, though he tried, his lungs, his arms and legs burning with effort.

He couldn't do it.

Damn it!

Ava!

Desmond woke with a start, his face damp with sweat, his pulse thundering in his veins.

Ava.

He turned to find her. She lay next to him on her stomach, the bedcovers kicked off, her sleeping body all lovely curves in the silver moonlight.

Just calm down. She's right here.

It had been three weeks since Desmond had told Ava his secret, and she was still there with him. Part of him continued to be amazed.

She'd gone to work every day, home to check on Wicked, but they'd spent every night together and every moment of the weekends. And they'd begun to do some "normal" things: going to dinner, to lunch, to see a movie. Their outings never lasted long, though; they couldn't keep their hands off each other for more than a few hours.

He'd bound her again and again, at home, at Pinnacle, loving the way she looked in the ropes, the way she yielded to him. Loving her response to being bound in front of a crowd, how it made her glow, as though the energy of all who watched was reflected in her body. But he didn't need the ropes to be with her.

When was the last time he'd been with a woman and not needed them? When had he ever had "normal"? It had never really worked with Lara, although he'd tried. That was part of what had ended the relationship, and he'd since realized he couldn't be with a woman while denying his desires.

He thought he'd understood that, anyway. Until Ava had made him see that as long as he kept any part of himself cut off he wasn't being true to who he was.

He'd run far too long like a coward from his past.

It was a relief simply to have her know. To know and not judge him, even if he still judged himself. He wasn't sure he'd ever be able to get past that. Maybe, with Ava, he'd find a way to.

It had been years since he'd let himself depend on another person for anything; he hadn't done that his entire adult life. And now he had allowed himself to hand over to Ava the key to his redemption.

How was it that with her, redemption seemed possible?

His gaze wandered over her bare flesh, her hair wild and drifting over the pillows. He reached out, took a curling tendril between his fingers, stroked the softness, that finely spun golden silk.

His gut tightened. He wanted to touch her. To take her in his arms. He needed to do it.

Needed to.

He reached for her, his fingers anticipating the heat of her body. His heart a wrenching weight in his chest suddenly, pulling into a hard, complicated knot.

He loved her.

Christ and God damn it.

He yanked his hand back, shook his head at his own folly. How the hell had he allowed this to happen?

The knot in his chest went hot, became as solid as the water in his dream, heavy, holding him down.

Cannot let this happen.

No. But it was too late, wasn't it?

He flipped the covers back and got out of bed, went into the bathroom, shutting the door behind him. He turned on the light, saw his image in the mirror, pale and drawn.

He couldn't calm down.

Turning on the faucet, he splashed his face with cold water over and over.

She's just a woman. Nothing to be afraid of.

But that was a lie. The question was, what was he going to do now? Because he couldn't allow this to continue.

He could not love her.

He did love her.

Fuck.

He reached into the shower and blasted the hot water, showered as quickly and as quietly as he could. His head was a buzzing cacophony of voices.

I love her.

I cannot love her. I can't love anyone.

Need to get away. Just get away.

Creeping back into the bedroom, he pulled clothes from the closet unseeing, got dressed. Scribbled a note and left it on the dresser. And with his heart going as numb as his head, he opened the front door, pulled it shut behind him. He got into his car and drove off, the crescent moon shining onto the stark, cold water of the San Francisco Bay, the stars glittering as hard as flint in the black sky.

Chapter Eleven

AVA STRETCHED, keeping her eyes shut against the morning light. It was Thursday, and she had to go to work. Why hadn't Desmond woken her? Maybe it was still early.

Opening her eyes, she turned onto her side, but he wasn't there. He must be up already. But there was no familiar scent of coffee in the air, no sound of the shower running. No sense of his presence nearby.

She sat up, looked around the room, felt the emptiness of it. And saw the small folded rectangle of paper with her name on it sitting on his dresser.

It was cold in the room as she walked across the wood floor, chilling her bare feet. She took the note back to bed with her, pulled the covers up to her chest before unfolding the small, forbidding bit of paper and reading it. His handwriting was neat, precise.

Ava—
I received a message early this morning and had to leave on business. I won't be back for several days, at least. I can't

be certain. Please lock the door when you go. I've left the
gate open so you can get your car out.

Desmond

She shivered all over.

What was going on? His note was so flat, so cold. But she
knew. Get her car out. The message was clear: Get out.

It didn't feel like much at first, knowing it was over. Shock,
maybe? But in moments she was shivering all over, and not with
the cold morning air. No, this came from somewhere deep inside
her body. It was more than his sudden disappearance, the terse-
ness of his note. It was an emptiness that went beyond the lonely
house. It was a certainty in her heart.

*So this is how it ends. Before we even really had a chance to do
more than begin.*

Shaking her head, she found her clothes, slipped into them, as
though the fabric would somehow protect her. But it didn't help.

Desmond.

It hurt, even thinking his name, as the shock wore off. Seeing
his things all around her. Knowing he was gone.

She didn't know what to do. Wait for him, try to talk to him?
But if Desmond had wanted to talk he would be there now. He
would have made some reference to when he'd be back, when
he'd get in touch with her.

She spotted his watch on the dresser, a platinum Rolex. Reaching out, she touched it, running her fingertips over the smooth
metal. Tears gathered behind her eyes. She wanted to let them fall,
but she couldn't do it. She bit her lip, hard, harder, until she tasted
blood.

Desmond, why?

Because he was too damn caught up in his past hurts to let himself love her. To be loved by her. She hadn't said anything, but
surely he had to know!

Anger simmered, hot and furious in her veins. And she was

shaking with it. He was gone. Gone! Right when she'd started to get it. To feel her own strength. To feel sure about what she wanted. To know that what she wanted was right. The bondage. The exotic sex. When she'd finally come to understand that perhaps she was good enough just as she was. But more than that. She had come to understand that she wanted to find love. And she'd thought she had, with him.

God damn him!

Her fingers tightened around the watch, until it bit into her skin, cold and hard. She drew her arm back and hurled it across the room. It hit the floor, a hard thump, no louder than her pounding heart.

A small sob escaped her and she clamped her lips together.

Yes, cold and hard. Like Desmond. Or like he pretended to be. Because if that was true, he wouldn't have felt enough to make him leave like this.

She shook her head, bit her lip once more against the tears that burned, wanting to spill over.

Why did she always want to cry when she was mad? When she was hurt? Enough with the damn tears!

Desmond.

She wasn't going to allow him to make her feel like this. Worthless. That was her sad old story, and she was fucking over it. She was better than that. She'd finally come to know that, deep inside, where it counted. Too bad Desmond couldn't see it, too.

His loss.

No, who was she kidding? She'd lost every bit as much as he had. And she couldn't stand it.

She could not stand it.

The tears scalded her eyes, burning her, but she swallowed them back once more, as hard as she could. She had to grip the edge of the dresser, her legs were shaking so hard.

What was all of this self-realization worth if she ended up like this all over again? With nothing. Nothing more than this absolute emptiness. With this pain in her heart that threatened to take her over, devour her.

Empty.

Aching.

Nothing.

Desmond.

She bent her head until her face pressed against the wood of the dresser, the edge biting into her cheek, and let the pain wash over her, let the tears fall. Only this time, she was crying as much for the man she loved as she was for herself.

Sunday morning Ava woke to the insistent ringing of the telephone. She sat up in bed, rubbed her eyes, peered half-blind with sleep at the caller ID.

Marina.

She picked it up.

"Hello?"

"Ava, there you are. I'm glad I reached you."

"I'm here. Is everything okay?"

"You tell me," Marina said.

"What do you mean?"

"Did you know Desmond was at Pinnacle last night?"

A sharp jab in her chest, burning, aching.

"He doesn't need my permission to do whatever he wants," she said quietly.

"Come on, Ava. I have some idea of what's been going on between you two. I introduce you two and you practically disappear, for more than a month. The few times I've seen you together at Pinnacle you're in your own little world, you and Desmond. Something important has been happening between you."

"Yes."

"So, why weren't you with him last night?"

"Because he doesn't want me to be."

"I don't believe that."

Ava brushed her hair from her face, burying her fingers in it, pulling tight. "No. I don't really believe it, either."

"Ava, tell me what's going on."

"He just . . . he got up and left me the other morning. Everything was going great. Better than great. We were . . . we'd gotten so close. Confided in each other. And then he was just . . . gone."

Marina was quiet a moment. Then, "You know, men can be idiots sometimes."

"Yes!"

"Well, that explains his odd behavior. Although I should add that he wasn't with anyone last night; he didn't play any of the girls. He sat in a chair all night, brooding. He would barely even talk to me. So, tell me, what do you intend to do about it?"

"What can I do? He left, Marina. He made his decision."

"He made a foolish decision."

"Maybe. That doesn't change anything."

"I've never seen Desmond look at anyone the way he looks at you, Ava."

"And?"

"And I don't think you should just let him go. He's been alone too long."

"And you haven't?"

Another long pause in which Ava had time to regret her words.

"We're talking about you and Desmond," Marina said quietly.

"Yes, of course. I'm sorry, Marina."

"No. Don't be. I have . . . my issues. Which makes me all the more certain that you can't simply let this go."

"I don't want to. I want to be with him. God, Marina, if he only knew how much!"

Her throat was so damn tight she could barely get the words out.

"Tell him," Marina said fiercely. "Tell him how you feel."

"Do you really think it'll help? He's so shut down."

"Do you love him, Ava?"

"Yes!"

The ache in her heart was a palpable thing, the pain in her chest threatening to choke her. She swallowed, hard.

"Isn't that worth a try? Love is so precious." Marina's voice broke. "Too precious to waste."

"Marina? Are you okay?"

"Maybe not. But you can be."

Could she be? It didn't feel like it. But she didn't want to run anymore. She had to be brave sometime. Had to face what she feared most: rejection.

"I . . . I don't know where to start, Marina. What do I say to him?"

"You'll figure it out. I know you will."

If only Ava was as sure. But it felt good to know someone had confidence in her. Maybe it was time to have confidence in herself.

She would do it: find him, talk to him. She had to try.

She was damn tired of allowing life to pass her by. And this was too important. What was more important than love?

"I'll do it. I'll talk to him."

"I'm glad. For you both."

Ava sighed, tangling her fingers in her hair. "There are no guarantees, Marina."

"No. That's the beautiful and terrifying part, isn't it?"

Terrifying, yes. The beauty would come only if she was able to get through to him. Only if he could love her.

Did he love her? She'd thought he did. She was about to find out. She didn't want to think about what she'd do if he didn't.

DESMOND TAPPED his fingers on the edge of his keyboard, trying to focus on the computer screen. But the words blurred together; nothing made sense.

Nothing had made sense to him since he'd walked out on Ava.

Not even why he'd left her like that. It had seemed so clear at the time; he'd *needed* to go. Even if he felt like an ass for the way he'd done it. An ass and a coward.

Christ.

She'd hate him. She'd have every right to. And he couldn't stand it.

He loved her.

Fuck.

The idea made him break out in a cold sweat.

But he couldn't have stayed. Couldn't have led her to believe she could count on him, rely on him, in any sort of all-encompassing fashion. He'd only let her down eventually. And he could not live with that. No, better to live with this searing pain that thundered in his chest night and day. The pain of knowing what he'd given up.

A dream image of Nessie flashed through his mind: her long, dark hair, her pale, staring eyes. Her sweet face expressionless. Lifeless.

That was what happened when he loved someone and failed in his duty to them.

He should never have let this attachment to Ava happen. But it had felt so damn good . . .

Ava . . .

No, don't think about her.

Do not think about her.

A sharp knock at his office door. Must be a delivery. But he wasn't expecting anything. He got up, ran a hand over his unshaven face, the stubble scraping his palm. Another long rap on the door.

"Alright, I'm coming. Just hold on."

He yanked the door open. And found Ava standing there.

Her blue eyes were enormous, glittering with hurt. And with anger. He took a step back before he realized what he was doing.

"I've been waiting, Desmond. Only you never came. You never called."

"Ava . . . I didn't mean to—"

"No, don't start making excuses. I don't want to hear it. All I want are the *reasons* why you did this to me. I understand your need for control. I understand you have pain in your past that drives your actions. But I never expected you to be . . ." She paused, her voice breaking. "I never expected you to be cruel."

Christ, her voice, her accusations, which were all too true, went through him like a knife in his chest.

"No. You're right. I have been cruel. I'm sorry, Ava."

"Well, that's a start, anyway."

He realized then they were still standing in the doorway, that it had started to rain outside, just a fine mist but wet and cold.

"Ava, will you come in? Talk to me?"

"You want to talk, Desmond? That's good. Because I'm not leaving until I get some answers."

Oh, she was angry. But she stepped into his office. He reached to take her coat from her shoulders, but she shrugged him off.

"I don't know that I'll be staying that long."

So much fire in her. One of the things he loved about her.

Don't think about that now.

But what else could he think of, with her standing before him, so angry and so fucking beautiful it broke his heart even to look at her.

You cannot have her. Just apologize. Do what you can to repair the damage.

"Ava, I'm sorry. You deserve better treatment."

"Yes, I do. But I love you anyway, Desmond."

Her eyes were absolutely blazing.

His heart hitched. He couldn't breathe for a moment.

"You love me?"

She took a step toward him. He could smell her perfume,

could see the tears trembling in her eyes. Fucking awful. So damn beautiful.

"Yes, I love you. And you love me. Don't try to tell me any different."

He bowed his head; it suddenly felt too heavy to hold up. "It's true," he said quietly. "I do love you, Ava."

"Then explain this to me. Explain how you could leave me like you did."

So much pain in her voice, and he felt like hell. He raised his gaze to hers, saw the tears pooled against that brilliant blue, like the clear water in a summer lake.

His chest knotted, twisted.

"I had to. I can't . . . I can't be responsible for you. For anyone. Not to that extent. One night, a few weeks of play, is one thing. But this . . . I can't do this."

"Desmond, that's bullshit. That's an excuse you use to run." She reached into her hair, her fingers gripping the golden curls. "God damn it, Desmond! You can't use that excuse forever. You can't use it with me. Just tell me what's really going on. Talk to me. Can't you talk to me, Desmond?"

"I did. I told you about Nessie."

"Yes, but that's only the beginning, isn't it? She's why you won't allow yourself to love anyone."

"I can't!"

"You won't."

"Damn it, Ava, it's more complicated than that! I cannot make any promises to anyone, promises I can't possibly keep."

"Is that what you think? That you're incapable?"

"Yes. That is exactly what I think. What I know. If I can't save the people I love, then I don't deserve to love anyone."

"I don't need saving, Desmond. I just need you to love me."

He shook his head. "It's never that simple."

"Stop it! Stop trying to convince me you're such a terrible

person. You may be damaged, Desmond, but you are capable of getting over it. You're just afraid to. All of this stuff, the power play, the need for control, it's all driven by your fears. And it may have worked well enough when you were just . . . playing with people. But it doesn't work once your heart is involved, does it?"

He took another step back, buried both hands in his hair. She was right. "Ava, how can you love me, then? How can you love such a coward?"

She saw the pain on his face. His eyes were a dull green glow beneath his lowered lids. And she hurt for him as much as she did for herself. Reaching out, she stroked her fingers over his cheek. He lifted his head, his gaze meeting hers.

She said softly, "I just do. That's the thing about love. It's that powerful, Desmond."

"You're stronger than I am, Ava, do you know that?"

He covered her hand in his, pressed it to his cheek. Then he drew her into his arms, his hands rough on her. He pulled her in tight, until she was pressed so close to his body she could feel his heart pounding in his chest.

"I've been a fool, Ava."

"I was trying to tell you exactly that," she said, laughing even as the tears spilled onto her cheeks.

"Christ, what would I do without you?"

"You don't have to do without me."

He pulled back, his gaze hard on hers, his eyes blazing. "I love you, Ava."

Her heart surged, filled, until she felt it might burst from her body. "I love you, Desmond."

He kissed her then, his mouth a soft press at first. She opened to him, sighed into his mouth as he parted her lips, pressed deeper, until he was kissing her so hard she was breathless, shaking.

He pulled away finally. "I'm so damn sorry."

"I know."

"I've carried these ideas with me for so long. I've been convinced that anyone I cared about was in danger somehow."

"It's not true. The only way you can really protect anyone is by loving them. It's taken me a long time to understand that myself, because of my own past. Love doesn't have to be perfect. And neither do you. Thank God, because I'm hardly perfect myself."

"Ah, you are to me."

He leaned in, brushed a kiss across her mouth. Lovely. Sweet. Perfect.

"Desmond, I have my own history, my own issues. And being with you has helped me work through some of it. I mean, it's been this long process, and I thought I'd already come through it. And then you pushed through those blocks that were holding me back during bondage play, and everything really opened up inside me. My Pandora's box, I suppose. And it hasn't been too bad, facing the old stuff, dealing with it. Because I love you. Because you love me. That's the last piece of the puzzle."

"Ah, Ava. Come with me. I need to make love to you in my bed. I need it to be soft and beautiful and sweet. Like you, my Ava. My girl."

She nodded, and he took her by the hand, led her upstairs. Outside, the rain fell, splattering the windows. The sky was a pale, pearly gray. And the sun was diffused, softened, as it shone through the glass.

They reached his bedroom, and he undressed her slowly, laying tender kisses on her skin as he removed each piece of clothing. And with every kiss she felt loved, cherished, adored.

Finally she was naked, and he shed his own clothes quickly. His arms went around her waist, tightened, and the press of bare skin to bare skin was exquisite. She breathed in his scent, as dark as the earth, that pure and clean. His mouth came down on hers once more, his kiss almost brutal but so full of emotion it made her want to cry again. But this time it was joy welling up inside her, chasing the pain away.

He lifted her, laid her on the bed, her body sinking into the down ticking, his body covering hers. She was wet, needy. But everything seemed to be happening in slow motion, as if in a dream, and she was in no hurry for it to be over.

His hands roamed over her skin: touching that sensitive hollow at her throat, her shoulders, then her breasts. His touch was as sure as ever but more tender than before. And she felt his love in every caress, even as his fingers tightened on her nipples. Pleasure was a languid current moving through her, taking her higher and higher. When he lowered his head over her stomach, his tongue stroking downward in long, lazy arcs, the anticipation was almost too much to bear yet too good to make him stop, to beg for him to hurry. She let her legs fall open for him. Then he was there with his warm mouth, licking at her sex, her swollen clitoris, his hands, his lips, and his tongue creating a steady pulse-beat of sensation moving through her like music. And in moments she was coming, crying out his name.

He made his way back up her body in a trail of hot, lovely kisses, until he was poised over her.

"I want you, Ava. Just like this. I want to be inside you. I need to be a part of you."

"Yes, Desmond . . . I don't need anything but you."

She felt the tip of his cock poised at the entrance to her body. He kept his gaze on hers as he pushed inside. A long shudder of pleasure made her moan, then he was deep inside her, his hips moving. Desire built and, with it, emotion. She watched his face, his hard features softened by pleasure. By love.

"I love you, Desmond," she whispered as he moved deeper, pushing sensation into her body.

"I love you, my Ava. My beautiful Ava."

His hand came up and his fingers curled under her jaw as he thrust, over and over, a slow, rocking rhythm. Inside her body a fire was building, blazing, until she came in a dazzling flash, so intense it hurt.

"Desmond!"

He cried out, tensed all over, came with her, his gaze on hers. So beautiful, his face, his green, green eyes. They clung to each other long after the last waves had faded away.

"I'll protect you always," Desmond whispered into her hair, his breath still a ragged pant. "Care for you. I understand finally that I can. You are mine, Ava. Truly mine. It's you who's taught me what that means."

"Yes, yours." She had never felt so much that she *belonged*. "It's what I've always wanted."

And it was true. She'd only ever wanted to belong, to be accepted. To be loved. Maybe she'd had to fight to get there with Desmond, but he loved her. Loved her! It was like some sort of revelation, simply to feel his love. It was like being safe for the first time in her life. Safe. Cherished. Loved.

Perfect.

PART TWO

Soothing the Beast

Marina and James

Chapter One

"SHIBARI IS the ancient art of Japanese rope bondage. But Shibari is about far more than binding someone, rendering them helpless. It truly is an art."

Marina Marchant scanned the faces of her audience as they sat in their folding metal chairs in front of the main staging area at Pinnacle. The workshops she presented were always well attended, and tonight was no different.

Except for him.

He sat at the back of the room, all dark eyes and brooding, rugged features, a scowl on his face. She thought it might be part concentration, part some sort of inner struggle. Interesting . . .

Why couldn't she stop analyzing him?

She cleared her throat and went on. "But beyond even the visual art involved in Shibari, the art of sensation, is the art of what's happening in the mind. Shibari contains symbols we can all relate to on some level. And I don't mean only those of us who are interested in erotic restraint, in extreme sex. The psychological symbols involved are fairly universal in Western and Eastern cultures. What does that sense of being held helpless in another's hands mean to anyone? At the very root of it is the need to be rendered powerless, no matter the individual's reasons. And those reasons are complicated, layered. Unique. That's what makes the experience so fascinating. And for some of us, irresistible."

She saw him lean forward in his chair, his dark, liquid eyes intense, and she had a profound sense of being watched. Not just looked at but watched very carefully. Examined. It didn't make her uncomfortable, exactly.

Not exactly.

He was too beautiful, this man. Masculine. Must be well over six feet, and shoulders like a pro football player's. The tattoo work she could see on his arms, peeking from beneath the sleeves of his simple black T-shirt, looked Asian in design: clouds, water. Gorgeously detailed work. The tattoos only seemed to accent how heavily muscled his arms were. And she did love tattoos on a man. Something so male about them. Something a little wicked.

Nice.

Don't lose focus.

She pulled her hair back from her face, the long, auburn strands catching in her fingers, and she had an odd surge of self-consciousness. She'd given this lecture dozens of times. What on earth was wrong with her? She let her gaze wander over the others in the audience, a mixed group, men and women of all ages. She'd always loved that one could never look at these people and know what secret desires hid beneath their utterly normal-looking exteriors.

She glanced at him once more, found his eyes still glued to her. She looked away, paused to sip from her bottle of water, before she continued.

"Power play is all about what goes on in the players' heads. Psychology. Regardless of how it might turn us on. Sex *is* psychology. What we desire, how we respond.

"I believe it's important to explore your own desires, your own responses to different stimuli, in figuring out what you want, why you want it. The ritual of Shibari should lead you to a greater understanding of yourself, but that will happen only if you take the time to see beyond the idea of simply being bound, or of binding someone else. Make it as much an inner journey as it is a physical experience, and you'll reach the deepest levels Shibari can take you to."

She continued with her lecture, recommended books to read on rope bondage and meditation, passed out a list of information resources. And he watched her the entire time, the beautiful man in the back of the room, his large body a powerful, enigmatic presence.

Who was he?

She wound up the lecture with an invitation to the Shibari demonstration she was giving the following month and a brief question-and-answer period. But she could hardly keep her attention on what she was saying. She kept seeing him in the corner of her eye, his short, black hair, his dark, watchful eyes. The small scar over one eyebrow, another along his jaw, making him seem even more purely masculine.

A surge of desire swarmed her body, warming her all over.

How long had it been since she'd felt this sort of attraction to a man? Certainly not since before Nathan . . .

No, don't think of him now. He has nothing to do with this.

No, but he was the reason it had been so long since she'd been able to look at another man this way. With lust swimming through her veins.

Stop it.

Just finish up, go home. Have a glass of wine and forget all about this man.

"Alright, I hope to see everyone next time. If you're interested in joining Pinnacle and exploring further, please see Carrie at the front door for an application."

As usual, several people approached her, and she answered a few last-minute questions as everyone filed out of the room. Everyone but him.

He stayed behind, standing by his chair, while she talked to people, while she gathered the stack of leftover handouts, put them in her purse. Finally he strode up to the front of the room—there was no other way to describe it—and came to stand before her.

She'd been right; he was well over six feet tall, broad and heavily muscled. And he looked vaguely familiar . . . and even more amazing-looking up close: large, dark brown eyes, his skin a smooth golden brown. His jawline was finely sculpted, broken only by the narrow scar that ran the entire length of the left side. His mouth was wide and generous, his face a bit too serious.

"Ms. Marchant?"

"Marina, please."

His teeth were white, even. Perfect other than a small chip right in front.

"I'm James. James Cortez." His voice was deep, as smooth as caramel with a touch of whiskey in it. "I've heard about you. That you're a Shibari master. I've heard how you use meditation and trance states in your work, that you have a degree in cultural anthropology, which interests me very much."

"My degree is in art, and I work as a private dealer, but I did study cultural anthropology. I nearly got my master's, but I . . ." Why was she telling him this? "What can I do for you, James?"

"I think you may be exactly what I need."

"I don't know what you mean." It didn't seem like any sort of standard pickup line. He was far too serious for that. "What is it you're looking for?"

He just stared at her for several moments, his dark eyes piercing. Then he said very quietly, "A way out of my own head, maybe."

She nodded, couldn't speak for a moment. God help her, he *smelled* right. Clean and sharp. Male.

"Are you asking me to play you?"

The idea made her heart pound, imagining him in the ropes. *Her* ropes.

"Yes."

She could see now that there were tiny golden flecks in his brown eyes. Like chocolate and honey.

"I . . . I don't play men. If you've heard so much about me, then surely you've heard that."

"Yes. I'm hoping you'll make an exception."

"And why would I do that?"

Other than the mad fluttering in her chest, the way her legs went weak standing so close to him, inhaling his scent.

Yes, that was exactly why she wasn't going to do what he asked. She couldn't stand weakness. Not in a man, and not in herself.

He moved in closer. She took a step back.

"I'll be honest and tell you, Marina, that I need what you have to offer. I need to find some peace. I've tried everything else: standard meditation, silent retreats, hypnosis. I've tried to find it in the ropes, but I haven't found anyone good enough, anyone who uses more than the ropes, the old bondage rituals. I need more. I need you to . . . help me."

James watched as her lush red lips parted, made a little *o*. He hadn't expected the woman to be beautiful. Capable, intelligent. But not this overwhelming beauty. The high cheekbones, the almond-shaped gray eyes that looked like crystal and smoke all at once somehow. The perfect, pale skin set off by the heavy curtain of dark auburn hair that waved around her shoulders. The tall, willowy figure that was as graceful as the way she moved her hands while she spoke.

He was being too damned poetic.

He was just . . . caught off guard. That was all.

Marina was shaking her head. "I can't help you." She picked up her coat and he reached out, helped to slip it over her shoulders. "I'm sorry. I really can't help you."

He held on to her coat for a moment, the black leather smooth and cool beneath his fingers. Her skin would feel like that: silky, poreless.

"I'm not your usual submissive boy. I don't need all of that. I just need the ropes. I need someone who can understand the head trip. Who can guide me."

"The ropes *are* the head trip." She looked angry now, her gray eyes throwing sparks. "Look, I don't play with men. I have my reasons for that. And it seems that you really don't even get what the power exchange is about, so why would I want to play with you?"

"Because I need you. And I assure you, I do get it. Try me and see." He needed her more than ever, now that he'd seen her. He needed to touch her, to run his hands through all that gorgeous hair.

But he wasn't supposed to be thinking about this in terms of sex. Sex had gotten him nowhere.

Impossible not to think about sex with this woman.

He should let it drop, find someone else.

He didn't want to do this with anyone else.

"Marina . . . I don't mean to be disrespectful. I only mean to explain that I'm not looking for the usual kind of domination dynamic. I'm looking for the trance state. I'm looking to get my head straightened out."

"Perhaps you should try a therapist." She picked up her purse, slung the strap over her shoulder. She was still angry. He wasn't sure why.

"I've done that. It didn't help." He moved in closer, put a hand on her wrist where a bit of bare skin showed at the edge of her sleeve. Her skin was soft and cool, just as he'd imagined, and he had to ignore the kick of desire in his gut. He said quietly, "I need to find that shadow place. I know you understand what I mean. Not everyone does. I can see in your eyes that you've been there. Can you tell me that's not true?"

She blinked at him, long, dark lashes coming down on her pale cheeks. "No," she said, her voice a little breathless.

"Then take me there. I can't do it alone." Her skin was burning now beneath his palm. "Come with me."

She was shaking her head, just a small motion, side to side, but she said, "Okay. Okay."

He smiled then, not in triumph but in relief. She couldn't have any idea what it cost him to have to ask for this. For anything. "Is there somewhere we can go to talk?"

"There's a bar down the street."

He nodded. "Thank you."

She paused, looking at him with those stormy gray eyes. There was something veiled behind them, but there was no way to know what it was.

"Why do I think I might regret this?"

He didn't answer.

She took a long breath, exhaled slowly. "I'm going to do it anyway. We'll talk, at least. I'll give you a chance to try to convince me to do what you're asking. I'm not sure why. But we can talk."

"A chance is all I'm asking."

"Oh, you're asking a lot more than that. Let's go."

THE AIR in the bar was warm, a little too close. Or maybe it was James who was a little too close, only inches away, it seemed, on the other side of the small, round table. A glass of red wine sat before her; she twisted her fingers around the stem of the glass, trying to work some of her edginess off. Why had she even come here?

"I appreciate you agreeing to talk with me," he was saying, sipping a glass of mineral water.

"I still don't know why I'm here. I don't know why I agreed to this. But since I did, go ahead. Tell me why you think you need me."

He rested his arms on the table, leaning in, and she caught his scent again, clean and dark all at the same time. Too good. She picked up her glass, sipped, trying to swallow the lust away. But being alone with him in the half-dark bar was only making it worse.

"I told you I'd heard about you," he said. "Your name is pretty well known in the bondage and BDSM circles. I've read about your lectures on the Internet."

"You . . . researched me?"

"I researched the masters of Shibari. You were one of a handful of thoroughly knowledgeable people in San Francisco. And the only one who really addresses trance states in any sort of detailed way."

"I have done a deep study of meditative spaces: Buddhist monks, the whirling dervishes of Turkey, Catholic nuns, even." She stroked the wineglass with her fingertips, concentrating on the smooth, cool glass. It was too hard to look at him; he was so intense. "I believe that same sort of trance state can be reached through bondage, if the people involved respond to it, are open to the idea. It's not for everyone."

"This is exactly what I'm looking for. What I think I need."

"Why? I get the feeling this is not some journey of sexual gratification."

"I can find sex anywhere."

She was sure he could. But he wasn't being cocky. "Tell me more."

"I've . . . been through some pretty rough experiences. I work as a news journalist. Well, I did, until two years ago."

"That's where I know you from. I've seen you interviewed on television. I've read your articles in magazines."

"Yes." He nodded.

"You've been all over the world. Written for *Time, National Geographic,* covered all the worst war-torn countries. You did that special on the lost children of Brazil, the street kids. And another on the Serbian refugees."

"Yes."

She saw his face shutting down just a bit and had the first glimmer of understanding of what he'd been through, doing that sort of work.

"You must have seen . . . everything."

"Yes." He glanced away, and she watched the rise and fall of his broad shoulders as he drew in a long breath.

"I'm sorry, James."

He turned back to her. "No, don't be. We all choose our lives, don't we? I did some good work." He stopped, drank from his glass, set it down a little harder than was necessary. "This is what I wanted to tell you. I have seen nightmares beyond anything you could possibly imagine. And I'm not saying that to glamorize myself or what I did for a living. No, just the opposite. Ugly is ugly. But this is the shit I need to get out of my head. Or . . . learn to think beyond. I don't know yet how it'll work. But I cannot meditate by any normal means. I can't quiet my mind. I don't really sleep . . ."

"God, James."

"And I don't want pity. I just want help. And frankly, it's hard as hell for me to have to ask for it. Can you understand that?"

His brown-and-gold gaze on hers, boring into her, glittering with need and pain and . . . she didn't know what else. And as much as the way he looked got under her skin, heated her all over, the expression on his face went right into her. Touched her in some deep way.

How could she refuse him?

"You think I can help you with these things?"

"I think you can take me where I need to go, if anyone can. Nothing else has worked. I've gotten close enough to get a taste of what's possible, in the ropes. But I've never been with anyone who knew enough about anything beyond the patterns and the knots. The power exchange has been there, but not intensely enough for me. I've never been with anyone who was strong enough."

"And you think I am?"

He cocked his head to one side, looked at her as though he was evaluating her for the first time. "I think you're one of the strongest women I've ever met, Marina."

She went warm again, the heat making her shiver, making her legs go weak.

Unacceptable.

But she wasn't going to turn him away. She couldn't do it.

"I . . . we would have to set some limits," she said, her throat dry. She swallowed, her fingers gripping the delicate stem of the wineglass. "There would be no sex."

"You're taking me on, then?"

"If we can come to an agreement."

I must be crazy.

"Of course."

"I understand you're no slave boy, and that's not what I'm interested in. I can't stand to see a man being weak." No, she'd seen far too much of that while Nathan was dying. "But I won't put up with you fighting me when we're in role."

"No, of course not. I want to give in. Even if it's difficult for me."

Impossible that this hulking man was saying these things to her.

She wanted nothing more than to bind him, to see him give in, to make him yield to her. Oh, too good to think about it, bringing a man like him to his knees . . .

"I'll contact you in a few days to make arrangements."

He nodded. "I appreciate it."

He put his hand out, as though he was shaking on a business deal. But his palm was a little rough, warm on hers. And it was as though she'd been shocked, a current of electricity running up her arm. She pulled her hand back, but it was too late; that current ran hot in her body. She crossed her legs against the subtle ache that had started between them.

No sex.

Yes, she'd have to stay in control. She could do it. She'd been doing this for years. And once she had him in the ropes, all that masculinity would be gone, or at least diminished, and he wouldn't seem so overwhelmingly . . . male.

Would he?

But she was going to do this, despite the warning bells going off in her head. She knew nothing could make James Cortez any less male to her. Any less masculine. Any less dangerous.

Oh, yes, he was a danger to her. To her sense of control. To the walls she'd constructed so carefully after she'd lost Nathan. And even knowing that, she was unable to resist.

She was about to take a tiger by the tail. And she intended to enjoy every second of it, right up until the moment when he would inevitably devour her.

Chapter Two

Marina woke to the quiet, misty light of the morning sun coming through the lace curtains of her bedroom. It was hard to tell what time it was; it was always foggy in San Francisco, it seemed, even where she lived, in the Castro district, which was sunnier than most other neighborhoods. But she had no idea how long she'd slept.

A glance at the clock told her it was nearly ten. She wasn't surprised; she'd been up until after two, her conversation with James Cortez running through her mind like a movie on an endless loop.

She couldn't stop thinking about him, about the things he'd told her, what he wanted from her. What she wanted from him.

She wanted to help him.

She wanted to touch him.

She wanted that surge of power that came with bringing a man of his size, his strength, to his knees, literally and figuratively. There was nothing like it. And she hadn't experienced that for years. Not even with Nathan.

Nathan had been sweet. Not that he was any less a man. But

he'd had a gentle nature, had been so naturally submissive. Not her usual type, but it was impossible not to love him.

Why couldn't she stop thinking of Nathan? And James? It was all tied together somehow.

Maybe playing with James wasn't the best idea. Yet she felt compelled. And confused. She was usually so levelheaded. This man had thrown her off balance, and she didn't like it.

But she still wanted him.

Throwing back the down quilt, she got up, padded across the floor in her thin white-cotton eyelet nightgown, found her thick fleece robe. Wrapping herself in it, she slid her feet into her slippers and went to the kitchen, where she started a pot of coffee, sliced some sourdough bread, and laid it in the toaster oven.

She loved this old Victorian house, had bought it with the money from Nathan's life insurance and spent an entire year renovating it. It had been a lot of work, but she'd needed the distraction. And everything was perfect, exactly as she'd wanted it. She'd had the old floors reconditioned, the crown moldings and tin ceilings restored, all of the brass grates and doorknobs polished. The kitchen she'd had completely modernized, but she'd kept the vintage look in the marble counters, the old iron stove she'd found at an estate sale. And she'd filled the house with a combination of Victorian antiques and more contemporary pieces, covered the walls in the modern and ethnic art she loved.

Her house comforted her as nothing else did. It felt real to her. Solid. More solid than anything else had since she'd lost Nathan.

A small stab of loss went through her. Would she ever stop missing him? It was different than it had been; it was no longer unbearable. It was simply omnipresent, that sense of having lost something important. She'd come to accept it. Maybe it would never go away.

Her coffee was ready, and she poured a cup, added too much sugar to it before pulling her toast out, buttering it, and putting it on a small china plate, as she did every morning. She found comfort in these small habits. She carried it all to the big white-washed wooden table by the window overlooking the street. The fog was beginning to lift already, exposing the city like a blanket rolling back.

She loved the architecture in her neighborhood, a combination of gingerbread Victorians, like her own, and the stucco structures built in the 1920s and '30s. And she loved the diversity of her neighbors. She could feel at home only in a community of people who accepted those in alternative lifestyles. Not that she walked down the street dressed in leather or carrying a whip. But there was an underlying sense that everyone was accepted here.

She ate her toast, watching the activity on the street below: people walking their dogs, filing in and out of the small grocery store on the corner, going about their daily lives. Why did she feel incapable of doing that herself today? She was too distracted.

She had to get James Cortez out of her mind. Or at least get her wandering thoughts reined in, under control.

Maybe she should talk to Desmond. He could usually help her get her head back on straight.

She poured another cup of coffee, took it into the living room, settled onto the cream-colored suede sofa, and picked up the phone.

Desmond answered right away.

"Desmond Hale."

"Desmond, it's Marina."

"Marina, how are you?"

"I'm fine. Well, I think I am."

"Can you be a bit more definitive, perhaps?" he teased.

"I know. I don't know what my problem is. That's . . . my problem. Why I'm calling." She paused, sipped her coffee. "Desmond, I think . . . I may be in trouble."

"What is it? What's wrong?"

"It's nothing that serious. I just . . . I've gotten myself into a situation. I've met a man, James Cortez. He's looking for a top, someone to work the ropes with him. And he's . . . he fascinates me more than I'd like to admit. There's some sort of odd connection there. But I'll admit it to you because the attraction is undeniable. And I think I'm in real trouble here."

Desmond laughed. "Don't say that like it's the end of the world. It's a normal occurrence for most of us."

"Yes," she agreed quietly. "But this is me we're talking about."

"Maybe it's time, Marina."

"Maybe."

He was silent for several moments. "You know, we can get stuck in these ruts. All of us. I was stuck. Until I met Ava."

"This isn't a rut, Desmond. I had a loss."

"I know, and it was profound. I understand that. But it's been four years. You haven't expressed any interest in men the entire time."

"That's because I haven't been interested."

"And now?"

"And now this man . . . I want to play him, Desmond. I'm going to."

"Well, that's good, then."

"Maybe." She shifted on the sofa, pulled a dark blue velvet pillow in close to her body. Why did her stomach ache?

"Marina, it can be good if you choose for it to be. I've learned that. Don't fight your desires. If you're feeling something, then let that guide you."

"Words of wisdom from a man who's newly in love?"

"That I am. It wouldn't be such a bad thing for you, either."

"It's hardly love. I've just met him."

"But it's something. It's attraction."

She nearly moaned aloud. "Yes . . ."

"And you're going to play him."

"Yes." God, that strong, golden body in the ropes . . . "Yes, I am."

"What can I do for you, then?"

Her hand tightened around the telephone. "Talk me out of it."

"I'm not going to do that. I think you should try this, play him. Be with a man. It's time, Marina. I know you've never really gotten over losing Nathan, but as trite as it may sound, he wouldn't want you to be alone forever. You know that."

"I do know it." She sighed, pulled the pillow in tighter over the vague ache in her chest. "I guess I just needed some validation that I'm doing the right thing."

"You won't really know until you get there, will you?"

"I suppose not."

Desmond's tone dropped. "Look, I understand what you're feeling. I've been through this, wanting something but not wanting to give in to it, to lose control. We understand that about each other. But sometimes that's the best thing we can do. Sometimes it's necessary."

"Desmond, Ava is the love of your life. This man, James, is . . . just a man. A stranger."

"He is now. But perhaps if you give it a chance . . ."

"Maybe that's what I'm afraid of." She had to stop, to take in a deep breath. "You know I wouldn't admit that to anyone but you."

"As long as you can admit it to yourself."

"I don't like it, Desmond. I don't like that I can't predict what might happen with him."

"Ah, we are the worst sort of control freaks, you and I."

She had to smile. "Yes, we are. And I like it that way. I'm perfectly comfortable being in control."

"Don't we tell submissives that they learn the most about themselves when they push their boundaries? And shouldn't that apply to us as well?"

"Oh, you're Mr. Philosophical now, aren't you?"

"Love will do that to a person."

"I told you, this is not love."

"Not yet. But you never know."

"Desmond!"

"Alright, I'll stop teasing you. But let me know what happens with this James person."

"I will. Thanks for talking to me. Even though you haven't been of any help."

"Well, you're welcome for that." He laughed again.

It was good to hear him so happy. And maybe he was right. Maybe it was time she sought some of that for herself. Not the big, important relationship he had with Ava, certainly. But maybe something . . .

"I'll talk to you soon, Desmond."

They hung up, and she stayed on the sofa, sipping the cooling dregs of her coffee. She should get up, do some work, even though it was Saturday. There were clients she should call, paperwork to file, research to do. Work should distract her.

It should.

She doubted it would. James's face was imbedded in her mind: his voice, his intensity. Even his need was a palpable thing to her, something that had burrowed under her skin.

Maybe she would send him an e-mail, ask him a few questions, clarify the negotiations for their first time together. Then she would put him out of her mind for the rest of the day, do something constructive.

Like get back into bed, pull out her vibrator, and bring herself to a lovely orgasm thinking about him . . .

She flung the pillow into the corner of the sofa. God, she had to get up, do something, anything! Had to stop thinking about him, fantasizing. She stood up, carried her coffee cup into the kitchen, set it in the sink. And she stalked determinedly back into her bedroom, pulled a change of clothing from her dresser drawers, yanked her robe off, then her short cotton nightgown. Naked, she stared at the bathroom door, contemplated getting in the shower. Getting dressed, working. And with a moan, she turned back to her unmade bed, sat down hard on the edge, pulling open the nightstand drawer. Inside was a selection of vibrators; she chose the most powerful, a large textured silicone piece in royal blue. Switching it on, she lay down against the pile of satin and brocade pillows.

James . . .

God, just thinking about him made her wet.

She spread her thighs and slipped her hand down in between them, felt the moisture there. Imagined it was his hand, his brown-and-gold eyes watching her. Oh, yes, to have him on his knees, watching her touch herself . . .

When had she ever done anything like that?

Didn't matter. All that mattered was that image of him, his massive body kneeling before her. Her hand spreading open the lips of her sex, the other hand pushing the buzzing phallus in, just the tip, teasing herself.

Pleasure like a rocket surging into her body.

James . . .

She teased her clit with circling fingers, let the vibe do its job, sending currents of desire through her, pushed it in a little deeper.

She'd order him to kiss her thighs, to move in between them, to lick her . . .

God . . .

She moved the vibrator in deeper, angled it until it hit her G-spot. Pleasure like some sweet wave making her feel loose and languid all over. And she pinched her clitoris, hard, imagining it was James taking it between his teeth.

She moaned, arched her hips into her own hand, into his hand, shoved the vibrator hard inside her. And cried out as she came in a sharp torrent.

"James!"

She was shaking, pleasure flooding her in a scorching tide. And his face in her mind, his scent in her head, surrounding her, devouring her.

Just as he would.

God damn it.

He's just a man.

But her shivering body knew differently. He was the first man to make her *feel* something in four long years. And those feelings were dangerously out of control.

She pulled the vibe from her body, switched it off, rolled onto her side. She was still trying to catch her breath, to catch her sanity.

She just had to play him, get him out of her system. It was nothing more than simple chemistry.

That and his *need*. So damn strong she couldn't resist the pull of it. Couldn't resist the challenge of fulfilling it. And him.

James.

Her body was heating up again already. No point in fighting it. She lowered the vibrator once more between her thighs, tensed as she touched it to her swollen clit, and gave herself over to desire.

JAMES'S HAYES VALLEY neighborhood was quiet; it was too early on a Saturday morning for most people to be up and about. But he'd woken at six, too restless to stay in bed. After trying to lie still for an hour, he'd gotten up, dressed, and left the house in search of coffee.

He went into the small café on the corner, ordered his usual latte, carried the paper cup back up Gough Street, passing the restaurants, shops, and galleries, all closed now. Later the street would be bustling with activity, which he usually preferred; it was why he lived in the heart of the city.

Today he didn't mind the stillness; he had too many thoughts running through his head. He'd approached Marina Marchant as a means of dealing with the constant buzz in his brain, but it had only gotten worse since he'd met her.

She was too damn beautiful; he couldn't forget her face. Fucking perfect, really. He'd never seen anything like it.

And he was going to let her tie him up.

He was getting hard just thinking about it, about her hands running the rope over his skin. His pulse flared with nerves.

Impossible that he was afraid of her. He wasn't afraid of anything. Except the nightmares that were his memories.

And maybe this woman.

He shook the thought off as he pulled out his keys, let himself into his building. It was a three-story stucco, too old for an elevator, but he never minded the stairs, and now they served to burn off a little excess energy. He crossed the small landing and opened the door to his apartment, which took up the entire top floor. He loved the open feel, with the old, wide-plank wood floors and vaulted ceilings. He'd furnished it sparsely, needing the space around him. And he loved feeling the movement of the city downstairs, even the sound of traffic. It kept him from thinking.

He was thinking now. Too damn much, too damn fast, too damn . . . Marina.

Kicking the door shut behind him, he crossed the open floor and went to his desk, turned on his computer, waited while it booted up, staring at the blue screen.

He had too much time on his hands this morning. He should work on his next book; he'd been promising himself he'd do it for more than a month but hadn't done much more than make some notes. He'd spent his time just wandering the city, being in his own head, trying to figure out how to deal with the ugliness in there.

That was the only way he could think of it: "the ugliness," as though it needed some official title. Flashes of all his travels, the suffering he'd seen. He'd tried a number of techniques to make it stop, but he'd never been entirely free of it.

The one thing he never played in his head was that last trip to Burundi.

God help him, he never wanted to see Africa again. And he never would.

Don't think of it.

Ever.

No, think of Marina, whether he wanted to or not. That fucking gorgeous skin. Flawless. The mouth like some sort of invitation. Her delicate hands. Even better that he had some idea of what those hands could do. She was *nawashi,* after all. A rope master. He knew enough about Shibari to understand what that meant. And to truly be *nawashi,* she had to be more than an expert with the ropes. She had to *get* it.

Had to, damn it. Because she was his last hope.

Sipping his coffee, he opened the file he kept his notes in for his current project, a book about the homeless in America, the first piece about the U.S. he'd worked on in years. But he couldn't bear to think about the starker, more tragic issues in the third-world countries in which he'd spent much of his adult life. It was too much; he could admit that to himself. That admission was what had enabled him to quit. Or maybe forced him to.

Stop thinking!

Yeah, turn his mind back to Marina. Why was he getting it all mixed up, anyway? Marina, his job, all the horrible shit he'd seen. Better to focus on her.

Marina.

He had a feeling about her, that she could be some sort of key. Stupid, probably. Maybe wishful thinking. Maybe that lust had kicked him like a punch in the gut the moment he'd set eyes on her.

But the lust wasn't the important thing. Or it wasn't supposed to be. The thing was the ropes, the ritual, the headspace.

Closing his eyes, he imagined once more the ropes sliding over his skin, binding him, holding him still. He knew he couldn't be still any other way. He had to hand over his power, and to really get where he needed to go, he'd have to hand it over completely. Something he had never been able to do before. But with Marina . . .

Oh, yeah, a lot was going to be different with her.

His computer dinged, and he clicked into his e-mail.

Marina.

He leaned in, scanning her message. A long note asking about his desires, telling him how she operated in a bondage scene. Insisting again that there would be no sex.

The woman was pure sex to him.

But alright, whatever he had to do. He could control his lust, couldn't he?

But it wouldn't matter, would it? Because she would be in control. And he would be rendered helpless in the ropes.

If he could only give himself over. If he could only allow himself that much release. Inconceivable. But with Marina, he had a feeling anything was possible.

He started typing his answers to her right away. Yes, he'd had experience in the ropes. Yes, bondage was sexual for him, and yes, it was also spiritual. No, he wasn't looking for pain play or humiliation; he wanted only to be bound, to have that relief from responsibility forced on him.

His pulse thrummed in his veins as he thought about his answers, typed the words. It was all becoming more real suddenly, that this woman was going to put her hands on him. That he was going to let her.

Too good. Like some sort of gift.

He couldn't wait.

Chapter Three

SHE HAD MANAGED to wait an entire week somehow. And tonight, finally, she would see him.

James.

Her whole body was vibrating with need.

Control!

Oh, yes, tonight would be all about control. And she would handle it. She always had.

She'd never felt this sort of overpowering lust before. Not for anyone else, ever. Not even for Nathan. That had been a slow, sweet simmer of desire; with James, it was more like an electric shock.

She'd showered, rubbed scented lotion into her skin, brushed her hair until it shone, all the time thinking about how the rituals of preparation were the same, whether as a Domme or as a submissive. Making herself perfect. As a gift for those in the submissive role. As a means to getting in touch with her personal power as a top.

There was power in being a woman, in the sexuality of it. And it was sexual when she was playing a man, even if she'd made a rule about no sex. But sex was power. Power she would use to take this strong man down.

She shivered, a delicate thread of desire spiraling through her system, making her breasts ache, her nipples come up hard.

Oh, yes, this was definitely about sex. But she would use it, channel it.

She would not sleep with him. Not let him touch her.

Oh, how she wanted him to touch her . . .

Groaning, she shook her head, yanked open her dresser drawer to choose her lingerie. Even though she hadn't been with a man since she'd lost Nathan, her drawer was full of red lace, black silk. She'd never been able to deny that part of her: herself as a sexual being. No, she'd simply chosen to acknowledge it by wearing sexy lingerie, using her collection of vibrators. Everything secreted away where she didn't really have to deal with it.

One meeting with James Cortez and the issue was brought to the surface with jarring clarity.

Maybe she just needed to get laid, for once?

She almost laughed as she slipped into a black satin bra and matching thong, the fabric cool against her skin.

She was not going to sleep with him!

Going to her tall antique armoire, she chose a body-hugging black knee-length skirt, slid it over her thighs, zipped it up, found a black knit top with a low, lacy neckline, pulled it over her head. When she went back to her dresser to find a pair of black seamed silk stockings, she caught her reflection in the ornate oval gilt mirror. She could see the arousal in her glossy eyes, her dilated pupils enormous, dark. Her cheeks were flushed. And she couldn't resist smoothing her palms beneath her shirt, over her stomach, her satin-covered breasts.

How long had it been since anyone had touched her?

Too long. Maybe Desmond was right. But there was more at stake for her than simply meeting her sexual needs. Too much. She couldn't risk allowing anyone to get that close. She'd lost too much to let that ever happen again.

It could just be sex.

Hot, animal sex and sweating bodies crushed skin to skin . . .

She really had to pull herself together. James would be there at any moment.

She dropped her hands, leaving her breasts aching. Needy. Going to her closet, she pulled out a pair of red patent-leather stiletto heels, slipped her feet into them, feeling more like herself. She loved shoes, had an enormous collection of them. Stilettos made her feel powerful. And that's what the evening ahead was all about. Power. Her personal power. Which she was not going to give up for any man, no matter how tempting he was. No matter how he made her feel, even this raging, heart-thumping lust.

Her hands went back to her breasts, and she closed her eyes, let herself feel that pleasure, let herself imagine it was James's hands on her . . .

The doorbell rang and she nearly jumped out of her skin.

Get it together!

She took a breath, smoothed her hair, and went to answer the door.

James stood on the other side, dressed in jeans and a black button-down shirt with a little white cotton peeking out at the neck. He looked good. He looked absolutely amazing, all dark eyes and golden skin. She'd forgotten how incredibly good-looking he was.

That scar on his jaw . . . she wanted to reach out and touch it . . .

"Marina." He smiled, his teeth white and strong.

God, she could swallow that mouth.

"Hi. Did you find the place okay?"

"Yeah. It wasn't a problem."

She realized suddenly she was standing at the door, staring at him. She stepped back.

"Come in."

Why were her nerves fluttering like a girl with her first prom date? She really had to settle down, get into her role. Do her job.

Don't talk. Don't put it off. Just do it.

"Do you need anything to drink before we begin, James?"

"Wow. You really go straight for the kill."

"If you like to think of it that way." She smiled at him, found her sense of balance in having thrown him off.

He nodded, smiled a little. It was flirtatious, almost a cocky grin, his dark eyes glittering. Then he seemed to understand what he was doing, and the smile vanished, his features going blank. Interesting that he could shut himself down like that. Probably some sort of survival instinct developed on the job.

"I don't need anything. Thank you."

"As I mentioned in the e-mail, I don't require that you call me Ma'am or Mistress. This is not about a slave mentality. Call me Marina."

"Yes, Marina."

His tone was perfectly civil, but there was nothing submissive in it. He would be a challenge. But she'd known that going in. Had loved that idea, really. No docile, sweet subbie boys for her. It would never have worked. Not like it was going to with James.

A long, hot shiver crept over her skin. She bit it back, steeled herself.

"Follow me, then."

She turned and walked down the hallway, trusting that he would do as she'd instructed, and heard the soft skim of his shoes against the hardwood behind her.

She opened the door to the guest room; she never let anyone into her bedroom, her private sanctuary. But she'd never had a man in this house other than Desmond and another male friend or two. Never a man she was playing. Never a man she had this sort of chemistry with. She had to brace herself against the small quiver of lust and trepidation that ran up her spine.

He's a bottom, like any other, male or female. He is here for the same thing all the women have been these last few years.

She motioned for him to follow her inside. She'd decorated simply: A canopied queen-sized bed in dark, antique wood dominated the room; she'd left the frame bare of any drapery, preferring the clean lines of the wood. A high dresser in which she kept her ropes and cuffs. A wide padded bench angled in one corner, with eyebolts placed here and there, through which she could run the ropes, or attach handcuffs or ankle restraints. More eyebolts in the high ceiling that she'd had installed for suspension work. But she didn't plan on doing anything fancy with James. He would have no appreciation for the aesthetic patterns. He just wanted the headspace. Something more basic, primal.

She bit her lip, watched him standing in the middle of the room. He was eyeing her a bit warily, some emotion flashing across his features; she wasn't sure what it was. Could it be fear? That didn't seem likely, and yet . . .

Just get started.

She nodded her chin. "Strip."

He smiled, that edge of cockiness fleeting, then quickly unbuttoned his shirt and pulled it off, revealing a plain white sleeveless undershirt. She'd always loved these shirts, had a sort of fetish for white cotton. On a man. On herself. She always slept in a short eyelet nightgown. And the way the fabric stretched across his muscular chest made her want to reach out and touch him, to smooth her fingertips over the shadows of dusky nipples visible through the fabric.

She could see his tattoos clearly now, all black and gray work on his left arm. An angel covered his shoulder, wings spread wide, and below it a female Asian figure done in glorious detail, all of it backed by clouds and waves.

Beautiful and strong-looking, just as he was.

"Where should I put my clothing, Marina?"

"Just lay it on the end of the bed."

God, he was pure male beauty and grace as he moved to the bed, pulled the white cotton over his head. And made her breath hitch. All that golden skin, taut and fine. His chest and shoulders were pure muscle, the kind of muscles a man got only from working hard at the gym. Heavy, solid. And a long scar running across his right side, along the bottom edge of his ribs. Like the scar on his jaw, it only made him more masculine. More beautiful to her.

She couldn't help herself; she reached out, touched a fingertip to the ridge of scarred flesh.

"What happened here?"

"Battle wound."

She raised an eyebrow.

"Oh, no. I wasn't ever in the military. But my job was . . . I saw a lot of action, a lot of wars."

"You don't want to tell me how you got this, though?"

"Yes. Sure. Okay." He shrugged nonchalantly, but she could sense his discomfort, could see it in the tight pull of his shoulders, his neck. "Machete. Indonesia."

She nodded. "You're really not going to talk, are you?"

He turned his head away for a moment, and when he turned back his eyes were dark, shuttered. "I came to you to get away from this stuff. I'll tell you if you want me to, but it can't be now. I don't mean to be difficult. Uncooperative. But I can't pull this stuff out right now and still be able to get away from it. Not tonight."

"Alright. I understand."

He nodded, kept his gaze on hers. But he wasn't challenging her. Not in the way some submissives did, testing the strength and will of the top. He was simply searching her face for her response.

"James, I'm not going to push the issue. You have a right to keep your pain private."

"Yes!" he hissed, his eyes shuttering even more.

"Don't be so defensive with me. There's no need."

He shook his head once quickly, a sharp motion. "This is . . . sometimes difficult for me."

"That's why you're here, isn't it? We'll figure it out as we go."

He nodded again, his features relaxing a bit. "Okay. Okay."

She watched him for several moments as he took a long breath, composed himself.

"Continue," she told him, motioning with her chin.

He kept that liquid, gleaming gaze on her, like melted chocolate lit with amber, as he bent to unlace his boots, kicked them off, the kind of heavy black boots she loved. Then he unbuttoned his jeans, a process that seemed to take forever, as though it was happening in slow motion. Finally he slipped them off. He wore charcoal-gray boxer-briefs under them. She could see the bulge of his cock beneath the tight knit fabric.

She wanted to see it all, wanted it *too* much. But she would have to get him naked to make him vulnerable. Vulnerability was the only way she was going to reach this man, make him break down. And he would need to break to get to that place he craved so badly.

She loved the idea. And hated herself a little for it. But not enough to stop.

You're giving him what he wants.

She licked her lips. "Everything."

His thighs were tight with muscle, his abdomen a classic washboard. And when he slipped his briefs off, his cock was hard, ready. Beautiful.

When she looked up she saw that he'd caught her staring, but it didn't seem to faze him. He held his head proudly, his shoulders tight. Only the cords in his thick neck, his pulse visibly throbbing, betrayed the intensity of his struggle.

"Lay facedown on the bench."

He nodded, his expression sober, a little hard, but he did as she asked. His back was all long lines, his skin gorgeous and smooth except for the tail end of the scar on his side. His buttocks were a perfect curve.

She clenched her hands, took a breath.

You know this routine. Take him down.

"James, I am going to bind your hands to the table before we do anything else. I don't want you to speak unless you are having some real difficulty, whether physical or emotional, or unless I ask you a question. Do you understand?"

"Yes, Marina."

She opened a dresser drawer and pulled out two short lengths of white rope, fashioned a pair of wrist hitches, and took in the sight of his body laid out before her, his arms over his head. The dark, silky hair on his arms, the silky tufts under them. The way the muscle lay beneath the skin. And desire crept, as stealthily as a cat, into her body, into her very bones.

She licked her lips once more, reached out, touched the back of one wrist. He flinched. But he held still as she bound his wrist to a bolt in the table.

His skin was like silk, as soft as any woman's yet more dense.

She could hardly believe her sex was filling, growing damp, simply from touching his wrist!

But she moved to the other side of the bench, bound his other wrist.

Just do your job.

She bent over him, laid a hand on the back of his neck, felt him tense.

"Relax, James. I know this is hard for you. But you must concentrate."

Concentrate, Marina!

And not on the luscious feel of muscle beneath her hand, the delicious idea of his inner struggle, which was purely erotic to her.

"You're going to do some breathing first. In through your nose, a long, deep breath. Then out through your mouth. I will breathe with you. Follow me. Do you understand what I want you to do?"

"Yes. I understand."

She could tell from his voice that he was all too present, even if she hadn't known already from the tension in his body. So many submissives began that spiral down into subspace simply from being tied up, from being told what to do. With James, every step would be a battle. But she wanted to see that struggle, to know how difficult it was for him to give himself over. To see how strong he was.

She leaned over farther, until her breasts were pressed against his back. Lovely. Her nipples were hard, her breasts aching. But this was how it was best done.

"James, feel my breath. Follow my rhythm."

She opened her lungs, drew the air in slowly, ordering herself mentally to calm, felt him pull in a breath beneath her, his chest expanding, his back rising to press against her body. A short hitch, then he did it once more. She could feel the fight in him, even with this simple task.

"You must give yourself over, James," she told him quietly. "You know what you have to do if this is going to work. Just do it."

"I'm trying."

"Let it go, James."

He wanted to. Lord knew he wanted to. But it was always a damn fight. And now there was Marina pressed up against his back and he was hard as a rock. Which made the process more difficult yet easier to accept all at once. He didn't understand it. Maybe he didn't have to.

He continued to follow her breathing, to try to sink into the rhythm.

"You're trying too hard, James," she said, her voice a low, breathy hum across his shoulders.

"I know."

"*Shh*. Keep breathing."

He tried. Tried to let go, to stop trying so damn hard, as she'd said. It wasn't working.

"Marina—"

"Shh."

"No, I have to tell you . . . this is . . . I want it to work. But I need more."

She was quiet a moment. "Yes, I think you do."

She moved away then, leaving a small chill on his skin. His cock was as hard as ever, throbbing.

She smelled like chocolate and spices. Good enough to eat.

He had to stop thinking of her that way. As though he could throw off the ropes and ravish her. But he could hardly think of anything else.

"James, I'm going to bind you very tightly. It's what you need."

"Yes."

It was. He couldn't do this any other way. Couldn't be taken over. And he *had* to be.

"Please just do it, Marina."

Was he begging this woman? But his need was knife-sharp; the need to empty all the shit from his mind. Need made more intense by his need to touch her. To fuck her. By the idea that he would be denied that. It didn't make sense to him. But it didn't matter.

He felt the fall of rope soft against his skin, then she really began to work, the ropes crossing over his arms, back and forth, binding them to the table so that they were entirely immobilized.

Yes, this was what he needed.

She worked quickly, efficiently, and soon she was laying the rope over his back, binding him tightly to the table. Then down over his buttocks, his legs, until most of the surface of his skin was covered in rope. There was just enough room to breathe, to twitch a muscle the tiniest bit. And no matter how strong he was, how badly he might panic, he could not move.

Comforting. Terrifying.

His body pulsed with lust, with nerves. And he felt a small, smooth opening sensation in his brain as he let go just a little.

It was fucking going to work, with her.

Oh, yes, he was losing his mind already, and all she'd done was tie him down.

But it was Marina. This incredible, beautiful creature whose scent made him wild with need. Who emanated a strength he'd never encountered before in a woman. And he was really going to do it. To begin to give himself over to her.

It was really happening. Finally.

Chapter Four

MARINA FELT his breath quicken, felt his body relax just the slightest bit, a small loosening of muscle so subtle she would never have caught it had she not been pressed so close against him. A small victory, but still, it was a start.

She let him just be in the ropes, kept up the breathing, lulling herself a little in the process. It lasted only a few minutes; then she felt a small, sharp jerk of his bound body beneath her.

He was fighting it again. Thinking too much.

"*Shh,* James. Let it go. Let it happen."

"I can't."

"You can. You're choosing not to."

"Maybe."

He took a deep breath, and she could feel him making the effort to relax. It didn't work. His skin grew hot as a small sweat broke out on the back of his neck.

"Marina. Fuck . . ."

"I think this is all you can do tonight," she said quietly.

He didn't say a word, unable to give himself over enough to

admit defeat. The muscles in his back were growing tighter and tighter, his breath quickening.

"I'm letting you out, James."

"Okay. Yes. I can't . . . please just do it."

She pulled at the knots, slipping the ropes through her hands, but he only seemed to grow more tense. He was panicking; she knew the signs.

"It's okay, James. We can try it again. Almost done."

He was silent, trying to be stoic. But his breath was a raspy pant, his back absolutely rigid.

When she'd removed the last of the ropes he held still for a moment, as though he was challenging himself. Then he sat up.

His face was flushed, his eyes dark and glittering. Dangerous. His cock was still iron-hard. He was almost too beautiful to look at.

He stood suddenly, startling her, his eyes flashing. She took an unconscious step backward. Then he was advancing on her, backing her into the wall. She didn't have time to think about it; all she knew was the heat coming off his naked body, the menace in his eyes that was pure sex. Power. The scent of him male and musky and making her wet, damn it. Then he had her against the wall, one hand on either side of her waist, pinning her there as thoroughly as his burning stare. He moved in, a harsh growl coming from somewhere deep in his throat. Her knees went liquid. She was absolutely soaking. In shock. In need.

There wasn't a damn thing she could do about it.

He leaned in, lowered his head until she could feel his breath warm on her face. She could almost feel his lips . . . almost . . .

"God damn it, Marina," he whispered. "I'm going to touch you."

"Yes . . ."

She tilted her chin, parted her lips. She needed to taste him, to feel his flesh on hers. She couldn't think of anything else.

He moved his head, and she felt the lightest brush of his lips. Oh, yes, too good, making her melt, making her sigh against his mouth.

"God damn it." His words were a heated whisper on her skin. Then he pulled back, ran a hand through his hair, turned away from her.

Jesus. What the hell had just happened? What had she allowed to happen?

She was no longer in control of the situation, and they both knew it.

She still wanted him to kiss her. She didn't give a damn who was in charge.

"James . . ."

"I'm sorry. Fuck. I shouldn't have done that. I should have . . . I'm sorry. It won't happen again."

What if I want it to?

What the hell was wrong with her?

"No, it's . . . okay." She paused, drew in a breath, tried to calm her racing pulse, the damp heat gathering between her thighs. "Get dressed," she told him.

Yes, back in charge of things, issuing orders.

Tell him to kiss you. To take you to bed. He'll do it.

She was really losing it.

But he had already pulled his boxer-briefs back on over his raging hard-on, was slipping into his shirt, his pants, every movement aggressive, jerky.

There was a heaviness in her chest as she watched him, something entirely separate from her desire for him.

Regret.

She wasn't giving him what he'd come to her for. Wasn't doing her job.

She could barely think, still. She would have to figure it out later, talk to him once she'd calmed down.

Hell!

He was fully dressed now, watching her warily from across the room. His shoulders were still heaving a bit with his shuddering breath. His face was completely shut down, except for the glittering eyes. They were all pupils, black as night.

"I have to go," he said, his jaw clenched.

"You shouldn't leave yet, James. I can't let you drive like this."

He shook his head. "I need to go. Now."

She moved toward him, saw him flinch as he had when she'd laid her hand on his shoulder earlier. "You know better."

"I'm fine. I never hit subspace. I'm fine."

She was quiet a moment, searching his face. "You know that's not true, James. Even if you only caught that first edge."

"I'm not going to argue with you, Marina. But I am going to go."

That danger was still in his expression. She knew she wasn't going to be able to talk him into staying. Hated that there was nothing she could do, that she had let her control slip so drastically.

She nodded her head, and he turned and stalked out of the room. Every nerve in her body ached to follow him, to say something more. But dignity demanded she let him walk away—hers and his. And she didn't think she could stand to watch him walk out the door.

She heard the skid of his shoes on the floor, the soft creak of the door, then the knock of wood against wood as he closed it behind him.

It was then that she let out her breath, her lungs burning.

She felt . . . lost.

How had she let things spiral so out of control?

Walking to the bench, she ran her palm over the surface. She swore she could still smell him in the room, *feel* him, as though something besides his scent lingered there.

She'd always believed people had a unique energy about them, a sort of signature. And his was pure power. Pure masculinity. She'd never come upon anything like it.

She'd never met anyone like James. Never met a man who made her burn the way she did now. Unbearable, this wanting. Desire like fire in her body: her breasts, her belly, her sex.

She slid a hand between her thighs, pressed there.

Need like a razor, cutting through all logical thought, through her need for control. Through everything.

Stalking across the hall and into her bedroom, she stripped off her clothes, yanked her most powerful vibrator from the drawer, took it into the bathroom. She stood before the mirror, naked, her skin flushed all over. Her nipples were two hard, red points of desire. Her sex was soaking wet.

Spreading her thighs, she reached down and pressed once more against her sex. It was slick, hot. Aching. Her eyes fluttered as she brushed her fingers over her swollen clit, then watched carefully as she parted her pussy lips, revealing that hard bud of flesh. She spread her thighs a little farther, turned the vibe on high, and lowered it, touched the tip of her clitoris, desire pulsing through her. She shuddered.

This was what she needed. All she needed. She didn't need a man.

James . . .

No.

She pressed harder, the buzzing working its way into her body, shivering through her sex. Spreading wider, she shoved the tip of the vibrator inside her, moaning, her body clenching.

Oh, yes . . .

She kept her eyes on her image in the mirror, moving the vibrating phallus in and out of her, pleasure building, cresting.

James.

No, just herself and some good equipment. That's all she needed.

She pumped her hips, used her hand to rub her clitoris as she angled the vibe into her G-spot. Her breasts ached to be touched; her pussy ached.

When was the last time she was fucked by a man?

She thrust her hips harder, pressing the vibe deeper, pinched her clit hard.

James!

Pleasure arced through her like an electric current. Sharp. Lovely. Excruciating. And her body burst, her climax almost painful. And she was coming, coming, James's dark eyes, his smooth golden skin, his beautiful cock in her mind.

When it was over she dropped the vibrator onto the bathroom counter. Her image in the mirror looked flushed: face, neck, breasts. Her eyes were enormous, absolutely gleaming. Her mouth looked as though he had kissed her, even though he hadn't.

Even though you wanted him to.

Yes, she'd have to admit that much. And more. She wanted James. *Wanted* him, as she had no one else for years.

Dangerous. Oh, yes, James was dangerous.

Or was he? This had to be pure lust, nothing more. Why was she so concerned? She hadn't allowed a man to touch her since she'd lost Nathan; perhaps it was time, as Desmond had said. She was, after all, a sexual being, just like anyone else. She'd denied herself long enough.

But was it fair of her to consider sex with James when it was her responsibility to feed his need for subspace, for peace within the ropes? Would taking things to that level be good for him? Or would it only confuse the issue? She couldn't think clearly enough where he was concerned to be certain she was making a rational decision. And of course much would depend on whether or not he wanted her.

He did. That much she didn't need to question. The lust raging in his eyes, his hard, beautiful cock, the way he'd broken the rules, taking over like that . . .

She wouldn't have put up with it from anyone else. But James . . . she had a feeling she'd put up with almost anything from him, let him do anything . . .

Not very Domme-like. But James was no standard subbie boy, either. Far from it. And that was exactly why she was so damn attracted to him. Or part of it, anyway. That and his smoldering dark looks, the energy that emanated from him. The heat.

She moaned, pressed her hand to her sex once more, picked up the vibrator again. And told herself as she lowered the buzzing instrument between her thighs that another orgasm would cure her need for James, knowing full well it was a lie.

THE DRIVE HOME seemed to take forever. The city was alive, as it was on any Saturday night, despite the late hour. Too many cars, too many people and lights, too much noise and confusion. James couldn't seem to think, to lose himself in the buzz, as he once could.

He *needed* to lose himself.

He needed to get the near taste of Marina's lips out of his mind. The feel of her hair brushing his skin. The scent of her.

His cock was still rock-hard, growing harder as he thought of her. He pressed a hand against the ridge rising beneath his jeans, willing it to go down. It didn't help. Not that he really expected it to.

Nothing was going to help.

She was too fucking beautiful. Too hot. Too female. Too everything.

That sense of power, her absolute control, was a huge turn-on. And seeing her fall apart when he tried to kiss her . . . he'd thought he was going to lose his mind. Knew that if he'd let it go one step further, it would all have been over. He'd have pinned her against the wall, torn her clothes off, and fucked her, raw and primal, standing up, pushing her flesh into the hard wall behind her while he drove his cock into her sleek body . . .

Jesus.

He was hard as iron now.

Just get home.

Yes, get home, stroke himself until he came so he could stop thinking about her.

He groaned, forced himself to focus on the road, on the line of traffic moving down Van Ness. He swung a right onto Gough Street, then another right into the alley behind his building, parked in the small garage he'd been lucky to find in this old city. He slammed the car door behind him, made his way up the stairs to his apartment, fumbling with the keys at the door. Finally he was inside, and he made straight for the shower.

He reached in and turned the water on, yanked his shirt over his head, kicked his way out of his boots, his jeans, his boxer-briefs. His cock stood like a sentinel of lust between his legs, pulsing with need. Stepping into the shower, he turned the hot water up; he needed to feel the burn on his skin. Then he grabbed the bar of soap, lathered his cock, even the touch of his own rough hands making him pulse harder.

He leaned into the tiles behind him and began to thrust. This was no slow, even pace; no, he was far too impatient for that. It was a hard plunge into his soapy fist, then another, and another, too fast and rough to keep any rhythm. And pleasure pouring through his system, Marina's hot little mouth in his head.

He could imagine her taking him into her mouth. But no. It was him shoving his cock between her lips, making her eyes water, with her on her knees. Sucking him, sucking him, while he fisted a hand in her hair.

Marina!

His cock gave one hard throb, come flooding between his fingers, spraying the wall of the shower. And he kept coming, his body shaking.

Marina . . .

Finally it was over. He leaned his weight into the wall of the shower, letting the water wash away his sticky seed. His cock was still half hard.

Closing his eyes, he drew in one deep breath after another, trying to calm down. But it was no good. He needed her. Fucking *needed* her.

Not okay.

He'd never needed anyone. Not like this. All he needed from her was her skill with the ropes, her knowledge of trance states, her ability to make him clear his mind of all the shit that had been layered there over the years. Years of war and violence and unbelievable emptiness. Everything he'd seen and felt, and especially everything he'd tried so hard *not* to feel.

He was feeling now.

God damn it.

Marina Marchant was his one savior. And his worst nightmare. A woman he could fall for. A woman he could feel for. One he already did.

Chapter Five

ANOTHER MONDAY MORNING, and it felt like a Monday, the sky outside the window of Marina's office on Union Street a dark, threatening gray. Downstairs, the co-op gallery she rented office space from was just opening. The streets outside were quiet, still, the only crowds at the coffeehouses that dotted the street, two and three to a block.

She loved her office in the old brick building. It was small, but she didn't need much space. Just her computer on the enormous antique desk in the bay window, a phone with multiple lines on which she brokered art for her upscale clients. The red leather-bound book where she kept her most precious information: her contacts around the world, people who knew the hottest up-and-coming artists, those mysterious folks who could find almost anything, no matter how ancient, how rare.

She could have worked from home, but she liked getting out of the house, liked being out in the world. It made her feel more connected, more plugged into the city, into life. But all week she'd been totally disconnected, had felt nothing from the city around her. Nothing but a constant obsession with James. Where was he? What was he doing? Why the hell hadn't he called her?

Nine days since James had left her house. Since he'd tried to kiss her. Since she'd let him.

He hadn't called, hadn't answered the e-mail she'd sent.

She should have been furious. With any other submissive she had agreed to train this would have been reason for dismissal. But she knew there was far more to his sudden disappearance than mere disobedience. This was much deeper. For James. For her.

She'd felt his fear that night. Felt her own. And she was more compelled than ever to explore things with him, the electric dynamic, the astonishing chemistry, the sense of connection, of knowing who he was. Of absolute wanting.

She couldn't remember feeling so frustrated in her life, so damn helpless, except when Nathan had died. She didn't like it any more now than she had then. Helpless was one thing she didn't do well.

It was the one thing that prevented her from calling him: She couldn't let him see her powerlessness. It would make it all too real. But she didn't know how much longer she could stand not to see him, talk to him. And it was her responsibility to follow up with him, after a scene that had ended badly. She shouldn't allow this lack of contact to continue. She owed him that.

That's what she told herself, anyway, as she reached for the phone and dialed the number she'd memorized, just as she had every angle of his face, the curve of muscles in his long back, the scent of him.

She picked up a pen and tapped it against the wooden desk as the phone rang.

He probably wouldn't answer it. She should leave a message, reminding him how important it was that they talk about what happened when she'd bound him.

God, the sight of his strong body in the ropes, his shoulders bunching . . .

"Hello."

"Oh." The pen dropped from her hand, clattering onto the hardwood floor at her feet. "James."

"Marina?"

"Yes."

He was quiet a moment. She couldn't seem to get her brain to work, to speak to him.

"Are you there, Marina?"

"Yes. I'm here." Her body flooded with relief, with heat. "I . . . we should talk, James."

"I know. You're right."

No apology. But she hadn't exactly expected one. Hell, she hadn't expected to talk to him at all.

"Meet me tonight." His voice was a little rough. Commanding. She couldn't believe the way her body was melting.

Get ahold of yourself!

"Tonight's not good for me," she lied, trying to maintain some semblance of control. "Tomorrow," she said.

"Yes, tomorrow, then. We should talk in person."

He was taking over again. *Damn it.*

"Yes. Tomorrow. Come to my place."

"We should meet in public, Marina," he said softly.

"What? Why?" She was getting annoyed now.

He paused, a long silence that seemed to stretch interminably. "Because I don't trust myself with you."

She melted a little, unable to help that she loved the vulnerability in his admission. That mixed with his commanding tone a moment before. It was too good. She didn't understand the effect it had on her.

"Alright, then."

"Do you know a bar on the corner of Gough and Hayes called Absinthe?"

"Yes, I've driven by it. I've never been in."

"Meet me there at eight, if you can."

Ah, a small concession, a bit of manners, rather than him giving in to her.

She loved it, that he didn't really give in to her. But that was all wrong, wasn't it?

"I'll be there," she told him.

Another long pause. Then he said, his voice still low, "I'm looking forward to seeing you, Marina. And dreading it."

Her stomach knotted. "What do you mean?"

"I can't explain it any more until I see you."

"Okay. I understand. A bit, at least. I'll see you tomorrow night."

They hung up, and she was left gripping the phone in her hand. She felt oddly elated and empty at the same time.

What would he have to say to her tomorrow night? Would he tell her why he couldn't see her again? Was that what this conversation would be all about? She couldn't stand the thought of that.

Have to see him.

Yes. See him, talk to him.

Touch him.

One more day. She could wait that long. But just barely.

JAMES WALKED THROUGH the light evening rain, passing the lit windows of the small shops, galleries, florists, and hair salons that lined Hayes Street. He didn't mind it; he loved the rain. And this was no torrential downpour. There was just enough of it to make the streetlights gleam on the pavement, to bring out that smell of old, wet concrete and musty wood that was found in certain old cities. Always in San Francisco. It reminded him that he was home. And now, after everywhere he'd been, all the things he'd seen, that was all he wanted.

Except the woman he was about to meet.

A quick two blocks and he arrived at Absinthe. Small hammering in his chest, wondering if Marina was there yet.

Absolute pounding when he saw her, sitting by the window, the streetlights outside washing her skin in silver. Her hair was a fall of dark red, heavy and lush. It looked like pure silk. Her fingers were wrapped around a martini glass. Two olives, he noted, as he made his way through the press of small tables. The place smelled of good vodka and the faint scent of burnt caramel from the lavender crème brûlée the bar was known for.

She's just a woman.

A woman who twisted him all up inside. A woman who would set him free, if he could allow it to happen.

Fuck.

Just sit, talk with her.

"Marina."

"James. Hi."

She smiled, her mouth a red pout that widened slowly. She had a dimple in her right cheek; he'd never noticed it before. And he felt . . . charmed by it. That was the only word he could find to describe it.

He pulled out one of the cane-back chairs and sat down. A waitress approached immediately, and he ordered a Scotch before turning back to Marina.

"Thanks for coming. I know I don't deserve it."

She was quiet a moment, watching him. She didn't look angry, but her eyes were a dark gray, flashing with some emotion he couldn't identify.

"You're right, you don't."

"Why are you making an exception, then?"

She glanced down at the glass in her hand. "I . . . don't really know. And maybe that's why I'm here. To find out."

He nodded. "I don't know what the hell I'm doing, either. I don't know why I left your house the way I did." He rubbed both hands over his thighs. "Fuck. No. I do know."

She looked up, that cool, gray gaze on his. "Tell me."

Where to start? How much to reveal? How much would

anyone want to hear about this shit? "Do you have a while? Because this is no short story, and I . . . I'd really like to explain myself. I'd like to try."

She nodded. "Go on."

Oh, she wasn't giving him much, was she? But she was here, willing to listen to him.

"You know what I did for a living. That I traveled all over the world, reporting on the most horrific events. I spent years in all the war-ravaged countries, all of those places that are forgotten about once the war is over. And it's never really over in those places, no matter what the governments say. I've been in El Salvador, Laos, Serbia, Iran, Africa."

He paused as the waitress delivered his drink, took a good long swallow, let it burn its way down his throat.

"After a while, you think you've become numb to it. You pretend, anyway. That's the only way to survive it. The things I've seen were . . . too awful to write about. Oh, I wrote my articles, then my books. But the worst of it just sits in my head. The worst of it I can't even talk about. And after a while it . . . builds up." He stopped, drank again, shrugged. But his fingers were tight around the cool surface of his glass, so tight it hurt a little. "I don't know, maybe it's different for other people who do this for a living. But this is how it is with me."

"It sounds terrible, James. I don't know how you did it. I couldn't have."

Had her eyes gone a little liquid, or was he imagining things?

"Someone had to do it. Someone had to tell those stories. Someone had to be willing not to forget about those people. Children and old men, the women the only ones ever left behind to care for everyone. Or try to, with no resources. They are so desperate, these people. You have no idea. Shit, now I'm starting to sound like one of those commercials asking for money for UNICEF. That's not what I wanted to say."

Marina leaned forward, put a hand on his arm. She wasn't angry with him any longer; he could see that. And he really had not meant to use this stuff as some form of manipulation. It was simply part of his truth.

Her touch was warm . . .

He went on. "What I want to say is . . . I want to explain to you what goes on in my head."

"Yes, tell me."

He looked into her eyes. He read sincerity there. No pity. He couldn't have gone on if she'd pitied him. This whole thing would never work if she did anything out of pity. Still, his stomach was in knots.

"You need to know this stuff is always simmering at the back of my mind. How it underlies everything I think, everything I do. That I got out because I couldn't take any more. And I'm not ashamed to say that."

"There's no reason why you should be. There's only so much anyone can take. And these other people, these other reporters, maybe their threshold is different than yours because they don't feel as much. And I don't believe that's necessarily something to be proud of."

"No. Neither do I."

She smiled then, encouraged him to go on with a nod of her head.

"I don't know if you can imagine what it's like, to witness that kind of absolute suffering."

"Yes. I can. Not on that scale, perhaps, but yes, I have been witness to terrible suffering." She glanced away but not before he saw her eyes going damp, glossy. It was several moments before she turned back to him. "And after, sometimes all we can do is . . . withdraw. From the world. From ourselves . . ."

"Marina?"

"No, don't mind me. I didn't mean to say that to you."

"But you did." He leaned in, and when she would have looked away once more, he took her hand in his, felt a small shiver go through her. But he held on. "What is it?"

She shook her head, silent.

"I saw it, Marina. I saw something in you when we first met. I mentioned it, that dark place. It was one reason why I knew we could . . . work together. Why I knew you would have some understanding of me, of what I was searching for."

"I remember," she said quietly.

"Tell me."

She shook her head again.

"Alright then. I'll tell you more. And then maybe you'll be willing to share with me whatever has hurt you so badly."

She looked at him, her eyes flashing, haunted, her lush mouth trembling the tiniest bit. He didn't let go of her hand.

"On my last trip I was in Africa. Burundi. I don't know if you've heard of it; most people know more about Rwanda. They had a war in Burundi for twelve years. More than three hundred thousand Burundians died. Half a million people became displaced. It's the same story as in so many other African nations. Poor drinking water, little or no food, no medical care. Rampant HIV. And even after the war was over, there was conflict between the ruling government and rebel forces. And it's always the innocent who pay."

He had to stop, rake a hand through his hair, but he kept his other hand clasped to Marina's as the images ran through his head: the lush greenery dotted with shacks made from plywood and thin panels of corrugated tin. The abandoned coffee plantations like some sad testament to the country's need. Odd flashes: A boy riding a bicycle down the street, a goat held tightly in his lap. A row of women dressed in brightly colored cloth balancing water jugs on their heads and pathetically thin children on their hips. A long line of military Jeeps kicking up dust. The red dirt road they'd been driving down when the world had gone to hell around him.

"James? Are you alright?"

"What? Yes, sorry. So . . . I was in Burundi, had been there for about a month, just gathering information to put together an in-depth piece. I had my connection there, an ex-military guy. He wanted a better life for his country. He really did. So he took us around, these three other reporters and me. And one day . . . in fucking broad daylight, we were driving down a road to this small village to visit a hospital and they stopped us."

His stomach pulled so damn tight he could barely breathe, couldn't keep talking.

Just breathe.

Long, deep breath into his lungs, and a reminder that it was over, he was home now, and there was not a damn thing he could do.

"James . . ."

Marina was leaning forward, her hand wrapped around the one he was holding her wrist with. He could see his fingers digging into her smooth flesh, turning the skin around it white, but he couldn't let go, couldn't loosen his grip.

He went on. "Fucking pseudo-military. I think. You can't always tell. They had uniforms. Machine guns." He picked up his drink and drank the rest in one swallow. The burn didn't help. He wanted another drink, but this would have to do. Because he couldn't stop now. "They pulled us over and talked to our guide. I didn't catch most of what they said, so I never knew why. I never fucking understood why they yanked us all out of that van and shot everyone at point-blank range. Everyone except me."

"Jesus, James. I'm so sorry. I know that's not enough. But I am."

Tears in her eyes, real tears, and he could barely stand it.

"They left me there, on my knees in the dirt at the side of the road, the others dead all around me. I could smell their blood everywhere. I just stayed there, waiting for them to come back, but they never did. After a while I got up. I put everyone into the van, went back to Bujumbura, the capital. I didn't know what else to do. Everything after that is a blur for a long time. Months, maybe."

"This was why you quit," Marina said softly.

"Yeah. Or maybe it was the last straw. I don't know." His stomach was going loose and warm. Was it relief? Or was he finally going to lose it? "All I know is I couldn't do it anymore. Couldn't have it in my face any longer. And let me tell you, I felt like a fucking failure. Like I was letting down all of those people I hadn't written or talked about yet. And every awful thing I saw on that trip, I put my notes away, couldn't even look at them, and I felt like I'd let the whole damn country down. I was racked with guilt for keeping my mouth shut about what was going on in Burundi. For what happened to those men I worked with. For not being dead myself. Classic survivor's guilt, I know. I went to therapy. It didn't help much. I can't shake it. I don't know that I ever will."

"I don't know if anyone really could. You'll never forget, James. And I think it's okay not to. I think you can still . . . honor those people by remembering. But you've got to find a way not to let it hurt you so deeply. Not to let it affect your everyday life."

"That's why I came to you, Marina."

He looked at her, his brown eyes full of pupil, nearly black except for a rim of deep gold around the edges of the irises. And Marina shivered inside, a warm frisson running through her, making her weak with an aching empathy, a need to make it better for him. He was so damaged but still so strong.

"James, I want to help you. But I don't know if . . . if I can be objective enough."

He signaled the waitress for another drink before responding. "I've been thinking about that."

"And?"

"What if the objectivity of the others I've worked with, the Dommes, the therapists, what if their objectivity was the obstacle rather than the key it's supposed to be?"

She searched his features, but his mouth was still set in a grim line, his jaw tight. She couldn't tell what he was suggesting, what he was thinking. "What do you mean?"

"What if what I need is for someone to . . . really go there with me? To be involved."

"Do you mean sex?"

"Yes. Partly."

Marina picked up her drink and swallowed as the waitress brought James another Scotch. Watched his throat work as he drank it down fast.

"You need me to engage, is that what you're saying, James? To let my guard down with you?"

"Yes, I guess that is what I'm asking."

She nodded. It made sense. She could go only so deep with him, expect him to open up to her, if she wasn't willing to do the same. Being the distant and mysterious Domme worked well enough with most submissives, but James wasn't entirely submissive, regardless of how his body responded to being bound, to being dominated by her. Far from it. And he had a very specific need. One she wanted to meet. And her wanting went beyond the usual satisfaction of her control issues, the hot spark of being in command. It was so much more with James.

It scared the hell out of her.

"James . . . what you're asking is not something I'm used to giving. Not something I've given anyone for a very long time."

"This is the thing you don't want to talk about."

His tone wasn't at all accusatory. Still, she felt shaky even contemplating telling him about Nathan. Felt almost a sense of disloyalty to Nathan, talking about him to another man. But perhaps James was right, that this was the only way.

She wanted to tell him. She dreaded telling him, talking about it. But everything felt different with James. His pain opened up her own, made her feel as raw as he must feel, simply hearing him, seeing him struggle to get the words out.

She hated it, feeling so wide open. Almost hated James for making her feel this way.

But she was going to do it.

Because everything *was* different with James: the way she felt about herself, the way she felt about him.

The fact that she *felt* for him. It was like being bruised all over. And just like some submissive girl, a part of her reveled in that pain.

She really must be losing her mind.

Closing her eyes, she drew in a breath, drew in the fragrance of James's Scotch, the acrid scent of her own martini, and beneath it all, something male that was purely *him*.

Drawing in another breath, she steeled herself, prepared herself to talk about the one thing she never, ever discussed. The pain that had shut her down so long ago, and that she now understood she'd hung on to for far too long. It hurt to even think about letting it go. But James was right. It was time to talk about her pain, her past.

Chapter Six

"This isn't something I talk about, James."

He nodded his head, waiting. His eyes were still two enormous dark orbs, no less shadowed than they'd been before he'd told his story. But the telling didn't always diminish the pain; she knew that.

"So, Nathan was . . . he was my partner. My submissive. My lover. He was . . . I loved him."

It was hard to say it, yet strangely, not nearly as difficult as she'd thought it would be, with James's hand still holding on to her, his gaze steady on hers.

"What happened, Marina?"

"He died."

James was quiet, watching her, his features softening. "I'm sorry."

"Yes, so was I. I've never finished being sorry."

"I know exactly what you mean."

"Yes, you do. Which is why I can tell you."

He nodded. "Go on."

"He had cancer. Pancreatic, so we knew it was terminal as soon as he was diagnosed. But it took eight months."

"How long were you together?"

"A little over two years."

"Not long enough."

"No."

She was crumbling inside, but only a part of it was grief. Some of it was a sort of coming apart, a continuation of the opening up, as though it were the walls she'd constructed around her heart that were falling apart, rather than herself.

"And since then?" James prompted. "You've shut part of yourself down, just as I have. But I think you haven't reached that point where you want things to be different, have you? Where you want to let it go."

"I think . . ." She had to stop, to consider what he'd suggested. "I think that recently I have reached that point. Made a few realizations. And it's because of you, so thank you for that."

"I don't know what I did. But you're welcome."

"I don't really understand it myself."

God, his gaze was so intense, as though he could *see* her, really see her, in a way no one had for a long time. Maybe never.

"I haven't been with another man since Nathan died. It's been four years," she told him, feeling oddly embarrassed by it. "I've played only women, until you. You've changed things, James. And this is no empty flattery. It's simply the truth."

He nodded. "You're changing things for me, too. And I think together, we can change more for each other. That we can accomplish some forward motion for us both." He leaned in, his fingers slipping between hers, grasping tightly. "Tell me you're willing to try, Marina. For you. For me."

Her heart was pounding. At the idea of making herself so vulnerable with James. At his closeness, the way his hand felt in hers. He was so damn strong, in every way, it was nearly impossible to see him as submissive.

She knew there would be nothing submissive about him in

bed. And if she agreed to continue with him, there was no doubt they would end up there, and very quickly.

"I want to."

Too badly. But she wasn't going to think about that now.

He smiled then, a sort of odd half smile that was charming, nevertheless. And with his gaze still on hers, his grip on her hand softened. He lifted it to his lips, laid a soft, sweet kiss across her knuckles.

Heat shot up her arm, making her breasts go tight, her nipples harden. And in her chest was a churning mass of emotion, heavy, intense. She glanced down at her hand, then back to his face. She saw emotion mirrored in his eyes. Emotion, and desire as powerful as her own. And the heat was electric, sizzling between them.

"Now, Marina?"

She could only nod her head. She was half numb, and yet more alive than she'd been in years.

Four years.

James let her hand go long enough to drop a pile of cash on the table, then he stood, held her chair, and helped her to her feet.

"I live down the street. Do you need rope? I have it. Or we can go to your place."

"It can be anywhere. Let's just go."

Her heart was pounding, her body pulsing with need. He took her coat from the back of the chair, helped her slip into it, took her umbrella from her, and led her out to the street. He pulled her to his side, holding the umbrella over them both as they walked quickly to his apartment. She barely had a moment to take in the old stucco building, the narrow wooden staircase. Then he was unlocking the door, leading her into the open warehouse flat. An enormous sofa at one end, handwoven rugs on the wood floors, shelves and shelves of books. But she couldn't focus on any of it. All she could see was him.

James.

"Where are your ropes?" she asked him, her palms itching to feel the texture of them, to bind him, to watch him struggle. Yes, she loved that about him, that exquisite struggle. It showed his strength rather than any weakness.

"In here. Come with me."

He held her hand tightly as he moved across the room, through a door, and into a large bedroom. The bed was in the very center of the room, which was broken up by heavy wood posts. The room was dark, the only light coming through the windows: moonlight, streetlamps, the glow from the storefronts on the street below. And all of it blurred and softened by the rain, which was coming down harder now, a steady pulse-beat that matched her own.

James dropped her hand and moved to a large dresser against one wall, a heavy wood piece, Asian, probably. He pulled open a drawer, pulled out a number of net bags, carried them back to the bed, laid them down on the dark cotton quilt.

"They're color-coded by length," he said, his voice a low, husky murmur. "Fifty-foot, twenty, ten. Some shorter pieces. What do you want?"

He straightened, looked at her, and her breath hitched in her chest. He was so damn beautiful, his face hard, challenging her, his strong jaw set. Yet there was something soft and loose around his eyes, that contrast showing his inner struggle to submit.

She went hot all over. Wet.

She couldn't think of the usual commands. Could hardly think at all.

He stepped closer.

Oh, no, can't think at all now.

"Marina," he said, his voice quiet. "Just do it. Don't plan it." He reached out, stroked one finger down the side of her face, kicking the heat up another notch, before dropping his hand to his side. "Let's just . . . go where it takes us."

"Yes . . ."

She licked her lips, kept her gaze on his. "Take your clothes off, James."

He nodded and began to strip.

She took one step back and watched him, every motion a graceful ripple of slowly revealed muscle. How could she have forgotten how sleek his body was? How utterly perfect. His abs were a stark play of shadowed surfaces, his shoulders impossibly broad. And the tattoos on his left arm stood out to her, even in the pale light from the street.

She reached out, almost touching his biceps.

"What is this?"

"The archangel Gabriel. For protection."

"And this?" It seemed important, somehow, to know. She let her fingers rest on his skin, ran them down his forearm to the Asian figure draped in patterned robes.

"The Chinese goddess Kuan Yin, goddess of mercy."

"And do the clouds and the water mean something?"

"They represent all things mercurial. The ever-changeable nature of life."

"Why?"

"You never know what to expect from the world."

"But you've come to expect the worst, haven't you? I think I saw that in you from the start."

"Only the expectation, the reality, of people having to go through hell on this earth is immutable. But you know that. It's why we're here now."

She couldn't believe they were having this philosophical conversation, with him standing half undressed before her, her body on fire for him. Yet at the same time, it seemed natural with him. But she was too distracted by him sliding his jeans down his thighs as he spoke, and in moments he was naked.

Ah, lovely.

His cock was hard. Too beautiful. Her mouth went dry, and she had to lick her lips, to steel herself against the sight of him: that gorgeous golden skin, the strength of his thighs.

She had to get her hands on him.

Just do it, as he said.

She turned and started emptying the net bags onto the bed. Rope fell in lengths of white, black, blue, red. She gathered a few pieces in her hands, gestured with her chin to one of the wide, square wood columns. He didn't say a word, just went to the column, stood with his back against one side, his legs spread just a bit, as though he was in military pose. His eyes were dark, flashing, his jaw set. As she drew closer she could see his pulse jumping in his neck.

She ran a length of rope through her hands, just to get the feel of it, as she often did. Her palms were damp. She wiped them on her skirt, one at a time, saw James's gaze flicker to the motion of her hands. Then she had the rope between her fingers, a long length in stark black.

She moved in, watched him flinch with some small satisfaction that was like a sexual surge in her veins, hot, stinging.

"Back up," she told him. "Right against the post."

He did as she said, and she stepped closer, until she could feel the heat coming off his body, even through her clothes. And that scent that was purely him, carried to her on the waves of heat.

She breathed him in, shivered, leaned forward, and brushed a kiss across his cheek. He trembled, just the smallest tremor moving over his skin, but he held his position. When she moved back, she could taste him on her lips. Her sex swelled, heated.

More.

Oh, yes. She planned to have more. But she had to bind him first.

Have to . . .

Reaching around the column, she took one of his wrists and drew it behind him, then the other. She started there, wrapping his wrists in a simple noose knot, then she began an uncomplicated crisscross pattern on his body. She was too anxious simply to have him bound to take the time for the delicate, complex series of knots required for true Shibari. No, with him she realized it was the symbol that was important rather than the ritual. He didn't need the slow buildup. Not tonight. He needed to be tied down. To have something to fight against. Something other than the demons in his head that tortured him so terribly.

Moving around his body, she let the ropes lead her, all the while watching his breath quicken, his nipples peaking into two dusky points, his cock hardening even more, going dark at the head. And she felt perfectly in tune with him, every surge of desire as though it was reflected in her own body, a mirror of his need. Or perhaps his was a mirror of her own; she couldn't tell.

It didn't matter. All that mattered was the rope sliding beneath her hands, and under the ropes, his silken skin, the taut pull of muscle as he clenched and unclenched when she touched him. Oh, it was too good to see his response. Even better to look into his eyes and find he was slipping into subspace. But not that quiet, sleepy kind of space so many others went into. No, with James it was all edge, intensity.

When he was bound tightly to the post, she stroked a fingertip over his shoulder. He flinched hard, and she leaned in, her mouth right next to his ear.

"What is it, James? Can you tell me?"

"I just . . . it fucking frightens me, how much I want you."

Her breath went right out of her lungs, her sex going wet, pulsing. And she pressed her body into his side, just falling into him. Her breasts were crushed against his arm, her hips against his flank.

"Jesus, James."

He groaned but didn't say anything else. She pressed harder, moved her body so that her nipples were up against his arm. They were so damn hard, they hurt. And she wanted to feel his skin against them.

Oh, yes . . .

She stepped back just enough to take off her sweater, her bra, leaving her in her tight pencil skirt, her opaque tights, her high-heeled black boots. She saw him turn his head, blink hard, his cock jumping. She pressed back in until the tips of her breasts brushed against the ropes, then, shifting, she could feel his skin between the ropes.

Oh, yes . . .

A sharp intake of breath from him, then his mouth was on hers. His lips were so damn warm and sweet with whiskey, still. And his tongue went right in, claiming her even though he was tied to the post, nearly immobilized. But she was suddenly under his command as much as he was under hers. Or perhaps she had been from the start. She couldn't think about it, couldn't figure it out. She didn't care, for once. She just wanted to taste him, to luxuriate in the silky glide of his tongue over hers, the feel of his plush lips sucking her into him. She pressed her body closer, his heart beating against hers, a wild hammer thundering from his chest into hers, and back again.

Her legs were going weak. She reached out, steadied herself with her hands on his shoulders. And her hips arched into his, until his cock was at the apex of her thighs, begging to be let in.

Yes, have to have him, to feel him there . . .

She pulled back.

"James . . ."

"Kiss me, Marina."

"I will. But, James . . ."

"Now."

"Tell me first. Tell me you're mine." She felt half crazed, totally out of control. She wasn't sure exactly what it was she was asking for.

His voice was low, gritty. "Yes, yours. But you're mine just as much."

She nodded. It was true.

"I need to fuck you, Marina."

A stab of lust, sweet and low in her belly. "Yes."

"But *I* will fuck *you*, Marina." It came out as a growl.

"Yes . . ."

She didn't care about being in control now. She wasn't thinking about any of that; that wasn't why she sank to her knees and took the tip of his cock into her mouth. But to hear him groan, that was what made sense to her now. To taste his swollen flesh, the pearly drop of pre-come warm on her tongue. She felt him fight the ropes, give in after a moment, and his body went slack as she lowered her head and swallowed him as deeply as she could, her throat opening to take him in.

She slid back, swirled her tongue over the head of his cock before taking him into her throat once more. He was panting now, writhing the tiniest bit, as much as the tight ropes would allow. And she felt a surge of power, but it was different from what she usually felt when she was topping someone. No, this was all about the power of being purely female. The power of bringing him pleasure. And it was heady, potent.

But she needed more. She needed him.

She let his cock slip from her mouth, and rose to her feet. His face was all hard planes, but his mouth was soft, almost bruised-looking. And his eyes were blazing, golden.

She reached out and touched her fingertips to his lips, and he sucked them in, sucked hard, hurting her just a little. She drew her hand back, stood watching him for several moments.

"James. I'm taking you out of the ropes."

"Yes," he hissed. "God damn it, yes."

She did it quickly, and in moments the ropes fell at his feet, and he was charging at her, all pure male, in a rage of desire. He was on her so quickly she didn't have time to think about it. He stripped her skirt off, her boots, her tights, ripping holes in them as he tore them from her body. Then her panties, which were soaking wet. He paused, held them in his hand, brushed them across his lips, making her shiver all over. Then he tossed them aside and gripped her arms, backing her onto the bed.

His hands were hard and hurting on her arms as he held her down. And she went down without a word as he bent his head to take one nipple into his mouth. He sucked, grazed the tip with his teeth, and she was moaning, panting immediately, pleasure shooting through her body. She was writhing beneath him. His hands went to her breasts, pushing them together, kneading the tender flesh, and she arched into him.

Every touch was hard, commanding, exquisite. She didn't want it any other way. She tried to wrap one leg around his waist, but he pushed her harder into the mattress, sliding his hands up until he had her wrists pinned above her head.

"Don't move, Marina," he said. "You are mine right now. Say it."

"Yes. I'm yours, James."

Had she ever said that to anyone else? Didn't matter.

"Kiss me, James. Fuck me. Please."

He laid his body over hers, pressed into her, his cock pushing against her belly. She spread her thighs, and his muscular leg slipped between them, right against the wet heat of her sex. He moved, his thigh sliding back and forth, and she wanted to come right away, pleasure pouring through her system. But she didn't want to come like this.

"James!"

He leaned to one side, yanked open the nightstand drawer so hard it crashed onto the floor. He swore, dug around, came back with a string of condoms, tore one off with his teeth. Then he got the wrapper opened, sat back on his knees. He fumbled with the condom, swore again, and she reached out to help him, and somehow, together, they managed to sheath his cock. Still on his knees, he drew her legs over his, so that her hips were raised, her sex open to him. He kept his gaze on hers as he swept his fingers over her pussy lips.

"Oh . . ."

"So damn wet for me, Marina."

"James, come on."

She raised her hips, opening more for him. And he smiled, baring his teeth like some wild animal. His hands went to her hips and he pulled her in hard, plunging into her in one deep thrust.

"Oh, God, James . . ."

Pleasure, hot and deep, like shards of glass: that sharp, that intense. She was shivering with it instantly, had never felt anything so damn good in her life. And he was pulling her in, over and over, his hips hammering into her in long, hard thrusts. Fucking her, fucking her. And they were both grunting, panting, making primal, wordless sounds. She could barely breathe. She didn't care.

He paused, his strong hands on her hips turning her over onto her belly, holding her down flat against the bed, pulling her legs apart. He laid his body over hers, pushed into her sex from behind. He pulled her hips up a little, angling her so that his hard cock was hitting her G-spot. And at the same time, he wrapped one arm tightly around her waist, possessing her. His hand went between her thighs, pinching her clitoris between his fingers.

She came in a torrent, shuddering, crying out his name. Pleasure arced through her like an electric current; she could almost smell the burn of it on her skin.

Inside her, his cock was a solid shaft, pushing ever deeper, driving her climax on and on. Then he tensed, groaned, and even through the condom she felt the heat of it as he came, his body clenching, writhing.

"Marina . . . Christ!"

He kept pumping into her, even as his cock went soft, and small climactic shivers ran over her skin in shimmering waves, as though she couldn't stop coming.

Finally they were both limp, weak, and he rolled onto his side, taking her with him. Her mind was numb, her body spent, shaking. Yet she still needed more; she couldn't seem to get enough.

It was almost unreal to her that this was James lying next to her, his chest heaving with uncaught breath. That he had just been inside her body. It seemed like some sort of wild dream and yet more real than anything she'd felt in a long time.

Outside, it was really raining, the drops hitting the windows in thudding little splashes. She could hear the sound of it running down a drainpipe somewhere outside the building. And faintly, the cars on the street below driving through puddles. It comforted her, made James's body next to hers feel as though he was keeping her safe. It was as though they were isolated from the rest of the world, the rain cocooning them away in his bed.

Still, something nagged at the back of her mind.

Don't feel too much. You know what can happen if you do.

Oh, yes, she did. And she'd never planned to allow that to happen again, to be so vulnerable. But with James it was unavoidable, unless she wasn't going to see him at all. She knew already she didn't have it in her to turn away from him. And after tonight . . .

What?

But it was too much to think about. She curled into his side, listened to his quiet breath, knew he was asleep. And let herself drift into that same nowhere place, where she could dream of the rain falling outside, touching her skin like his fingertips, his soft lips. Like the words he'd spoken to her.

You are mine.

Chapter Seven

JAMES WAS AWAKENED by a soft shuffling and the sudden absence of heat. He opened his eyes and saw Marina's shadowy silhouette in the diffused, early-morning light as she got out of bed.

She was beautiful.

He'd been with plenty of beautiful women. So why did she make his heart lurch in his chest?

He lay quietly as he watched her get dressed, his eyes half-lidded. She was graceful, every movement like a dancer's. He'd seen it before, the way she handled the ropes, even her drink. And last night . . .

Last night she'd taken him somewhere he'd never gone before. Something about her. Had to be. Because it was more than the ropes, although that had been a catalyst. But he knew it wouldn't have happened with anyone else. The dynamic between them just worked. And he'd felt a sort of slipping away, as though when she had him bound, he'd given himself permission to let the rage build. And when she'd let him out, she'd allowed him to vent that rage on her, in her body. But once he'd touched her, it wasn't rage anymore. It was converted to something else. To sex. To . . . something *more*.

Damn it. He wasn't making sense, even to himself. All he knew was that he felt better. Lighter. And he wanted to do it again. Wanted to fuck her right now, just drive into her body over and over. Wanted to make her come, watch her fall apart beneath him the way she had last night.

He was hard again. But she was so quiet, so thoughtful, in the dim morning light; he didn't dare disturb her. And he wanted to see what she was going to do, if she would leave without saying good-bye.

Why the hell did it matter?

It just did.

When she was dressed she paused, looked around the room, her gaze resting for several long moments on the windows.

It had stopped raining. And it must be early; the streets outside were nearly silent, other than the occasional passing of a car. Finally she turned, moved toward the bed, and he opened his eyes, let her know he was awake.

"James, I have to go to work."

"Okay."

"I . . . we can talk later, if you want."

"Do you want to?"

She seemed surprised that he'd asked. "Yes."

"Good."

She was too close for him not to touch her. He reached up and pulled her onto the bed so he could kiss her. Her mouth was soft and lush, and his cock twitched.

Yes, to have her right now. To strip her down and wrap his arms around her. Push into her body as he had last night. But he'd take his time, explore her.

She pulled away. "I really have to go."

"Do you want me to get up? Walk you back to your car?"

"I took a cab last night. I'll get one on the corner."

"I can drive you."

"No, don't get up."

He could feel her shutting down, separating herself from him. He didn't know why she was doing it. He didn't know why he cared.

"How late do you work?" he asked her.

"I don't know. Each day is different."

"I'll call you tonight. See if you're home."

Why was he pressing the issue?

"Alright."

He twined his fingers in her hair, and her face softened for a moment before she pulled away. "I really do have to get going."

Then she was gone.

The bed felt too big to him, suddenly. And he was still rock-hard. Needing her.

He reached down and brushed his fingertips over the swollen head of his cock, breathing in the scent of leftover sex from the night before. His body arched into his touch, and he wrapped a hand around his rigid shaft, began to stroke. Pleasure shivered through him: his cock, his balls, his belly. And in moments he was thrusting into his fist, as he'd thrust into Marina last night. Just fucking her, fucking her, her body soft and yielding beneath him.

His climax came crashing down on him, pleasure like pure white heat, making him jerk hard into his hand, come shooting onto his stomach.

Marina . . .

Yeah, he didn't know why he cared, why he couldn't get her out of his mind. Why this God damn driving need couldn't be sated by jacking off.

Why he wanted to just *be* with her, as much as he wanted to fuck her, wanted her to tie him up again.

Crazy.

He'd call her tonight, ask if she would see him. And he'd figure things out then, after he talked to her. He'd spend the day calming down, getting his head back on straight. Because *this* was crazy. He'd known the woman three weeks. And it shouldn't matter if it had been three months. Three years. A man like him wasn't built for relationships. He'd never been in that headspace. Not with his kind of job. Not with the kind of risks he took.

A job you walked away from, left behind.

But that didn't mean *he* was any different. Did it? Or was Marina simply a different kind of risk?

MARINA STARED at her ringing cell phone, watching the screen light up with James's name. Her heart fluttered in her chest. Like some schoolgirl. She felt foolish. But she smiled as she picked up the phone, flipped it open, the anticipation of talking to him chasing away the doubts that had plagued her all day.

She took a long breath before answering. "Hello?"

"Marina."

Pure pleasure, hearing him say her name.

"Hi, James."

"You're there."

"Yes, I finished at six tonight."

"How was work?"

"It was fine. Good." She got up from the sofa and went to stand by the windows, watching the evening fog roll in like a soft, gray blanket. "I found a piece I'd been looking for for one of my clients for months. A Mexican painter, a surrealist. This client wanted a particular piece, a very large canvas. I was lucky to track it down." She could still see the painting in her mind, the image that had been e-mailed to her from the dealer in Lisbon. The bold strokes and slashes of color, the disturbingly beautiful distorted forms. Something frankly sexual about the piece. Or maybe that was simply where her mind was, after last night. Last night . . . She shivered. "God, I'm sorry, James. I'm babbling. I guess I still have work on my mind."

Or she was so spun by the sound of James's voice in her ear, by the memory of him pushing into her body, she couldn't think straight.

"No, it's fine. I like hearing about your work. We haven't really talked much about it. How long have you been an art dealer? How did you get into it?"

"My degree is in art; I think we talked about that before. I've been doing this for over ten years. I worked in galleries before that, since I was very young. Ever since I left home."

"When was that?"

"The summer I turned eighteen. A week after my birthday."

"Your parents didn't find that disturbing?"

"They were both gone by then. It was just me and my sister, Elizabeth."

"I'm sorry. What happened to them? If you don't mind my asking."

"No, it's fine." She reached up and traced her fingertips over the cool glass of the window, her eyes on the darkening sky. "It's been a long time. My parents were in an accident when I was a baby. My grandmother raised us. She was good to us, saw that we had everything we needed, but I've never been particularly close to her. She still lives in North Carolina, where I was raised."

"And your sister?"

"She's in New York, an interior designer."

"Ah, you have a lot in common, then."

"Not really. She's twelve years older than I am. She was always more like an aunt than a sister. We don't talk much."

"I'm not close to my family, either."

"Where are they?"

"It's just my dad. He left San Francisco a good ten years ago; he's retired in Puerto Vallarta with wife number four. We get along well enough. Well, Dad and I do. I don't like the wife much. But he seems happy."

"So, you were raised here?"

"Yes. I got my journalism degree at U.C. Santa Cruz, but the city has always been my home base."

"I love this city. I haven't left since I arrived."

"And when was that?"

"I must have been twenty-two, twenty-three. I studied at the Academy of Art here, right after I finished my associate's degree."

"So, it was always art for you."

"I did branch off to study cultural anthropology, initially. Then a few years ago I went back to school for it, but I . . . I never got my degree." She didn't want to talk about why she'd dropped out of school. Didn't want to tell him it was because Nathan got sick. She didn't want to get into that with him. Not now. "But I've always loved art. I have no talent for it myself, and always wished I did."

"The Shibari is art," he said simply.

"I suppose it is, yes. There is an aesthetic to it. There's form and balance, and even color choice, in the ropes, in the contrast of it against the skin."

"So, you are an artist, of sorts."

"Well, maybe. But I think that's a stretch."

It was nice, talking to him like this. As though they were normal people.

Weren't they?

It had been a very long time since she'd felt normal.

She realized suddenly that her sense of being separated from the rest of the world had nothing to do with her sexual proclivities, with her interest in rope bondage. It was that she had separated herself, had made an effort to hold herself apart, ever since she'd lost Nathan.

Four years was a long time to feel like an outsider. Long enough, maybe.

"Are you still there, Marina?"

"What? Yes, I'm here. I'm sorry, what did you say?"

"I said I want to see you. I need to see you."

Yes, she needed to see him, too. Absolutely needed to. And

that felt like an enormous risk to her. Acknowledging it, even to herself, made her shaky inside, a combination of overpowering lust and undeniable fear.

"Tonight, Marina? Can you see me tonight?"

"Yes."

Could it really be that easy?

Oh, no, can't resist him . . . impossible.

Impossible that she was feeling this way about him. About anyone. Impossible that she was allowing herself to. But she was right, he *was* irresistible. The only question was how far she was willing to take this. How much was she willing to risk? And if her desire for him drove her to surpass that boundary, would she be able to stop it?

"Marina." His voice was a husky murmur that sent a shudder of desire through her, heating her up inside. "I can't wait to see you."

God, what this man did to her! She could hardly think, her mind melting away on a sea of desire.

"Um . . . when?"

"As soon as you're free. Now. You tell me."

Yes, get some semblance of control back.

"I have a few things to do." *Liar. Again. The control thing is all crap now, isn't it? All you want to do is see him.* "How about nine? And come here, to my place."

"As you wish," he said.

Yes, that was better. Even if his tone was far from subservient. But she didn't want that from him, did she? No, she wanted strength, wanted his struggle, wanted the power of his anger in her hands, wanted to be the one to shape it.

"I'll see you in a few hours, then."

She hung up before he could reply. Before he could stir her up any further. There would be time for that once he arrived.

She groaned. He would stir her up, stir her blood, stir her mind. And she would be helpless against it. It didn't matter which one of them was in the ropes.

Hell.

But she wasn't going to turn away from him. She couldn't.

Taking in a deep breath, she flattened her hand against the chilly window, trying to ground herself.

Just let it happen. See where it goes.

Why did she feel that with James she was being driven toward the edge of a yawning chasm, and if she wasn't careful, she would go toppling off, flying into . . . nothing? A dark place she didn't want to know about, one she'd done a very good job of ignoring for the last four years. A place of loss, of loneliness.

But she would see him. Be with him. She had to. She would deal with the fear later. Deal with the fallout, if there was going to be any.

She slid her palm down the glass, feeling the chill of it on her skin, creeping over her wrist, up her arm. There would be fallout. Had to be, with everything James was already making her feel. How much more would she feel before it was over? She was afraid to know.

She was more afraid to stop.

EIGHT FIFTY-FIVE, and her pulse was hammering in her veins. She'd dressed all too carefully in a knee-length pencil skirt, her high black boots with the narrow heels, a body-hugging black top, a blood-red garnet on a long silver chain around her neck. Sexy clothes. Things she wore when she was in Domme role. They hadn't really addressed playing tonight, only talking. But if she didn't get her hands on him—or feel his hands on her—she really would lose her mind.

She paced the kitchen, sat down at the table, where a small potted geranium bloomed in the center in a Chinese porcelain bowl. She reached out and stroked the soft petals with her fingertips, the red blossom releasing its spicy fragrance. With the petals still between her fingers, she looked out at the dark street. There was a full moon; it hung in the sky like a luminous disk of pale gold, like some sort of guardian over the city, ever watchful.

She should watch herself tonight, with him. But she felt completely unable to do it. If she was going to allow him near her—and there was no question that she would—it meant a struggle to maintain any semblance of control. She was okay when he was in the ropes, if not quite as solid as she should be. But once she let him out . . .

Her sex gave a sudden, hard squeeze.

Oh, yes, once she let him out he was the one in command of the situation. Of her body.

A small shudder went through her: fear and lust again.

When the doorbell rang, she jumped, accidentally pulling two petals from the geranium plant. She swore under her breath, stood, smoothed down her skirt. With her heart an uneven patter in her chest, she went to answer the door.

He looked as great as ever. Better, maybe, now that she knew the taste of his mouth, the hard planes of his body pressed against hers. He was smiling at her, an honest expression she found irresistible.

Just like everything else about him.

She wanted to take his smiling face between her hands and kiss him. She wanted him to sweep her into his arms.

Stop it.

What was wrong with her?

"James, hi. Please, come in."

"You look beautiful, Marina."

"You don't have to say that just because we slept together."

"I don't have to say it at all. But I happen to think you're beautiful." He'd stopped just inside the door; he was staring down at her, his gaze dark, glittering. Intense as ever, as though there were some deeper meaning behind whatever he was saying. "Surely I'm not the first man to tell you how beautiful you are."

"No, but . . ." Why was she so flustered? "I just . . . thank you. Come in; I'll get you something to drink. What would you like?"

"Are we playing tonight?"

"I don't know."

Her pulse sped up.

Please, yes.

"Just water, then." He smiled again, his teeth a white flash between his lush lips. She wanted to run her tongue over his teeth . . .

She turned and led him into the kitchen; it felt safer than the living room. All too easy to make out on the sofa.

When was the last time she'd made out with a man on the sofa?

She gestured, and he sat at the table, looking larger than ever in her apartment, sitting in the white-painted ladder-back chair. She went to the refrigerator, returned with a bottle of San Pellegrino and two glasses with ice, set them on the table.

James picked up the bottle. "Allow me."

He poured for them both, and she sat down in the chair next to him.

Too close.

Not close enough.

"So," she began, "you wanted to talk about last night."

"Yes. Last night. About what's happening with us in general. About what happens to me when . . . when you tie me up. I want to tell you. It feels . . . significant."

"Tell me, then."

He paused, watching her, and she felt as though he could see right inside her, could see how her body heated under his gaze, how damp her panties were already, with him simply sitting next to her.

But he was talking again and she had to concentrate.

"When I came to you I wanted something very specific. To hit subspace, to go really deeply in, to lose myself. To find peace."

She nodded. "We discussed all of that at our first meeting."

"Yes. But I didn't know exactly what it was I needed until it happened."

"Are you saying you've found that peace already?"

"In a way. But it didn't happen the way I expected."

"What do you mean?"

He ran a hand through his dark hair, leaving it a little mussed and spiky on top. "I was looking for a way to find a sort of mindless space, an escape. But what I needed, ultimately, was to face the shit going on in my head. The part I didn't want to face. The anger."

"I felt that in you last night."

"I hope I didn't frighten you."

"No, not at all. You seemed to be able to channel it."

He leaned in a little, and she caught the male scent of him. Something about the way this man smelled . . . She took in a slow, deep lungful, careful that he not see what she was doing.

Lovely.

"Marina." His voice was low, a little rough, urgent, making the tiny hairs on the back of her neck stand up as he reached over and wrapped his hand around her wrist. "I need to go there again. With you. Tonight, if possible. I know I am not in a position to make demands."

Oh, if he only knew.

"No, I mean . . . it's fine. I'm glad I'm able to help."

"Marina, stop it."

"What?"

"Stop trying to remain so damn aloof. We both know you're not so indifferent. This is not a pro job, for God's sake. I feel something, with you. Something powerful. I don't even know what it is. But this dynamic could not happen unless we were on the same page. And I'm pretty damn sure I'm not making it up, that this is not something my mind has invented. This is the power play, but it goes beyond that usual kind of being in sync. Tell me you don't feel it, too," he demanded. "Tell me."

He was gripping her wrist hard, and she had to resist the urge to pull away. It was all too intense, suddenly. But he was right.

"Okay. Yes. There is something happening. And yes, I feel it, too. Of course I do."

He sat and stared at her, unblinking, his eyes liquid gold and chocolate brown in the bright light of the kitchen. She couldn't look away.

"I need to do it again." He said it once more, quietly.

She nodded her head once, stood. He came up with her, still holding on to her wrist.

"Take me there, Marina."

Chapter Eight

JAMES WATCHED MARINA as she worked, bent over him, moving her hands as though in some sort of dance: kinky, beautiful. She'd stripped him down with her own hands, and he'd been hard before she laid the first rope on his body. Now he was bound to the long, narrow bench in her guest room. He was on his back, so much rope on him he was immobilized. He felt that sliding sensation as his mind let go, yet he was acutely aware of Marina at his side, her soft hands on him, working the ropes, the occasional stroke of her fingertips against his skin.

Fucking amazing, what this woman's touch did to him. And even as conscious thought began to slip away, his mind to loosen, the awareness of his state of arousal anchored him in his body, holding him to the earth.

He took one last look at Marina, the fall of auburn hair around her shoulders, her cool, crystalline gray eyes, the silken curve of cheekbone. The softness and concentration of expression on her face. He felt her watching him, and watching over him. As soothing as she was stimulating.

He was going warm all over, his skin heating, as it often did when he was bound. It crept over his body and into his head, and he opened himself to it. He felt himself drifting and had a moment of panic, that fear of letting it all go, but Marina was right there.

"James, you have to let it happen if this is going to work. Do your breathing. Come on, follow my voice, my breath. You know how to do it."

She wrapped one hand around the back of his neck; her palm was warm. His cock grew harder, but it didn't distract him from what was happening in his head. If anything, it made it easier somehow.

Her voice was soft, nearly a whisper. "Good, James. You're going down."

He sank into it, into subspace, letting his vision blur, fade into blackness, his mind emptying even faster than it had with her before. Her hand was still on the back of his neck, keeping him in his body, so that his mind was free to roam.

The places came first in a jumble: Baghdad, San Salvador, Angola, Timor, Bosnia, and finally the red dirt road leading out of Bujumbura.

There was a small herd of goats, a brown-and-white kid kicking up its heels as it followed its mother, the only happy creature he'd seen in Burundi—hell, anywhere he'd been in Africa—and it made him smile.

That was the last time he'd smiled for a very long time.

The Jeeps racing up the road from behind them. Three of them, driving up alongside their van, the rapid demand over and over for them to pull over. So many of them, dressed as soldiers, spilling from the Jeeps almost as though they were clown cars. Except there was nothing funny about it. It was hard to tell if they were government troops or guerillas. Didn't matter. Things happening in a blur after that: yelling; he didn't know what they were saying, just the certainty that this was going to be very bad.

They were pulled from their van, forced to their knees on the side of the road, lined up like paper targets in a shooting gallery.

Brian Reynolds first, being pushed face-first into the red dust, a booted foot on the back of his head, then the first gunshot, God damn it, and Reynolds was dead.

His gut clenched.

God damn it!

Blood everywhere, the metallic smell of it, mixing with the dust. Fucking helpless, not a damn thing he could do, just watch out of the corner of his eye as they shot their Burundian guide in the head. Then squeezing his eyes shut while they killed Foster and Garman, waiting for his turn.

It never came.

Blood everywhere, and none of it his. Those fuckers driving off, just leaving him there with his hands clasped behind his neck.

But no, it was Marina's hand at the back of his neck.

"James, it's okay," she whispered.

No, it was not okay. It was fucking not okay!

He tried to bolt, but the ropes held him. Held his body so damn tightly he couldn't move, but he fought them anyway.

"*Shh,* James. Just breathe."

Didn't she know he couldn't breathe? He could not fucking breathe!

Rage tore through him, twisted his gut into a tight knot, poured through his system, hot and white. Like lightning in his veins.

He. Could. Not. Breathe.

He gasped for air, but his lungs were so damn tight. Didn't matter; he should die right here. He'd missed his turn.

Struggling against his binds, his muscles strained until they hurt. Pain all over his body, the rope biting into his flesh. He was breaking a good, hard sweat.

He'd missed his fucking turn!

But no, that was ridiculous. Was that really what he'd felt all this time? What he'd been hiding from himself?

God, he hated those motherfuckers, those murderers! Not a

damn thing he could have done about it, with their guns pointed at his head, the long machetes in their hands.

Not a God damn thing.

He yelled "Fuck!" and opened his eyes, found Marina watching him, her brows drawn together.

He was panting, dazed, but the rage was melting into a hot pool. It simmered in him still, but the ropes helped him contain it. But only for so long. It had to go somewhere eventually.

He said through clenched teeth, "Okay, Marina. Let me out."

He thought she'd argue with him. That she'd be afraid. Hell, he'd be afraid, if he were her right now. But she just nodded, and in moments he was free.

He wasn't even hard anymore. He just . . . *needed*.

With a growl he grabbed her, pulled her tight, and closed his mouth over hers. Her lips were sweet, so damn sweet, and he opened her up with his tongue. She was going loose already, and he was hard again instantly. He ground his cock against her, started to tear her clothes from her body.

Have to see her, touch her, fuck her.

He could feel her trembling, could feel her desire coming off her like waves of heat as he stripped her bare. Then he thrust a hand between her thighs, found her wet.

"Christ, Marina."

"Come on, James. Come on . . ."

Lord, to hear her beg like that. To hear her need, almost screaming at him, drowning out the shit in his head. Yeah, just be with her, inside her body, feel her need, feed his own. Feast on her.

He pushed her down on the bed, spread her thighs, and lowered his head between them. He took her with his mouth; first with his lips, then with his tongue, drawing it over her wet hole, the hard nub of her clit, sucking on her flesh: clit, pussy lips. She was grinding into his face and he wanted her to, wanted her writhing as she was now, making little mewling noises.

He pulled back long enough to demand of her, "Come, Marina."

"Oh . . ."

She spread her legs wider for him and he dove in once more, sucking, licking, using his hands, pressing two fingers inside her, her pussy like wet fucking silk. He worked her hard, thrusting with his fingers, curving them to rub against her G-spot. And she was moving her hips, really shoving her beautiful pussy against his face, loving it, needing it.

Then she was coming, her insides clenching around his fingers, her hips pistoning, and there was a rush of liquid, soaking his hand, his face, sweet and hot. And still he worked her, still she came, calling his name.

"God, James! James, James . . ."

Finally he couldn't stand it any longer. He left her long enough to find his pants, to pull a condom from the pocket and roll it onto his cock. He was rigid as steel, his own touch as he slipped the condom on almost too much as he watched Marina on the bed, her breasts flushed, her mouth soft and loose. Her hair was everywhere.

He laid down on the bed beside her, rolling to his back, pulling her on top of him.

"Fuck me now, Marina."

A small smile from her, a touch of triumph in it.

"You are not in control here," he told her quietly.

The smile was gone immediately, replaced by something softer, more yielding. And she went loose in his hands as he gripped her hips hard, guided her onto him, her long legs straddling his body. One sharp thrust upward and he was inside her, impaling her. And he held her tight as he pumped up into her.

"Fuck me, Marina," he told her again, and she began to move, her hips arching as she took him in, ground down onto him. So damn good, pleasure rolling over him like thunder. And she kept at it, riding him, bucking and lunging like some wild thing, riding his anger as much as she was his body.

He reached up and took her nipples between his fingers, felt them harden, watched as they went a dark red. He pinched, she cried out, her head falling back, her lips parting. He pinched harder.

"James, fuck!"

"Am I hurting you?"

"Yes . . . please . . . hurt me."

He twisted that tender flesh harder, pulling, pinching. She was grinding against him, her pussy holding his cock like a gauntlet of pure pleasure. And he felt the anger flooding out of his body and into hers, then dissipating, fading away.

She was coming again, that hot sheath clenching his cock, milking him. And he thrust deeper, fucking her, fucking her. Needing to hurt her just a little.

"Oh . . . James, God . . ."

His climax hit him like a blow to the gut, pleasure ramming into his system, his body convulsing. He was coming so damn hard, pumping the anger into her as he came. He was shuddering all over, and it was so damn good, almost too good, almost painful.

Only when it was over did he see how his fingers had dug into her hips, leaving dark red marks on her pale skin. But there was something beautiful about it. Something about it making her *his*.

She collapsed onto him, her lithe body stretched out over his. He felt dazed, light, as though his brain had been wiped clean.

No need to think about anything at all right now.

Fucking bliss.

He lay with her for a while, maybe dozed for a few minutes. When she sighed he turned his face, held hers in his hands, kissed her. She was pliant, still. And there was something about seeing her that way, feeling that yielding, that made his cock stiffen again. But there was no more animal in him. He just wanted to *be* with her. To touch her. Just . . . touch her.

He'd think about what the hell that meant later.

"Marina. Come into the shower with me."

"Yes . . ."

They got up and he took her hand. "Show me where."

"This way."

She led him across the hallway, through what he realized vaguely must be her bedroom, which felt oddly intimate to him. Just seeing her space, the place where she slept. Light filtered in from the hallway, dimly illuminating the room, and he glanced at the big bed covered in a deep, plum-colored silk and piles of pillows.

To have her in her bed. Oh, yes, he would do that. But later.

Marina turned on the light in the bathroom, all pristine white tile and thick lavender towels, brushed pewter fixtures. An enormous ornate, pewter-framed mirror hung above the sink, and he caught their reflection in it: her disheveled hair, the flushed, glowing skin on both of them, their interlocked hands.

He reached in and turned the hot water on, let it run for a few moments. Marina was quiet, and he had a sense that she was in subspace, that he had put her there by taking command of her body. And he felt a sort of tenderness toward her. Something about the fact that she had given herself over to him. He understood it was something she had seldom done before, if ever.

Precious. That's what she was to him at this moment.

His heart hitched in his chest, but he couldn't think about it, didn't want to stop to figure it out. Instead, he pulled her into the wide shower stall, under the warm spray, and she went with him, held still while he wrapped his arms around her. Laid her head against his chest. And even though they didn't exchange a word, he knew she felt what he did. That they were both allowing this unusual moment of intimacy.

But he was still thinking too much. Better just to be quiet inside. To enjoy this, whatever it was.

Marina leaned into him, his chest a solid wall of comfort beneath her cheek. When was the last time she'd felt this sort of safety? When had she allowed herself to be a woman, with a man? It had been so long. And until this moment, she hadn't understood how much she needed it.

Lovely, just to stand there, the water coming down like a warm rain on her skin. Her nipples still tender, brushing against his chest. And his arms around her, holding on to her. That sensation itself nearly made her want to cry. That and . . . something else.

James.

Yes, it was him. *Him.*

God, too much to think about, especially now, in this state of mental disarray.

She turned her face up to his, found him looking down at her, his dark eyes highlighted in gold. A few drops of water clung to his long, black lashes.

He was beautiful. So beautiful, in a way she'd never found in any other man. He was deep. Kind. Honest. And despite everything he'd been through, despite his pain, there was a purity about him.

Something inside her was opening up. And she was letting it happen.

She stood up on her toes, pressed her lips to his. And her heart beat a quickening rhythm as he opened to her, slipped his warm, sweet tongue into her mouth. His arms tightened around her, crushing her. And it felt good. It felt safe.

Her heart ached with wanting, and he met that need with his hard, silent kisses.

She pressed closer, and he kissed her and kissed her, lips and tongue and hot, wet skin. She'd never felt anything more wonderful in her life.

They stood beneath the water, kissing, touching. His hands went into her hair, slid over her face, her shoulders. Then lower, over her breasts. And as he cupped that full flesh in his palms, her body heated once more, her sex going wet, a steady pulse of desire thrumming through her veins.

He pressed closer, his erection a solid shaft of warm flesh against her belly. She wanted him. Needed him. Yet it was in some slow and languid way. She knew she didn't need to hurry, that he would be there.

"James . . ."

He pulled back, his gaze on hers, his expression serious. Calm.

"I'm taking you to bed, Marina," he said. *Told* her.

"Yes. Please."

He shut the water off, led her from the shower, dried her body with one of her thick towels. Yet there was nothing submissive in what he did, even when he went down on his knees, running the towel over her legs, drying her feet, one at a time. No, it was more that he was caring for her.

He dried himself quickly, then took her hand once more. He stopped at the foot of her bed.

"In here, Marina."

She could only nod her head, her mouth dry. She knew this was important, that he would take her in her own bed. But she couldn't stop to think about it. She simply wanted him, needed to be close to him, to feel his body. For him to take command of her.

He wrapped his hands around her waist, pushing her down onto the bed. The raw silk of the bedcover was a little rough against her skin. She watched him standing over her, the pure masculinity of his form, backlit by the light shining in from the bathroom doorway. She loved the rounded curves of muscle: his wide shoulders, his chest. The dark nipples, the narrow line of hair below his navel leading to his engorged cock.

She loved his cock; it was as beautiful as the rest of him was. All golden skin, the swollen head a bit darker, the gleaming drop of pre-come on the tip. She licked her lips, moved her gaze back up to his face, which was soft in the shadows. His mouth was so lush. Even more so to her, simply knowing the feel of it, the taste of it.

God . . .

Her body pulsed, heated, her sex soaking wet.

She reached up for him, and he came to her, lowering his big body over hers, and she felt absolutely enveloped by him: his scent, his hot skin, the weight of him pressing down on her. And once more she had that sense of being in his hands. Of him being in charge. And she loved it.

He was kissing her again, his mouth soft on hers, his lips plush, wonderful. His tongue slipped into her mouth, seeking, demanding. And she opened for him: her lips, her thighs. He eased a hand between them and began to stroke.

"Ah, James . . ."

"Do you like that, Marina? You're so wet for me."

"Yes. Yes, I like it. I need more."

"I'll give you more, in my own time. In my own way."

"Yes, James."

Whatever he wanted. It didn't matter. As long as he was touching her. As long as he was with her.

He pressed a finger inside her suddenly, and she gasped.

"Good, Marina?"

"Yes!"

He began to pump, and she ground her hips into his hand as pleasure rocked her. Her entire body was tight with desire, humming. Tighter and tighter. Higher and higher as he pumped into her, one thumb pressing mercilessly onto her clit.

"James . . . Oh . . ."

"Are you going to come?"

"Yes."

She was panting, right at that keen edge.

"Not yet."

He pulled his hand from her, kissed her so hard it bruised her. But she wanted it, needed that brutal kiss.

"James . . ." She panted against his lips.

"Shh."

He turned her over, onto her stomach, lifting and moving her effortlessly, and she had a sense of the sheer power of him. Yes, to

be taken from behind . . . by *him*. Her sex clenched hard in anticipation.

With an arm around her waist, he pulled her onto her knees,
used a hand to spread her legs wider before dipping back into her
dripping sex.

"So ready for me, Marina . . ."

"Yes, James. Come on. Please."

"Please what?"

"Please fuck me, James."

"Is that what you want? To be fucked?"

"Yes, please . . ."

She needed him, so badly she could barely stand it. Her sex felt
wide open, exposed. Hungry.

"Here, Marina?" His voice was rough as he pushed two fingers
inside her; they slipped in like silk, pushing pleasure deep into her
body.

"Ah . . ."

"Or here?"

His hand slid back, to that tighter hole, her own juices making
it slippery, wet. She moved her knees apart.

"Anything. Yes. Whatever you want. Just do it."

"Do you have lube, Marina? Condoms?"

"In my nightstand."

He reached into the drawer, dug for a moment. Then he moved
behind her and she heard the tear of the foil condom packet. Her
sex was absolutely quivering with need. She hadn't had a man in
her ass for years; it was something she'd never let a submissive
man do to her, ever.

But James was far from submissive. And her own head was
floating, light, as she sank ever deeper into subspace. As she gave
herself over—mind, body, and soul—to James.

His hand once more at her anus, his finger covered in lube. He
rubbed in small circles, and it was exquisite, pleasure humming
through her body, into her sex.

"Ready, Marina?"

"Yes."

She arched her back, lowered her face into the pillows, and gave herself over.

He pressed his finger against her hole, nothing more than a gentle pressure for a moment. Then he slipped it in, just the tip. But it was enough to make her go right down, her mind emptying out, her body humming with sensation.

"Good girl," he whispered to her. "I think you can take more." He sank his finger into her body, and it slid right in.

"Oh . . ." Pleasure, a small whisper, shimmering like light in her system.

"Come on, baby," he said, encouraging her, and she pushed back against him, taking his finger deep into her ass. "Yeah, that's it."

He moved his finger inside her, and in a moment he added a second one. She took it easily, her sex dripping, her body seizing in pleasure, needing more.

"Christ, you're so hot and tight. I need to be inside you. I need to fuck you."

"Please, James."

She felt his body behind her, his hands spreading her ass cheeks wide, then his fingers at her anus once more, slipping in, then out, before guiding the head of his lube-covered cock to the opening.

"Are you ready?"

She couldn't wait. She pushed back against him, taking him in. And she was filled, with his flesh, with desire, with the need to please. She was empty of thought, full of sensation: pleasure intensified by what was going on in her head.

Yours.

He began to move, a slow, gentle pumping of his hips. He felt so good, so right. So right that she should be beneath him, commanded by him. Belonging to him.

Yours, James.

His hand came around and teased her clit. She barely needed it, his cock in her ass driving pleasure deep into her body. It spread, her sex, her breasts, swelling.

When he drove harder she couldn't help but groan aloud. But none of it mattered. She was out of control. She was a being made of nothing but sensation: his cock moving in her ass, his fingers pressing onto her clit, his scent all around her. His body taking control of hers. And all of it beautiful and safe and astonishing if she let herself think about it.

She didn't.

Instead, she let him fuck her, until it hurt, until the pleasure and the pain were an indistinguishable mixture in her body. It was all one: exquisite, excruciating. And they were coming together, shivering limbs, hot, panting breath, divine pleasure like liquid heat taking her over.

He was taking her over.

James.

Yours. Forever.

Chapter Nine

SHE WOKE TO the morning light, the gentle rhythm of James breathing beside her, his eyes closed, his body peaceful.

His profile was all clean lines, all except the scar running over his jaw, but that only added to the pure masculine power of him somehow. She wanted to reach out and touch him. But she couldn't do it. Just watching him lay there, in her bed—her bed!—was too lovely, too overwhelmingly beautiful. Too much of what she wanted.

Yes, to have him here with her like this. To wake up to him every morning. To climb into bed with him at night. To let him command her body so that for once, she could let go.

She remembered how he had taken her the night before, how her body had responded, how her mind had responded. How her heart had opened to him. So raw, so vulnerable.

Too much!

Her heart hammered. She tangled her fingers in the sheet, absently stroking the satin trim, comforting herself in some small way. But it didn't help.

She could not do this. There was far too much to lose. Better to stop now, right here. Not to let things go any further. He wasn't a good risk; he had issues of his own, and they ran deep. He was with her to work through those issues, then he would move on. It wasn't as though he had made any proclamations to her of love.

Fear like ice, stabbing into her chest, twisting her up inside. Tears stung her eyes.

Good God, she loved him!

She watched his sleeping form, let that liquid feeling creep over her for several moments, going warm and weak all over.

Weak.

She could not do this!

Shaking, she climbed from the bed and went naked into the bathroom. Turning on the hot water, she got into the shower, let the heat of it pound onto her shoulders, and wept.

She hated this, feeling so fragile, so much in danger. This was exactly what she'd been avoiding since she'd lost Nathan.

How long had it been since she'd cried? Oh, she'd cried for endless months when Nathan had been diagnosed, when they realized he was terminal, and for hours, days, weeks at a time, when he'd died. She'd cried until her face hurt, until she was numb all over. For a long period of time she had ceased to exist, other than her endless tears. And she had sworn never to cry again.

She would not do it now. She would not allow this.

Quickly, she washed her hair, washed the scent of him from her body, got out, and carefully applied her makeup, dried her hair, wrapped herself in a robe. And steeled herself as she went back into the bedroom, found him watching her from the bed, a smile on his sleepy face. She could barely stand to look at him.

"There you are. Come back to bed, Marina."

"I have to work."

"Can you be an hour late?"

She shook her head. "I have a phone conference with a client at nine."

Lying to him yet again.

"It's seven-thirty."

"I need to put some information together. I really have to go."

He sat up, the covers slipping from his body, and he moved naked across the room until he was standing before her. He took her chin in his hand, making her flinch.

"Marina, what is it?"

She pulled away, turning to open a dresser drawer, and dug through, pulling out a pair of underwear, a silk chemise. Her jaw was so tightly clenched she could barely get the words out around it. "I just . . . have to work."

"That's crap."

He was right behind her, his hands on her waist, turning her to face him. His expression was fierce, his dark eyes burning with emotion.

"You want me to go, is that it? That's fine; you do what you need to do. But don't bullshit me, Marina. Be honest with me. Tell me what you want. What you need. That's what this has been all about between us, hasn't it? Until right now, anyway."

She swallowed past the knot forming in her throat, as much from his nearness, the scent of sex on his naked skin, as from the hard tone of his voice.

"Yes. You're right. I . . . I need some time. This has all gotten very . . . intense."

"Yeah, it has. But that's why it's so good."

"Maybe."

"Why are you doing this to yourself?"

She wanted to cry again. But she wouldn't allow it. She could only shake her head. She couldn't look at him, her gaze wandering instead to the foggy view outside her bedroom window. So gloomy out there. So gloomy inside.

"I'm sorry, James. I just have to . . ." She stopped, shook her head, squeezing her eyes shut. "Please just go. Okay? Just . . . go."

He took a step back, his body tensing as though she had hit

him. Maybe she had. His face was dark, shutting down at high speed, his jaw hard, tight. Unbearable.

"Yeah, fine. I'm going."

He moved away, disappeared into the guest room to find his clothes. She stood in her bathrobe in the middle of her bedroom, her ears painfully tuned in to every sound: him closing the guest-room door, the creak of the wood floors as he moved down the hallway, the quiet thud of the front door closing behind him. The moment he was gone the tears came, and there wasn't a damn thing she could do about it.

Wrapping her arms around her body, she sank onto the foot of the bed and cried until she was dry inside.

It was after nine when she looked at the clock. Her face felt swollen and tender. Her head was heavy, numb. She couldn't cry anymore. She couldn't think.

But no, she *had* to think. Was she going to walk away from him? Could she? She was grieving as though she already had. And maybe after the way she'd treated him this morning, it would be too late already. But that would be for the best, wouldn't it?

Wouldn't it?

What the hell was she going to do now?

Leaning over the side of the bed, she picked up the phone on the nightstand. She should call Desmond, talk to him. He was always the calm voice of reason. Or he had been until he'd met Ava six months ago. Now he was lovestruck. Dumbstruck. No, talking to Desmond was a bad idea. She would have to handle this on her own, just as she had all these years. And Desmond would only talk her into going to James, telling him she loved him.

Impossible.

She could not do it. She couldn't risk feeling like this again, not for one more day. Look at what it was doing to her already, loving James.

God, she loved him! And it was like a knife in her chest.

Because she could not allow this to happen. Not again. Never, ever again.

Dropping the phone, she curled up on the bed, her head on the pillow where James had slept so recently. She breathed him in, breathed in the pain of knowing it was over. And gave herself permission to feel it, to let the pain rack her body, just for this one day. And after that, she would shut it all safely away, in that dark, locked compartment in her heart where she stored everything that hurt.

JAMES SAT AT an outdoor table at Absinthe, his hands cupped around a cappuccino, watching the waning afternoon light and the world go by without him.

More than two weeks had passed since he'd last seen Marina, her torn expression, emotion making her eyes huge in her pale face. He'd thought she would call him the next day. Or that weekend. But he hadn't heard a damn word.

He'd had no idea that anything could hurt as much as this did. More than the broken jaw he'd come home from Manila with. More than the machete injury he'd gotten in Indonesia. More, even, than the drifting remnants of what had happened in Africa.

He never knew loving someone could hurt like this.

God damn it!

He gripped the steaming mug, burning his fingers on the hot porcelain. It didn't matter. Nothing mattered now.

He loved her, and what was the fucking use? She'd turned away from him, leaving him to wait, the pathetic rejected lover. It felt like hell.

It felt like death. That same sort of loss. Crushing, tearing at his insides.

But this time there was something he could do about it. He could damn well try. No one was holding a machete to his throat now. He was not going to kneel in the dirt and fucking take it.

He took a long gulp of the coffee, not caring how it scalded his tongue, his throat, on the way down. And it felt like he was being jarred awake after being in some kind of emotional coma for two weeks. What the hell was wrong with him that he'd waited this long? Was he crazy? He fucking loved her. Why the hell should he sit there and let her walk away?

He tossed a ten-dollar bill down on the white tablecloth and made his way through the other tables, hit the sidewalk almost at a run. In moments he was back at his apartment, keying open the garage, climbing into his car. He gunned the engine as he pulled onto Hayes Street. It was another gray day in San Francisco, which had always seemed a bit romantic to him. It had made him feel only more removed from the world, more sad, these last weeks.

Yes, it was time he took charge of his life. And that meant taking charge of Marina long enough to tell her that they were supposed to be together. He would make her see it.

He drove through the city, making for her place as the sun set. Saturday-evening traffic was heavy, and it seemed to take forever to get to her side of town. He pulled up, finding parking right in front. The lights were off, and there was no answer when he pounded on the door.

Maybe she was working? He knew she often did on the weekend. Getting back into his car, he drove toward Union Street. Parking was more difficult there, and he ended up three blocks away, but the walk through the cool evening air helped to work off some of his energy, some of the pure fury he felt. Fury at himself for allowing her to walk away.

Her office was dark when he arrived at her building, the gallery on the first floor already closed. He paced the sidewalk, thinking. Where the hell would she be?

He grabbed his cell phone, dialed her number, and his heart stuttered when he heard her voice, but it was only her voice mail.

Damn it.

He hung up without leaving a message. What he had to say to her had to be said in person.

He made his way across the city once more, heading toward home, frustration burning hot in his veins. Where was she?

When he got to his place he couldn't seem to make himself go inside. Too stifling in there. Too quiet. Instead he walked up Hayes Street, passing the shops and restaurants in a blur of light and sound: people talking, laughing. He felt more like an outsider than ever. He turned onto Gough Street, his legs working hard as he made his way up the hill, then down a side street onto Van Ness. Long, hard strides, but never hard enough to get his mind to calm, his thundering heart to still. But it was better than sitting around his place by the Goddamn phone, like he'd been doing lately.

The city was coming alive around him: neon signs, the flashing streetlights. The streets were always full of people in San Francisco; it was a walking city, a nighttime city. And he was glad for all the activity, the life of the place. It energized him, distracted him a little from what was going on inside his head. But he never quite stopped thinking about her. He didn't think he ever would.

He must have walked for an hour before he got back to his street. He checked his watch. It was after nine now. And he knew exactly where he needed to go.

Back into his car, then he pulled out into the street and drove through the seemingly endless traffic until he reached the Potrero Hill district. He found parking in the back lot behind the old brick structure. He was nearly bursting by the time he reached the door.

Calm down.

He showed his membership card to the doorman, heard the sounds of the trancelike music drifting through the curtained doorway leading into Pinnacle. But he wasn't there to play. Oh, no, he had serious business, if he could only find her. He didn't even know why he thought he'd find her there; it was some weird sense that told him he would.

He moved through the main floor of the club, barely taking in the red lighting, the heavy pieces of equipment lining the room: the crosses, spanking benches, racks, and leather-padded tables. It was early enough that there wasn't too much activity yet. He hoped he wouldn't run into anyone he knew. He was hardly capable of carrying on a normal conversation.

He climbed the wrought-iron spiral staircase to the next floor.

The bondage room. This was her place.

She was at the far end of the room, standing by one of the large wooden bondage racks, her hand resting on one of the support columns. She was alone.

He had to catch his breath. Her hair was a sheaf of red-and-gold fire waving around her shoulders in the dim amber lights. She was dressed all in black, her high-heeled boots, her tight black leather skirt, and leather corset making her skin all the more pale. A jet pendant hung from her slender throat. When she turned her head, he could see the shock in her eyes, the red slash of her lip-sticked mouth making a small *o*.

She was the most fucking beautiful woman he had ever seen.

In a few long strides he was next to her. She stood frozen, watching him with fearful eyes. It hurt to see it, the anxiety, the tension. He never wanted to make her feel like that. But hell, he wasn't the one doing it to her. She did it to herself.

"Marina."

God, she couldn't believe he was there! Her palms went damp, her throat dry. She couldn't breathe, couldn't speak. It hurt too much, seeing him. Seeing the fury in his eyes, the desperate, hard set to his mouth.

At the same time, she was weak with relief.

She hated feeling weak.

He reached for her, his large hand wrapping around her wrist. She flinched, but she didn't have it in her to pull away.

"Marina, we need to talk. We're going to talk, whether you like it or not. Come with me."

"Where?"

She was trying hard not to notice that she was shaking all over. Pain was building in her chest. The pain she'd tried so hard to ignore these last couple of weeks. That she'd done a lousy job of pretending wasn't there, hovering over her, day and night.

"Come up to the roof with me. It'll be quiet up there this early."

She hadn't agreed to go, hadn't had a chance to protest, to say anything, when he pulled her with him, across the long room, up the wooden staircase, through the heavy door that led to the roof garden.

It was cool up there, the night damp, but it wasn't the cold that was making her shiver. It was as though simply seeing him had unlocked the floodgates of emotion she'd held so firmly in check. The tears were gathering in her eyes already, and they'd hardly exchanged two words. Her head ached. And she felt helpless against him. Helpless to turn away from him.

She didn't want to admit, even to herself, how horribly she'd missed him.

He led her to a patio table, his hand still tightly gripping her wrist. Once there he let her go, but he stood only inches from her. Neither of them sat down.

She could smell him. Could feel the anger and the love radiating from him. Oh, yes, there was love there. She'd known it the morning she'd asked him to leave her house. Had known it the night before when he'd kissed her so tenderly in the shower. When he'd taken over her body in her bed.

His voice was hard, sharp. He had a right to be angry. "Talk to me, Marina. And make it count."

Her pulse was a wild flutter, making her dizzy. She couldn't think with him standing so close to her!

"I . . . I don't know what to say, James."

"Oh, yes, you do. I want an explanation. I want to know how you could walk away from me, from what we have!" He moved in even closer, and she had to bite her lip against the tears. "Tell me what the hell this is about for you."

"I think you know what it's about," she said, her voice a strangled whisper.

"Yeah. It's about Nathan, isn't it? But that was four years ago. How long are you going to punish yourself? How long are you going to deny yourself?"

She shook her head. "No, that's not it. It's not about Nathan."

It was about *him,* James, about what she felt for him. What she didn't feel capable of dealing with.

"Isn't it?" He ran a hand through his hair. His eyes were blazing; she could see them even in the dark, the roof garden lit only by a few scattered wall sconces, by candles in hurricane lamps on the tables. "Do you think I don't understand? Me, of all people. You know damn well I do. You feel just as much guilt over Nathan's death as I do over what happened in Africa. Survivor's guilt. We all feel it. But you know what? It's okay that we're still alive. And what's the fucking point if we're not going to really live? Do you think that's what he would have wanted for you? I don't think so."

"No, of course not. He wasn't like that." She was getting angry now. How dare he try to tell her how she should feel? And yet a small part of her knew he was right. That he got it. It was just too hard to face.

"Then why are you doing this? To yourself? To me, damn it!"

Oh, his anger was like heat, scorching her. But behind the anger was passion. For her. That was what drew her, and what scared her to death.

"It's too hard for me, James. I can't . . . I can't go through another loss like that. I don't have it in me."

"Marina. There are no guarantees in life. I can't say I won't get hit by a truck tomorrow. But God damn it, how can you do this, manifest the loss you're so afraid of? You're making it happen. It's not fair!"

"Life isn't fair, James! Life wasn't fair when Nathan died of cancer at the age of thirty-five. It isn't fair now that I love you, and you can be taken from me just as easily."

He looked stunned. Hell, so was she. Had she really said that out loud?

She watched as a series of emotions crossed his features, as his face softened. He reached out and stroked her cheek. "I didn't expect you to admit that to me so easily."

She let out a hard, croaking laugh. "You think that was easy?"

"God damn it, Marina."

He grabbed her and pulled her in close. She fought him, *had* to, but he only held her tighter.

"Marina, stop it. Stop struggling."

She tried again to twist out of his grasp, the tears coming hot and fast.

"No, James. Don't make me do this!"

Her arms flailing, she made one last effort to pull away.

"Marina. Damn it, girl. You love me. You fucking love me! And I love you. It's going to be okay. I love you."

The strength went right out of her, hearing him say the words. She sagged against him, long sobs coming from somewhere deep and dark inside her, pouring out against his strong chest as he held her.

"I didn't want to do this, James. I didn't want to love you. But I do. And I'm so scared."

"I know. So am I. But we're here, and we're together. I never thought it would happen to me. I never thought it could be this good, and this torturous. I never understood until I met you. Until I loved you. But I'm not stupid enough to turn away from it. To turn away from you. I can't do it."

He held her, let her cry it out against his shoulder, her fingers digging into the muscle there as she hung on to him. It was too much, everything she was feeling: old pain and loss, the fierce love she had for James, from which she could no longer hide. She was overwhelmed by it. Helpless against it. But that's what it came down to, wasn't it? She couldn't deny what she felt for him, couldn't make it go away. It was too strong, too real.

Finally she told him, feeling ashamed, "You're so much braver than I am."

"Maybe. Maybe not. This feels like the hardest thing I've ever done. And the best. The most right."

Everything inside was melting, the pain and fear and love, blending together, until it was a pool of emotion. And she knew she had to simply *feel* it, the good and the bad.

After a while the tears stopped and she lifted her head.

"James."

"What is it?" He was stroking her face, her cheeks, her eyes, her lips, with his fingertips. He was being so tender with her, so careful.

"It couldn't have been anyone but you."

His eyes shone, gleaming and dark. "No one else for me, either. No one but you, Marina."

He kissed her then, so softly, just a sweet brush of his lips. She wanted to cry again, because it felt so lovely, so right. She couldn't get enough of his mouth. Of the sweet taste of him on her lips, the feel of his flesh on hers. She pressed closer, and his arms went around her, held her tight, then tighter, his lips crushing hers. He kissed her until she was breathless, weightless. Until she was melting all over. Until the pain faded away and all that was left was love.

He pulled back and whispered to her, "I need to be alone with you."

"Yes, please. Not here. Take me home, James."

He smiled at her, held her hand tightly as they went downstairs. His hand was at her waist protectively as he put her into his car. He got in, turned the engine on, and they moved into the night. But the darkness was no longer inside her.

He held on to her hand during the drive. They were both quiet.

And she felt an odd sense of calm, despite the beating of her heart, her fluttering pulse. But it was pure excitement, anticipation, her response to his fingers wrapped around hers. To knowing he loved her.

They reached his apartment, and he never let go as he led her upstairs, through the front door, past the wide warehouse windows, and into the bedroom. A soft, diffused light shone through the windows from the streetlamps and the moon outside, casting shadows in amber and silver. He took her to the big bed and began to undress her.

He whispered into her ear, his breath warm against her skin, "I love you, Marina. I love you."

She was in awe. Of him. Of everything she felt. Her throat was tight with emotion, but it was all good. Wonderful. She smiled as he drew her coat from her shoulders, as he stroked her bare arms with his palms.

"Such beautiful skin. Have I ever told you that?" There was awe in his voice, too. Adoration. "I could touch you forever. I plan to."

"Forever, James?" Her heart was pounding.

His gaze steadied on hers. "Yes. Forever."

"Ah, James . . ."

His thumb brushed her cheek, his expression softer than she'd ever seen it. Then, leaning in, he trailed his lips over the rise of her breasts beneath the leather corset. Her body burned for him, her limbs growing weak. She buried her hands in his hair, held him to her breasts as he kissed them, her nipples coming up hard.

"James, I need you."

He pulled back, looked into her eyes. "Tell me, Marina."

"I love you." Tears gathered behind her eyes. But the sadness was gone. "So much."

His hands were in her hair, pulling her in, then his mouth was on hers, his tongue opening her lips, drawing her into his mouth. He tasted so sweet, felt impossibly soft. Like silk and sugar.

His hands were everywhere, it seemed, pushing her skirt down, reaching behind her to unlace her corset, pulling it from her body.

"I can't get enough of you, Marina," he murmured to her as he ran his hands down her thighs, helped her step from her panties. "Never enough."

She helped him out of his clothes, touching his skin everywhere she could reach: his chest, his shoulders, then his stomach, wrapping her arms around his wide back. He was smooth and golden, over steel-hard muscle. How could a man made the way he was be so gentle? But he was, every touch reverent, lovely.

"James . . . no one has ever touched me the way you do. Your hands . . ." She had to stop for a moment, her throat tight with emotion. "No one has ever touched me inside the way you do."

"Marina. Baby." He moved down her body until he was kneeling on the Persian rug. He kissed her stomach, and pleasure surged through her body in gentle waves. "Love you, baby," he whispered against her naked skin. "*My* baby."

She was shivering all over, her sex damp with need, her breasts aching. He moved his mouth lower, brushed his lips over her hip, down her thigh. She couldn't take it, couldn't wait.

"James, please . . ."

He rose to his feet, took her in his arms, and pushed her down onto the bed, laid his body over hers. His skin was like satin against hers, naked flesh to naked flesh. Amazing, that sensation alone. And he smelled so good, like *James*. She lifted her head, opening her mouth against his throat, licking and sucking, tasting him. He moaned, and she eased her thighs apart, letting him settle his big body between them, and she felt his erection pressing at her opening. A new surge of desire shivered through her, over her skin, deep into her belly.

"James . . . I need you inside me. Please."

With both hands he lifted her body, moving her up the bed until she rested against the pillows. And he leaned over to pull a condom from the night-table drawer. Kneeling over her, he tore the packet open with his teeth, pulled the latex sheath out.

"Let me . . ."

Taking it from him, she rolled it over his hard cock, loving the solid feel of his flesh. Loving his quiet moans.

Then his hands were on her hips, raising them, pulling her closer. His gaze was on hers, his eyes dark, lit with gold in the dim light. Lit with love. And as he entered her, she felt everything at once: his body driving into hers, his silken skin, his hands warm on her flesh, emotion shining through his eyes. And most of all the way her body surged to meet his, needing his touch, needing to know how real he was, how solid. How he loved her. How she loved him.

She melted into him, wrapped her legs around him. He was whispering into her ear.

"I love you, baby. Love you, love you . . ."

And she knew it was true.

"I love you, James."

Pleasure surged, soared, lighting her up inside. And when they came together, it was like the slow spread of pure desire flowing from her body into his and back again. They shuddered with the force of it, the heat, calling each other's name over and over. And they clung to each other, warm sated flesh upon warm sated flesh. Ultimate pleasure. Infinitely precious. Inexplicable, undeniable. Love.

And no matter what happened, all of those things that were beyond her control no longer mattered. What mattered was their love for each other, living in the moment. And the moment was wonderful. Whatever happened, what she had with James gave her all the strength she needed. She didn't need to be afraid anymore. She loved, and was loved. And she knew she was safe at last.

Getting down and dirty with Eden Bradley

Tell us about your first time. How did you start writing erotica and what was your first Black Lace book?

I've been writing erotica for over twenty years. It was just short stories at first, and I didn't think to do anything with them – I was simply compelled to write. It wasn't until early 2000 that I started writing with publication in mind, and at first I was writing 'steamy' romance (hot, but not quite erotic) because that was the only real market at the time here in the US. But soon the e-publishers started up, and erotic romance was selling like mad! That was all I needed to start writing what I truly wanted to write – erotic fiction.

My first Black Lace book was *The Dark Garden*, a BDSM novel. As to where that story came from…much of it was inspired by my own experiences in the BDSM arena. I wanted to write about kink from a true perspective (or from my own personal truth, anyway). I wanted to show readers the depth of connection that happens during this kind of extreme sensation-play and the roles involved in domination and submission, the psychology behind it. Because of my own history with these things, this was an important book for me to write.

When did you feel like you could show people your writing and that you could actually be an erotica writer?

I got involved in the online writing community pretty early on. I had a critique partner I showed everything to. I also am an administrator at the largest romance writers' discussion forum online, RomanceDivas.com, and there's a wonderful community there, so I've always had other writers to share and discuss my work with. The writers I've networked with have been incredibly helpful and supportive – they made me feel I could do it right from the start, and there are so many I have to thank for helping me on this journey.

Where does the inspiration for your ideas come from?

From many places. Sometimes a song will create a mood that gets me thinking about a story idea. I've been inspired by places I've traveled to, like New Orleans or Seattle, by people-watching at a café. And because I'm actively involved in the BDSM lifestyle, many of my ideas come from real life experiences – fleeting moments, whole scenes, the emotion of a relationship.

Tell us about your writing process? Is it the same for every book you write?

My process has changed over the years. I do more advance planning now. Since I write very much character-driven stories, most of that planning is about character development. I start by asking myself all sorts of questions about my characters: What do they look like? What do they do for work? What kind of car do they drive?

What is their family and relationship history? Sometimes even the smaller details help shape who they are.

Where do you feel most comfortable writing and why?

I'm a bit of a prima donna when I write! I have to be at home at my desk, in my comfy chair, wearing my fuzzy slippers (leopard print, of course!). I used to be able to take a laptop to a café and write, but lately I need to be free of all distractions in order to focus.

I moved from California to Dallas, Texas a few months ago, and I have the most beautiful office here! My office is in what was intended to be a dining room. It has gorgeous polished wood floors, and my desk sits in front of the window overlooking our pretty street. I have two big book cases filled with books, my great-grandmother's hand-painted rocking chair in a corner and art on the walls (I'm a huge art geek). The space is airy and open. I love it!

We're used to reading about ménages in erotica. Would you ever collaborate with other authors on an erotica book?

I have collaborated on a continuity series (stories written by multiple authors set in the same world). It's a post-apocalyptic series called *Wasteland*, written with authors R.G. Alexander, Crystal Jordan and Lilli Feisty. Each of the stories are ménage relationships. It was an exciting project to work on, but it does take some extra time to build a 'world bible' for everyone to work from so we don't confuse anything. I would be willing to do it again if my schedule loosened up enough to allow it. And having great personal chemistry with the other authors is crucial.

Do you have any favourite erotica books?

I love *The Siren* by Tiffany Reisz – I wish I'd written that book! Also Portia Da Costa: *Entertaining Mr Stone* has just stayed with me – a powerful story.

If you could spend a weekend with one other writer, past or present, who would it be and why?

I would love to spend time with Tanith Lee. Her use of language is so gorgeous, and her work has had an enormous impact on my writing voice. I'd love to ask her questions about my favorite book of hers, and about her writing process. I'm sure I'd babble like an idiot if I ever got to meet her!

Do you think anyone can write erotica? And do you have any advice for anyone starting out?

In addition to having the driving *need* to write which helps you to survive this very challenging industry, I think writing sex has to feel natural for you or your discomfort will come through on the page – and that can be erotic material in general or a specific act or topic.

As with any genre, read some of the best out there and dissect it as you go, to figure out what makes it great. Then just write. Learn to create story arc and character arc that's driven forward by the sex itself – this is what makes well-written erotica, otherwise the sex is superfluous.

What's your relationship with your readers like?

I love my readers! That's my favorite thing about going to the conferences where I get to just hang out with them and talk about books. One of my closest friends started out as a reader. And I'm always interested to know what they want to read about and what kinds of promotions are the most fun for them.

To find out more about Eden, follow her on twitter:
@EdenBradley

Hungry for more?

Read on for extracts from Eden Bradley's
forthcoming new novels

The Seduction of Valentine Day

and

The Darker Side of Pleasure

Coming soon from Black Lace

BLACK
LACE

The Seduction of Valentine Day

Chapter One

THE COSTLY SCENTS OF the finest imported champagne and custom-blended cologne fill my nostrils as I straddle his prone figure on the big bed. I love these beds at the Beverly Wilshire—plush and lovely, with soft Egyptian cotton sheets. Only the best for Enzo Alighieri. Including me.

"Fuck me now, my Valentine," he says, his elegant, Italian-accented voice rough with desire. "You know just how to do it, *mi tesoro.*"

"Ah, Enzo . . ." I sigh in pleasure as I lower myself onto his erect cock.

I have always loved Enzo's cock. The skin is a deep gold, as it is all over his body, which is still fine and beautiful, no matter his age. He is strong, well muscled. And he has the stamina of a twenty-year-old. Which is the only way he manages to please his wife, his mistress, and me. And he does please me.

I squeeze the walls of my sex around his cock and he moans a little. Pleasure is swarming my system already and I smile down at him, moving my hips, grinding onto him.

"Touch me, Enzo."

He reaches up and takes my breasts in his hands, plumping them, kneading them, playing my hardened nipples between his fingers.

"Oh, yes . . ."

I reach back and slip my hand between his thighs, caressing his balls. He loves this. He loves my every touch, to hear my panting breath, to watch me come. Oh, yes, I know exactly what he loves, what he needs. It's my job to know. And I am nothing if not a perfectionist.

He pumps up into my body, shafts of pleasure filling me, spreading, making me shiver. One of his hands has snaked down and is teasing my clit, tugging, rubbing, pinching. He knows how to make me come. After all, we've been together nearly a decade, Enzo and I. My mentor, my friend. My client.

Why is that the most important part? But I don't want to question it as his thrusting hips take on a more urgent rhythm. His breath is a panting gasp now, and I feel him tense beneath me.

"Ah, just another moment, Enzo. Give it to me . . . I know you can do it."

"You will be the death of me, Valentine," he says, his voice rough.

But he does it, pistoning into me, his clever fingers never leaving my throbbing clit, my swollen nipple, until I'm coming in a flood of heat onto his thick, lovely cock.

"Oh, yes . . ."

I throw my head back, let it wash over me. And he tenses beneath me, cries out, his hands going to my hips, his fingers digging into my flesh.

And I catch that scent I adore, the scent of arousal, the

scent of come, beneath his expensive cologne. And underlying it all, the scent of money.

I LEARNED ABOUT SOMETHING called suspension of disbelief a number of years ago in one of my English lit classes. This is when a writer must make the reader buy into the unusual long enough to be drawn in and believe in the world the writer has created.

It's something like that with my line of work. Our clients must suspend their disbelief long enough to believe the girl likes it. My particular "talent," if you want to call it that—my particular perversion, really—is that they don't have to do that with me. The truth is, I love it.

This is my dirty little secret. Because this is supposed to be taboo among the professionals of my world. Call girls. Prostitutes. Hookers. It doesn't matter what you call us. The fact is, I get paid for sex. And it's the only kind of sex I can get off on.

Who knew a nice Jewish girl from the Valley could end up here? Well, half Jewish, anyway, my father being a lapsed Catholic. And maybe I've never been all that nice.

I grew up in Van Nuys. Van Nuys is possibly the most generic, boring place on earth. Middle class, cardboard-box houses that all look the same, block after block. The entire area looks as though a dull film has settled over it.

My family was at the lower end of the middle class. Not that we were poor. We always had a roof over our heads, food on the table. My father, a construction foreman, worked a lot, but he spent his money anywhere but at home. My mother never did much other than drink. Strange that he wasn't the drinker. Jews don't tend to be drinkers. Not that it ever stopped my mother. But my life has been a combination of the utterly dull and the most perverse, in every way, on every level. Classic hard life story, I know, but that's my story. Or it was. Too fucking bad.

I make a lot of money. Enough to keep me very comfortable in my Hollywood Hills home. Enough to pay for the expensive clothes I buy at Barney's and Kitson, my weekly facials and massage at the spa. Enough to pay for the breezy little Mercedes I drive, if it hadn't been a gift from a happy client. This is why I do it.

Actually, that's a lie. It's what I tell myself when I'm not in the mood for the kind of deep, soul-searching honesty that keeps me up at night. How I justify it in the most basic, simple terms.

The truth, or part of it, anyway, is that I began in this business because I needed to distance myself from what I was before. From that lower-middle-class Jewish girl from the Valley whose mother was always passed out on the couch, surrounded by a sticky puddle of whatever she was drinking on the floor, the overflowing ashtrays. Repulsive. I won't even allow my clients to smoke around me. If they don't like it, they can find another girl. I'm at a point in my career where I can make a few demands of my own, and I do.

I am someone else entirely now.

I look different. I *am* different. No one from my old life would even recognize me. And truly, I wouldn't care if they did. My life before this is almost in another dimension, in my mind. I like it that way.

I don't look like the average girl from the Valley. My one gift from my mother is a fine-featured, beautiful face. I don't mean to be vain; I am beautiful. People who pretend not to know these things are full of crap. I have long legs, a great body, hard and tight, even this close to thirty. My brown hair, highlighted in gold and caramel, hangs in layers almost to my waist. Most men prefer long hair on a woman, so I rarely cut it. My eyes are green, without the colored contacts the other girls wear. High cheekbones, a full, lush mouth. My ass is superb. I've been told so often enough. But what really gets them is that I love what I do. I love sex. I don't care who I'm doing it with. I just like to fuck. I like to suck cock. I love the anonymity of these men not knowing who I really am. I get off on it.

But there's one catch. I have to get paid.

I have never had an orgasm with a man unless he's paying to have sex with me. My first trick was like an epiphany. The moment he handed that wad of cash over into my greedy little hand, my body started to heat up, my legs began to shake, and I was coming almost as soon as he touched me. That's when it became magic for me.

Which brings me to Italian film producer Enzo Alighieri.

He was one of my first clients. Enzo found me at this cheap call girl outfit where I got my start. And he knew right away I was different from the other girls there. He told me I was too beautiful, in his lovely Italian accent. I adored him on the spot. Not the way a normal woman might adore a lover. It was never that complicated. I liked him the moment he walked into the room. So sophisticated. Elegant. And he's sexy. He really is, even at nearly seventy now. He has that commanding air about him; I'm sure everyone else in his life kowtows to him. Everyone but me. He lets me get away with anything.

I understand perfectly well that I'm nothing more than a sort of pet to him. A project. And a priceless piece of ass. He often tells me so. But it was Enzo who took me under his wing, got me out of that dump of a whorehouse in Hollywood, and made me go to school.

Yes, school. Because if you're going to be what amounts to a modern-day American geisha, a 21st-century courtesan, you must be well educated, just as the geishas are. Just as the old Venetian courtesans were.

In addition to having studied history, literature, business, and political science, I now know how to play golf and tennis, although not too well. Men prefer to win, don't they? I read the *Wall Street Journal* and *Forbes*. I've studied massage therapy, I know wine. I've learned to speak German, a little French and Italian, and even a few words of Japanese and Arabic, both of which are a necessity in my line of work.

The Middle Eastern rich have tons of money. More than the usual wealthy do, and they aren't at all shy about spending it on whatever brings them pleasure. I admire that in a person. They're the ones who fly the girls to Miami for a week, to Europe, even. Give us entire wardrobes of designer clothes. They like to have a lot of girls at once. I don't mind. We all get paid, regardless, and it makes the workload a little easier. And the food is always superb. Unfortunately, I'm thinner than most of them like, so I don't get those dates the way some of my friends do. But once a man is with me, he'll always come back for more.

They can always tell, my clients. Even the most selfish, the most dense. They know right away that I'm into it, that my orgasms are the real thing. And these men are the sexual sophisticates of the world. They've had first-class ass in every corner of the planet: the pros in Amsterdam, Paris, Berlin.

I know I sound crude when I talk about these things, but this is a crude world. I'm not bitter, I swear it. I see the beauty in the world, too. I've spent far too much time around the rich and privileged to be blind to beauty, not to appreciate it. I love the ballet, could watch it for hours. I could wander every museum on earth and never get enough. My current obsession is art history, and I've been taking classes off and on for the last few years, soaking it all up. This is something I do purely for me. I may be a classless kid from the Valley, but I've learned about the rest of the world, seen enough to develop a real appetite for the finer things in life. And for me, art has become a necessity.

There is the gritty side to my lifestyle, of course. Even the girls at the top of this food chain can get into trouble. There was Trina, a gorgeous girl, new to the business, who was kidnapped and taken to some godforsaken place in Southeast Asia and never heard from again. These things happen, and when they do, when we working girls hear about it, it scares us, even if we pretend it doesn't. This job, as luxurious as it is, is not entirely without risk. But we keep doing it anyway, don't we? Some sick part of me gets off a little on the cheap thrill, I'll admit to that.

I don't like fast cars, in particular, and you'll never catch me climbing a mountain. My thrills are all of a sexual nature. Which makes me the perfect woman for this job. I am embedded in this life for the long haul. It suits me to a T. It makes having a "real" relationship entirely impossible. But the circumstances of my life since childhood have made that impossible anyway, so I've never minded. What other sort of life would I have? What would I even want? No, I'm perfectly fine right where I am.

THE SUN IS BEGINNING to lower in the sky as the cab exits the freeway and turns onto Grand Avenue. I love this time of day: the pale light turning the sky an ethereal shade of gold, like an iridescent film over the deepening blue. It's even lovelier now, in the fall, when that bit of moisture in the air, that first hint of the coming cooler weather, adds a pearly glow to everything. But it's difficult to really enjoy it; it's after seven and I'm running late. I hate being late, especially to meet a client. It's unprofessional. But the traffic was horrible, as usual in Los Angeles.

We pull up in front of the Dorothy Chandler Pavilion and I pay the driver. My cell phone goes off as I step out into the warm evening.

"This is Val."

"Val, it's Bennett. I'm not going to be able to make it tonight. A problem at the office."

"Oh, I'm so sorry. Shall we meet later?"

"No, no. This is going to keep me busy all night. But you shouldn't waste the tickets. It's opening night."

"I do love *La Traviata*."

This opera is the story of a prostitute. Why wouldn't I love it? And I've become a huge opera fan, thanks to Enzo's expert guidance.

"Enjoy it, then. I'll call you to reschedule in the next week or two."

"I hope you will, Bennett. I'm so sorry you have to work tonight and miss this."

"You can tell me all about it when I see you. Ah, there's my other line, I have to go."

I flip my phone shut, turn it off, and get my ticket at the will-call window, feeling a lovely sense of freedom at having the night off. Being able to enjoy the opera without having to be "on."

Of course, this also means no sex for me tonight. But for once, spending the evening on my own sounds even better. I realize I've been craving some time away from work lately.

Strange for me. But I have been doing this most of my adult life. I suppose it shouldn't come as a surprise. When was the last time I even took a small vacation—three years? Four?

Inside, the theater is cool, lovely in its stark modernity. The lights are bright, making me blink. I really would love a cocktail, but nearly everyone is seated already; I'd hate to be locked out of the first act.

An usher, all gangly legs and leering eyes, shows me to my seat. Not that I mind. A woman in my position can't afford to be offended by male attention. And I wore this champagne bias-cut silk dress to show off my lean curves, my pale skin. I don't have much in the way of cleavage, but the boy eyes the low neckline, anyway. My nipples have gone hard from the air-conditioning, so perhaps there's something to look at after all.

I slide in, murmuring apologies to those already seated as I go. The seats are fabulous: third-row center. I settle in, leaning down to set my small bag at my feet.

And that's when I catch a scent in the air, something masculine, sophisticated. I sit up and turn my head to see who is sitting next to me. I'm trained to be attuned to men. I can't help it.

He smiles. A gorgeous smile. His face is beautiful. That fact is what I notice first, and it's a few moments before I see that his features are a bit irregular. But still beautiful, in the most masculine way possible.

He has dark brown hair with a few natural highlights, cut very short, a little spiky on top. Warm hazel eyes, a full mouth, a strong, clean jaw. Broad shoulders in his designer suit. Nice. And he's young, maybe thirty-five. Too young for my tastes. So why is my body heating up? Why do I want to touch his mouth, just put my fingertips to his lips?

Stop it.

I make an effort to smile back, then turn away, looking at my program. But I'm not really seeing it, the faces of the cast members, the synopsis a blur. I can't stop noticing him out of the corner of my eye.

He seems entirely relaxed, something you don't often find in a man of his age. This makes him all the more intriguing. And there is a strange sense of anticipation, of tension. It's almost as though I can feel the heat of his body next to me. And I am hyperaware of that scent. Crisp and dark at the same time, like the woods with a faint wash of citrus.

I roll my program up in my hands, my fingers tightening around the glossy paper as I look around the auditorium. Why can't I calm down?

Finally, he turns to me and asks, "Are you waiting for someone?"

"No. My friend had to cancel."

"Ah, mine did, too. Well, my mother, not my friend."

"Oh." I don't know what else to say. I can always talk to men. It's my job to talk to men. Among other things. What on earth is wrong with me?

"I'm sorry, I didn't mean to intrude," he says, mistaking my tied tongue for offense.

"Oh, no, it's fine. I'm sorry, I was . . . distracted. It's lovely that you come to the opera with your mother."

"She loves the opera. I've learned to enjoy it, although it's taken years. But I like *La Traviata*. I like the tragedy of it."

"Most operas are tragic," I say.

"Yes, but no one does tragedy like the Italians."

I smile. "True. Unless it's the French."

We sit quietly for a moment, and that's when I notice he's looking right at me. I don't mean that in any sort of romantic terms. But I'm used to men seeing me as an object. That doesn't offend me. It's a requirement of my occupation. But when a man really looks at me, sees *me,* I notice.

This man is obviously far too nice a guy to be talking to a woman like me. Not that my clients aren't good people. But this nice man thinks he's flirting with a nice woman. If he only knew.

But that doesn't mean I can't enjoy it, does it? Just an evening of innocent flirtation. It's fun being a bit of a tease now and then, something I rarely get to do. When you get paid for sex, everyone knows up front what you're there for, even when a client simply wants me to be arm candy at an event. Of course, even those evenings usually end in sex. It's far too easy for the guy. I'm right there, paid in full. Why wouldn't he want to have sex with me? Or a quick blow job in the car, at the very least. I am every bit as good at being a companion as I am at sex. But it's nice to play at it for a little while. To simply be myself, to savor this sort of attention.

The house lights dim, go dark, and the orchestra begins. I let the music wash over me, trying to ignore this man seated only inches away. This man who I have no business flirting with.

The opera is wonderful, the woman singing the part of Violetta is beautiful and incredibly talented, a lovely, pure soprano. But I'm unable to become lost in the story. I am much too aware of his scent, his presence. I swear I can feel the heat emanating from him like an invitation.

I glance over at him, looking for a moment too long, and he turns and smiles at me.

I look away, flustered now. Embarrassed.

When was the last time a man managed to fluster me?

I force myself to focus on the music, on the costumes. It

really is a wonderful production, the sets colorful, dynamic, the costumes gorgeous. And the singing is superb.

Hours later, or so it seems, the lights come up. Intermission. God, I need a drink. I rise quickly and make my way to the lobby bar.

It's crowded, as it always is during the intermission. Voices, laughter, mingled with the clink of ice in glasses, the flash of jewelry. I look around, scanning the crowd. I realize that I'm looking for *him*.

I realize that I have turned into some sort of foolish schoolgirl. I shake my head in disgust.

A voice just over my shoulder. *His* voice.

"It's impossible to elbow your way to the front at these things, isn't it? Let me order a drink for you."

"Oh, no, that's not necessary."

His gaze catches mine. I can see flecks of green and gold in his eyes in the bright lights of the lobby. He's taller than I'd thought.

"I'd like to buy you a drink."

I feel momentarily stunned. Whatever is wrong with me? "Well. Alright. I'd appreciate it. A Tanqueray and tonic."

"Don't go anywhere," he says, giving me a wink.

I watch as he makes his way to the bar, shifting into the crowd. Utterly confident. Polite. Graceful.

There is a certain kind of man who moves that way. Men of power. Men who are entirely assured of themselves. A small shiver runs through me.

He returns in only a few minutes, handing me the drink and a paper napkin. I notice he's drinking scotch on the rocks. I can smell it, a nice blend.

"Thank you. I'm Valentine Day, by the way," I tell him, giving him my full name. My clients know me only as Val. Only

Enzo gets to call me Valentine. Only Enzo knows my last name. But my name is *mine*. I have to draw the line somewhere.

He takes my hand in his. "I'm Joshua Spencer."

A current flashes up my arm, shafting deep into my body. Heat. Desire. I pull my hand back, trying not to do it too quickly, trying not to appear rude.

"So," I ask, pausing to sip my drink, covering my discomfort, "what do you do besides taking your mother to the opera?"

"Professionally? As in 'what do you do'?"

He's grinning, but there's nothing mocking in it; he's just being nice.

"Professionally, personally. Whatever you'd like to tell me."

"My job is fairly boring. I'm in real estate development. A family business."

"I don't think that's boring at all."

He shrugs. He has the broad shoulders of an athlete. Nice. "It doesn't make for exciting discussion unless you're also in real estate. Are you?"

I can see he's teasing me, but I like it. "No. I'm definitely not in real estate."

"Ah, good. Because I really hate to talk about work."

"Tell me something else, then."

"Something else?" He pauses. "I play hockey twice a week. I'm on a team. I run sometimes in the mornings. I don't have time for much else. The occasional play. Or the opera with my mother. Or without my mother, as the case may be." He flashes a boyish grin. "And I love art. I like to go to the Getty at least once every couple of months. I'll see whatever's there."

"I love the Getty."

He steps closer, his voice lowering, as though we're having

a private conversation. Perhaps we are. Another shiver runs up my spine, long and slow and warm. Exactly as I imagine his touch would be.

He says, "Let me guess. You like the Impressionists. Paintings from the more romantic eras."

"I do like the Impressionists, especially those who came into the game a little later. But I'll admit what I really love are the Neoclassicists. Leighton, Alma-Tadema, Collier. Waterhouse, of course."

"Ah, but still romantic." He gestures with his drink, then takes a sip. I watch the muscles in his throat work as he swallows.

I smile. "Yes, I suppose they are. But I'm afraid my taste in art isn't very sophisticated. I like it to be pretty."

"A feminine trait. Not necessarily a bad one."

He moves in a step closer, a few inches, really. But I feel as though we are in our own bubble, apart from the crowd around us.

"What about you? I'd guess you like something completely masculine, the more modern artists. Pollack? de Kooning?"

"Actually, I prefer the surrealists. Hockney. Dalí."

I nod my head. I love a man who knows art; it really makes me swoon. Or maybe it's just him?

"So, what do you do for work, Valentine?"

I freeze for a moment. I have a few standard answers I use in order to sidestep this question. But suddenly my mind is a blank. The lies won't leave my mouth. I lift my drink, take a long swallow, letting the gin go to work, loosening my insides. I still have no idea what to say.

The house lights flash.

"Time to go back in," he says. "Let me get rid of these glasses."

He takes mine, holding it between his fingers along with his, brings them to the rapidly emptying bar while I stand there, feeling a bit lost. Then he's back at my side, his hand going to the small of my back as he guides me through the theater doors.

His palm is warm through the thin silk of my dress. And my sex is going so damp from this nearly innocent touch, I'm almost afraid to sit down. To try to hold still for another hour or more, next to him in the dark.

I manage to do it. But the entire time I am more aware than ever of his tall, muscular body next to mine. I don't dare to look at him. I don't have to. I can feel him. And I'm soaked the entire time.

Torture.

When the show is over we stand and I feel awkward again. Do I simply leave and say good-bye?

"Did you drive?" he asks.

"I took a cab."

"Let me find one for you."

His hand at my waist again as we walk out of the theater. I can hardly stand for him to touch me. To touch me but not *touch* me.

At the curb he waves a taxi down.

"I won't be so rude as to ask for your address, so you'll have to tell the driver where you're going. But I hope you'll call me."

He pulls a business card from his pocket and slips it into my hand, grasping it with his fingers for a moment. He's looking into my eyes, and even in the dark I swear I can see a dim green and gold glow in his. He is too beautiful, this man.

I want him to kiss me. I want to pull him into the cab with me. I want to take him home and fuck him. But I do none of this.

"Thank you for the drink. And for the conversation."

He gives my fingers a final squeeze. "It was my pleasure. Call me, Valentine."

I smile, nod, and he hands me into the cab. He shuts the door, and I give one last shiver.

The cab pulls into the night, and we are immediately stuck in traffic. I don't dare look behind me to see if he is standing there.

Joshua.

I clear my throat, smooth a hand over my hair. His card is in the other hand. I should tear it up. Toss it out the window. But instead I slip it into my bag. I can throw it away later. That's exactly what I should do. Anything else would be ridiculous. Unrealistic. And life has taught me to be realistic. I am the poster child for accepting reality, no matter how ugly. It's this beautiful, nice man who's thrown me off balance.

I know what I should do. But I close my purse, my fingers tightening on the metal clasp, as though I am still holding the card in my hand. As though I really can call him tomorrow, go on a date. One in which I don't get paid.

I'm not the sort of woman who can afford to indulge in this kind of fantasy. I will toss the card the moment I get home.

Won't I?

Chapter Two

I LET MYSELF INTO my house, the heavy wood door swinging shut behind me. The moment my feet hit the small rug in the entry hall I step out of my gold stiletto heels, curling my toes, enjoying the warm flow of blood. I love the way my legs look in a good stiletto, but they hurt like hell.

I flip on lights as I make my way down the short hall and into the living room, flopping onto the long dark-brown leather sofa and lying back against the Indian and Moroccan pillows piled there.

I love this house. It's a big Spanish style with an open floor plan that makes me feel like I can breathe. So different from the oppressive environment I grew up in. But I don't want to think about that now. No, now I just want to enjoy my house.

I've been decorating for the last four years, ever since I bought the place. It's my favorite thing to do. Besides sex. I love picking out individual pieces. Exotic imports are my favorite; I have a lot of heavy, carved pieces from India, Spain, Southeast Asia. My artwork is a mix of those same ethnic cultures and a few pieces from Japan. I love the stark esthetics of modern Japanese art; it's soothing. And all the dark, rich colors put together feel homey to me. I adore the exotic fabrics of these countries: the embroidery and damask, the dark, earthy tones mixed with bolder accents. And then there's my collection of orchids.

I know, I hardly seem the type. But there's something special about orchids. They seem so fragile, but they're stronger than they look. I can't help but admire that. And they look like the darkest, loveliest part of a woman. I'm not the first person to make the comparison.

A small collection of orchids sit on the window seat built into the wall of windows facing west, into the hillside, so they don't get too much sun. I have a particular fondness for the white varieties, but I have some in shades of purple, from pale lilac to deep amethyst.

But enough about my flowers, my house. What I really want to think about is Joshua Spencer. I eye my satin bag, sitting on the table in the entry hall. My fingers itch to take that card out. To feel the papery smoothness between my fingers. To dream of the impossible.

Because being with a man like him, being with any man when it's not a business arrangement, is entirely out of the question. These things do not happen to girls in my industry. And I've been in it far too long to delude myself.

Almost ten years. Has it really been that long? I was barely twenty when Enzo found me, and thirty is on the horizon. I suppose I should retire someday. But not yet. No, retiring now would mean giving up the only sexual satisfaction I can attain. Why would I even consider doing that?

Because maybe then I could have a normal life, a small

voice tells me. But no, not me. I will never be normal, whatever that is.

I'm brooding now. I hate when I get like this.

I get up and pad across the cool floors into the kitchen. Pale red granite on the counters, brass pots shining on hooks over the sink, a few more of my precious orchids on the windowsill. It's a great kitchen. Too bad I work so often at night; I love to cook. I love to experiment with Thai dishes, delicate French sauces. But right now all I want is another drink.

I pull the gin out, a glass, some mixer. The ice cubes hit the side of the glass, the sound seeming to echo in my quiet house. I don't mind. I like the peace. I mix the drink, take a long sip, then another.

I don't like myself when I drink. It makes me feel pathetic. But I need it tonight. All these broody thoughts. All because of *him*.

I am suddenly questioning myself. Just because I want a man. But it's more than mere want. No, it's not wanting in the usual way. It's this ridiculous yearning, craving, that won't let me go. My body is stirred with desire.

I take another gulp of the gin. No use in giving in to this kind of desire. Not even here by myself. It never works.

Damn it.

Throwing back the rest of the drink, I feel the alcohol buzz into my system, and head toward the bedroom.

Just get to bed. Forget about him.

I unzip my dress and wriggle out of it, hang it in the closet. Naked, I reach into my nightstand drawer and pull out a gummi bear from a plastic bag I keep there. Silly, I know, but this has been my bedtime comfort since I was a kid. I pop it into my mouth as I crawl into the big carved four-poster bed from Indonesia, beneath the heavy silk duvet cover done in shades of pale blue and deep chocolate brown. Soothing colors. But as I lay there in the dark, I don't feel soothed. Even the gin hasn't done its job. And I'm not enough of a drinker to get up and have some more. Not after growing up with my mother.

Shit, I really do *not* want to think about her right now. No, better to think about Joshua Spencer. About what I can't have. Makes it all the more tempting, doesn't it?

He's tempting enough all on his own. Those eyes, like amber flecked with malachite and silver. He has long, dark lashes. Lashes any girl would love to have. It's the one thing about his face which looks completely innocent. The rest is all rugged bone structure, and that lush mouth that looks too purely sexual to be at all pure.

Just thinking about him is making me hot all over, my nipples going taut, my sex damp. I squeeze my legs together beneath the weight of the covers. It doesn't help.

What would his skin taste like beneath my tongue? What would his cock look like, feel like in my hand? In my mouth?

I take in a deep breath and imagine his scent on the air. And I'm absolutely drenched now, the naked lips of my sex swollen and needy when I brush my fingertips over them.

I really do need another drink.

Instead, I roll over and reach into the drawer of my nightstand, pull out the big, phallic vibrator my friends Regan and Rosalyn gave me for my last birthday. I rarely use it. It's of very little use to me. But I need something, need it badly enough to try.

I lie back on my pillows, switch it on, and lower it between my thighs. And in my mind is Joshua Spencer's face.

I can feel the buzz of the vibrator as I touch it to my aching clit, and there is that lovely, momentary shock of pleasure. But as soon as I feel it, it's gone.

No.

Think of him. Joshua.

Imagine what he'd look like without his shirt on: strong pecs, arms heavily muscled from playing hockey. Washboard abs.

I lick my lips, try the vibrator again. And once more, that one delicious moment before it dissipates.

Concentrate.

His pants have to come next, revealing strong thighs. And in between them, his beautifully erect cock. Yes, now my mouth is watering. Smooth golden skin, the purple head glistening with pre-come. And I take him into my mouth, the swollen head hitting the back of my throat, the scent of him, of desire, filling my mind.

I run the vibrator over my clitoris once more, savor the thrill of sensation, the image of Joshua's cock going down my throat, sucking him, hearing him moan. But that's not where I need him most.

Moving the big vibrator farther down, I part my thighs as if for a lover. I'm so damn wet I don't need any lube. As wet as though there was a pile of cash on the night table, waiting for me. Oh, yes, my pussy gives a hard squeeze at the thought.

Joshua.

Yes, think of Joshua . . .

Think of him entering me, his cock slipping inside as I spread a little wider to take the tip of the vibrating shaft into me. A shiver of sensation, the low thrumming buzz of the pink, plastic machine. I angle to hit my G-spot, and another shock of pleasure shafts deep into my system.

Oh, yes . . .

Joshua . . .

His face, his fine hands. I'd looked at them at the opera. He has big hands, beautiful skin, yet a real man's hands.
Strong looking.

Oh, yes, touch me . . . fuck me.

I plunge the plastic shaft deeper, and the vibration is really starting to get to me. I pump my hips, thrust it deeper,
using the heel of my hand to press onto my hard clit.

And soon I sense that first raw edge. Pleasure ripples
through me in long, undulating waves. Almost there.

Joshua . . .

Oh, yes, his cock driving into me, his mouth on mine. He
tastes like good scotch: that smooth, that silky. His tongue in
my mouth, his cock deep inside me, and I'm nearly coming
now . . . *ah, yes . . .*

My hips arch into the vibrator, my sex clenches . . . and
then, nothing.

No!

I bury the vibrator deeper, angle it harder, and my climax
starts again, that heaviness weighing down on my belly, simmering, spreading. But once more it tapers off, disappears.

Fuck!

I almost want to cry. But I take a deep breath, picture his
face again.

His mouth is one of the hottest things I've ever seen. Yes,
imagine that mouth between my thighs, licking my damp slit,
sucking on my clit, hard and steady, just the way I like it. And
his big hands gripping my hips, holding me down.

Yes . . .

Warm and wet and sucking . . .

My body is shaking so damn hard with the need to come,

I can barely hold the vibrator. I grip harder, thrust it in and out, moving my hips in time. There is sweat on the back of my neck, between my breasts, between my thighs. If he were here with me, he'd be slippery with my sweat, his face buried in my soaking wet mound, loving my shaved pussy.

A long surge of pleasure running through me. My elusive orgasm builds once more, higher and higher. I squeeze my eyes shut tight, see his face, his tongue in my mouth and in my pussy at the same time, his cock plunging into me, his hands on my breasts, squeezing my nipples.

Oh, yes!

I reach for that peak, pleasure shivering through me, and poise on the edge.

Joshua!

I tremble, begin to come.

Ah, yes . . .

And it's gone, as if it never existed. And I am defeated once more.

God damn it!

I really do want to cry now. But I knew this is how it would end. It always does. I am always left panting and weak with unmet need.

Too bad I can't pick up the phone, call one of my clients. But we never, ever do that.

I want to throw the vibrator across the room. But I set it on the night table and throw the covers back instead, get out of bed and walk naked to the kitchen. I'm having that damn drink.

I pour the gin and take it back to bed with me, sitting up against the pillows, my body still shivering with need that will not be met tonight. And along with it, that sense of revulsion

I have on those rare occasions when I allow myself to drink like this: to comfort myself, to *use* the alcohol. But I'm drinking it anyway.

The moonlight is coming through the heavy paned windows, washing the room in silver. Everything looks surreal in the moonlight. Everything feels surreal to me: the aching desire in my body, the memory of the opera tonight. It's almost as though none of it ever happened. Maybe it didn't. I almost want to get up again and look for his card in my purse.

But it may as well have never happened, for all the good it'll do me. Because I cannot become involved with this man. Impossible. Fucking impossible. This is the condition of my life, and I have to accept it. I *have* accepted it.

God damn it.

THE SUN WAKES ME. I squint into the light, roll over, and pull my pillow over my head. I swear my sex is still quivering with need. So hard I have to squeeze my thighs together, trying to make it go away. No use.

I dreamed of him last night. I don't remember much, just a dark writhing of naked flesh, his face, his mouth. My fingers reaching out to touch it, those lush lips, then him taking my fingers into his mouth, that exquisite moist heat.

God.

I really need to stop.

I need to work, is what I need to do.

I roll out of bed and check my messages. One from Deirdre, letting me know Louis wants to see me. Apparently he tried to reach me last night, but my cell was off while I was at the opera. My regulars can usually reach me directly, but they know what to do if I'm not available enough for them: call Deirdre and have her get me, or find them another girl.

Deirdre is my madam, I suppose you would call her, although we who work for her call her The Broker. She's a cold woman, but she does her job incredibly well. She is elegant, sophisticated, has connections in the highest circles. She's more than fair to us. We make plenty of money for her; she should be. And she's not the type to resent the private gifts our clients give us: jewelry, designer clothes, even extra cash. She knows that her clients are satisfied when her girls are happy.

So, it's to be Louis today. I'm happy about that. I adore Louis. He's one of my favorites. He's sweet to me, and the most sensual of lovers. The fact that he's blind probably has something to do with that.

I don't pity him, which is why he asks for me, again and again. He's a strong man, a smart man; there's nothing to pity if you look beyond his inability to see. And he's ridiculously rich. His gifts to me are always extravagant. In fact, the car I currently drive was from Louis after a particularly long weekend of debauchery at his weekend house in Palm Springs. But today I need him more for the sex than anything else.

My body is buzzing again, alive, ready. In the shower I run my hands over my slick skin, between my thighs, and shiver with anticipation.

Yes, think about Louis, my client. Don't think of Joshua Spencer.

But of course he is all I can think of.

I'm to see Louis at lunch today, so I don't have much time. I put my makeup on, even though he can't see it. I always look my best. I would never consider leaving the house if I didn't. A woman in my position can't afford to risk that.

I dress in a soft knit wrap dress because it feels lovely and it'll be fun for him to take off. And beneath it, a lacy bra and G-string. Louis loves me in a G-string. He likes to go down on me, to fuck me without having to take it off.

I slip into a pair of heeled sandals and grab my purse and my keys. Outside it's warm and sunny, the air filled with the tangy scent of the eucalyptus trees that grow all over these canyons. I love living in the Hollywood Hills. There is an utter sense of privacy here, yet I can feel the hum of energy from the city below. Maybe it's all in my head. But I love it. It is the exact opposite of the deathly dull environment I was raised in. And as much as I hate to think about my past, I like to revel in the sensation of that utter contrast.

My slick little black Mercedes coupe is in the driveway, and I slide in behind the wheel. It starts with its customary purr. Taking in a long breath, I inhale the new leather scent, mixed now with the scent of the trees outside.

I hit the button which opens the gates to my property and back out of the drive, shifting as I swing down the road. It's a short drive to Beverly Hills and I'm early, but I want to stop and pick up a loaf of Louis's favorite bread at this little Italian bakery in my neighborhood.

I'm there in only moments. The bakery smells like heaven, and I realize I'm hungry. I hope a lunch date means lunch today, along with the sex. I should have eaten a little something before I left the house. I'm not thinking today. I can blame it on my slight hangover, but I know that's not what it's about.

I really need to get Joshua out of my head before I get into bed with Louis.

You see, this is one reason why a relationship doesn't work for a woman in my position. It makes us lose focus.

The guy behind the bakery counter asks what I want. He's

one of those pretty gay boys, all smooth skin and wide, glossy eyes. He's flirting with me, anyway, which is one reason why I adore gay men. My body heats up a little in response; I can feel my nipples going hard just watching his mouth move as he asks me what I want.

God, I'm in bad shape. My dear Louis is going to get the fuck of his life.

I get my bread and leave, make the short drive to Louis's house. Although calling it a house is a bit absurd. This place is a mansion, of the classic Beverly Hills variety. A large colonial, with soaring white columns, a large, circular drive with a fountain in the middle, the water splashing, gleaming in the sun.

Louis's valet, Thomas, answers the door. His face is expressionless, as always. He knows exactly who and what I am. If he has an opinion about it, it never shows on his stony features. He leads me to the back terrace overlooking the garden and the pool. The table is gorgeously set with china and crystal, a lovely centerpiece filled with enormous Casablanca lilies. Their perfume would be a bit overwhelming if we weren't outside.

Louis's gardens are beautiful, and it's a shame he can't enjoy the view. But he's had his gardeners plant fragrant roses, rosemary, tuberose, everything that smells good, so that the air is always perfumed.

He is already seated at the table, but ever the gentleman, he rises as I step outside, a moment before the first click of my heels on the patio.

"Louis, how lovely! I didn't expect to see you today. I'm so glad you called."

"I'm glad you were available. I had a cancellation and hoped you would make time for me."

He reaches out and I put my hand in his. That first tingle, just from the warmth of his touch. I truly like Louis. He's a wonderful man, a longtime client, so gentle, so kind. Far too alone.

"Sit down, Val, and eat with me. Are you hungry?"

"Yes, I'm starving. I brought some of that Italian bread you like." I hand it to his valet, who will take it into the kitchen and have it sliced for us.

"I thought I smelled it. You're an angel, Val."

He settles back into his chair gracefully, as he does everything. He is a large man, a bit bulky, yet still elegant in his demeanor. He's not particularly attractive, but that doesn't matter to me. He has an average face, his eyes covered with dark glasses. Good teeth, thinning brown hair. But it's his hands I love. They are the most sensitive hands, as though he can almost see with them. They really are his eyes, I suppose. His touch is entirely unique. Incredibly knowing, tender.

I give a long shiver of need.

Lunch is served, a nicely done salad with grilled salmon, a little white wine. I don't bother to ask about the vintage; Louis is a gourmand and I know it will be superb. It is.

As we eat we chat about his business, how tired he is of it, how he'll retire soon. Louis has been threatening to retire as long as I've known him. But he won't do it until he must, I'm sure. He needs to feel needed, useful. That's part of my job.

I reach out and touch his hand.

"Have you had time to digest, Louis?"

He smiles, turns toward me. "I ate lightly on purpose, Val. Just enough to fuel me."

"Then take me inside and fuck me. Please?"

"Such dirty talk, Val."

But his smile broadens, and I really can hardly wait. I'm throbbing all over simply anticipating it.

He stands and I take his hand, and he leads me into the house. His bedroom is on the first floor, a large room with an enormous bed in the center. One of those grand affairs you'd expect to find in a mansion, with four ornately carved posts soaring toward the vaulted ceiling. Everything is done in creamy shades on silk and velvet, the lovely textures that make his world come alive. Beautiful against the dark wood.

He sits on the end of the bed and I go to him, pull his hands to my face. He spends a moment exploring my features, as he always does.

"I'll have an extra gift for you today, Val, for coming on such short notice."

"Oh, I intend to," I joke, making him smile once more.

His fingers dip between my lips, and I pull them into my mouth, sucking on them. My dream from last night flashes through my head: Joshua Spencer's wet mouth wrapped around my own fingers, pulling, sucking. Ah . . .

I am soaked already.

"That's so good, Val," Louis tells me, his voice gone quiet. "But I want my cock there."

"So do I," I tell him, dropping to my knees and opening his trousers to release his hard flesh.

Louis's cock is a nice size, perhaps a bit larger than average. Only half hard now, but I'll take care of that quickly enough.

I lower my head and blow on it. I know he loves that, the feel of my warm breath on his flesh. His cock stirs, and I smile to myself. There is such a sense of power in what we can do to a man. They truly are powerless at times like this. I could ask him for anything. But all I want is his touch today, his cock. And of course, the knowledge that I will be paid for my services. But today it could be a dollar.

I lean closer and breathe him in. He is all clean soap and a hint of aftershave. His skin is sweet as I take the head into my mouth. I linger there, curling my tongue around his hardening flesh, teasing him. I hear him moan above me.

"Ah, that's it, Val." A gentle hand goes into my hair, and he runs his fingers through it. "So soft," he murmurs. "Your hair, your mouth . . ."

I pull him in deeper and begin to suck, curling my hand under his balls, fondling them gently.

"You're going to make me come too soon, Val. You know how much I love that."

I pull back for a moment to ask him, "Do you want me to stop? Or do you want to come in my mouth, Louis?"

"If you keep talking to me like that, I'm going to come all over your face, you minx." He chuckles.

He's really a good boy. A little bit of dirtiness goes a long way with him.

"Tell me how you want it, Louis."

"I want you to suck me for another minute or two, then I want to lick you. I want to feel you come. And then I want to screw you, come inside you."

Yes, a good boy. He never says "fuck."

"You're the boss, Louis. Your wish is my command."

I bend over him once more and really go to work, sucking hard, sliding his shaft in and out of my mouth, taking him deep into my throat, until he's moaning, squirming. Until I know he's nearly coming. I stop.

"Ah," he groans. "Perfect. Now I need to touch you, Val."

I stand up, and find I'm a bit shaky on my feet. And when

he runs his hands over my body, goose bumps rise all over my skin. He smiles a little when he feels the soft texture of the dress. Untying it, he slides it from my body, his hands somehow never leaving my flesh. He explores me slowly, his fingers running over the lace of my bra, making my nipples harden into two stiff peaks. Then he moves lower, brushing the small lacy triangle between my thighs. I let out a sigh.

"Eager today, Val?"

"I'm so ready for you, Louis. Touch me and see."

He does, a gentle glide of fingers beneath my G-string and over my aching slit.

"Very nice," he says, his voice rough with lust, making me smile.

His hands move back up my body, to my breasts, and he squeezes gently. Unfastening the clasp in the front, he slides the bra from my shoulders, and I feel gloriously free, almost as though the air itself is caressing my skin.

But in moments it is Louis's clever hands, soft on my flesh. His touch is so gentle, and from another man I might find this frustrating, but with Louis it is always lovely. That slip and slide of his fingers over my skin, circling my nipples until they hurt. God, they hurt.

"Suck on them, Louis," I plead with him.

He does just that, leaning in and taking one hard nub of flesh into his mouth. Ah, warm and wet and sweet, that sweep of his tongue. And I'm shivering, pleasure pouring through my system.

He moves his mouth down my body, circles my waist with his soft hands, pulling me around and laying me down on the bed so that my legs hang over the edge. He goes down on his knees, and I tremble all over, waiting for his mouth between my thighs. A moment later he parts my legs wider, teases at the edge of the lacy G-string with his fingers, then pulls it aside. Using his tongue, he teases the very tip of my hardened clit, and I'm shivering, clenching already.

"Yes, Louis. Lick me."

His tongue flicks against my clit again, then moves lower, licking at my swollen pussy lips.

"Inside, Louis. Please."

I arch my hips, and he obliges, his soft, warm tongue dipping inside me. Pleasure seeps into me like water, like the heat of his wet mouth.

His hands are on my thighs, making little circles on my skin. I love when he does this; it's a dual sensation, as though I am being touched everywhere, making my skin hot, sensitive. It's a lovely sort of distraction from what he's doing to my pussy, so that I won't come too quickly.

His fingers trace a long line down the insides of my legs, to my ankles. His fingertips skim the bones there, tickling a little, as his tongue laps at my clit, gently, featherlike, until I can hardly stand it.

"Make me come, Louis. Make me come in your mouth. You know I love that. You know you love that."

He moans, his tone as gentle as everything else about him. And he licks me in a slow, steady rhythm, his fingers now teasing at the lips of my sex, adding to the sensation, layer upon layer. Pleasure swarms my system, and as the first wave of climax shivers over my skin, Joshua's face appears before me. And I let him be there, let it be *him* licking me gently to orgasm as the waves come crashing down on me. Pleasure courses through me, sharp, sharper, with Joshua's beautiful face in my mind, Joshua and the knowledge that it's Louis between my thighs. My paying client.

I'm coming harder and harder, can't seem to stop. I'm

shaking with the power of it, and Louis is moaning now along with me.

Finally it's over. He lifts his head.

"That was spectacular," he says, his voice low.

"Yes it was," I agree. I don't have to tell him why. "You're going to fuck me now, aren't you, Louis?"

"You are a very dirty girl, Val," he says, chuckling. "But yes, I am."

I sit up and help him out of his clothes, taking a few moments to run my hand over his skin, making sure to keep that sensory contact with him while I grab a condom from my purse on the floor by my feet.

When he's naked I pull him down on the bed and climb on top of him, slip the condom over his cock, then hold myself over his body, tucking the head inside me with my fingers. I leave just the head there for a moment, savoring that first sensation of fullness, needing more. I need to come again. Once wasn't nearly enough, not today.

Louis's hands are on me once more, cruising over my skin, making me shiver. His fingers tease my nipples, and I lean into him, almost wishing for once that he would tug on them, pinch them. But that's not Louis. And I'm here for his pleasure. My own is secondary.

I press down onto his cock, a little at a time. He groans, thrusts gently up into me.

"Yes, that's good, Val, so good."

I'd love to really ride him hard, to fuck him like I would Enzo. I'll do it with Louis sometimes, but I know he likes these long, slow fucks the most. I force myself to keep it slow, to tease him, to tease myself. My body is full of need, my sex pulsing once more. And his fingers brushing my nipples are driving me mad; they're so damn hard. Joshua's face in my mind again, his mouth coming down to cover my nipples, pulling them in, sucking deep inside his mouth.

Oh, yes!

I tilt my hips, pressing a little harder on Louis's cock, a little faster. I can't handle slow anymore.

"Ah, you're a wild one today, Val," Louis says, but there's no admonishment in his voice.

"I need it today," I tell him truthfully, my words coming out between sharp, gasping breaths.

I move faster, grinding my mound into him. He's panting now, his hands on my breasts a little rougher than usual.

"Oh, yes, Louis. Touch me, yes . . ."

He pumps up into me, his fingers brushing my nipples, and that's all it takes. I come, hard, pleasure gripping my body in long spasms. I'm moaning, gasping. And Louis tenses beneath me, groans aloud, his hips jerking.

My climax is short and sharp, the sensation stabbing into me. When I stop shivering I look down at Louis. But all I can see behind my orgasm-glazed eyes is Joshua's face.

The Darker Side of Pleasure

CHAPTER ONE

BONDAGE. THE WORD REVERBERATED THROUGH Jillian's head, through her body, making her muscles tense and quiver.

Her stomach clenched as she pulled her sporty BMW into the driveway after a long day at work. She peered up at the sleek, modern expanse of redwood and glass her husband had designed for them six years ago, right after they'd married and moved to Seattle.

She took a deep breath and forced her hands to stop gripping the steering wheel. Tonight was the night. The night she and Cameron were going to start trying to put their marriage back together.

She yanked a little too hard on the parking brake, then grabbed her purse and the pretty pink shopping bag that held the new lingerie she'd bought for the occasion. Cameron was right. It had been ages since she'd dressed up for him. Hell, she'd been sleeping in the guest room for months. Not that that was his fault. It was her. She knew that. She just couldn't stand to be so close to him, with so much distance between them. It hurt too much.

Her nerves jangled as much as her keys did when she opened the front door. "Cam? You home?"

No answer. She exhaled on a sigh of relief. She needed some time to make herself ready. Not just physically, but emotionally, too—even though they'd talked about this almost a week ago. Maybe she'd had too much time to think about it. She did have a tendency to overanalyze things. She let her purse fall to the hardwood floor, gripped the lingerie bag, and headed down the hall.

Stripping off her clothes in the half-dark bedroom felt like a ritual, somehow. The house was quiet. The soft glow of twilight filtered through the Japanese paper shades that covered the ceiling-high bedroom windows. There was the faint scent of him in the air, that sense of intimacy in the room where they'd slept up until she'd moved into the guest room a few months ago. But they hadn't made love for too long before that. And on those rare occasions when they had, she felt as though she weren't entirely present in her own body, as if she were watching it from the outside. But tonight was supposed to help change that. The idea made her stomach clench up again.

She stepped into the slate-tiled bathroom and blasted the hot water, wanting the sheer force and heat of it to wash her nerves away. This was her own husband, after all. She closed her eyes as she moved beneath the spray and let the water sluice over her, trying to steer her mind down a more positive path.

Cameron. He'd been so young when they'd first met,

only twenty-one. She was an old lady of twenty-five at the time. But he was so mature for his age, so somber and responsible. And there was always something of the darkness about him that made him seem older than he was. Perhaps it was the tattoo that circled his right biceps, a sinuous circle in a dark tribal design. Maori, he'd told her. She loved it. She'd loved his tall, lean, yet muscular body. God, he had the greatest abs she'd ever seen on a human being. And she loved the way his straight, coal black hair fell into his eyes, even the dark-framed glasses he wore for reading.

That's how Jillian had first seen him, in her English Lit class in college. He was bent over a book, and he glanced up as she passed a printed handout to him. And those smoky gray eyes peered up at her—eyes fringed in thick, sooty lashes any woman would envy. Those startling eyes and that serious expression on his angular features, yet his mouth was lush and sensual, a stark contrast.

He still wore those glasses. And even after all they'd been through, a small shiver of excitement would course through her whenever he put them on. If only he had come to bed early enough to read, while she was still awake, while she'd still been sleeping in their bed.

But no, she shouldn't think about that. Tonight was for new beginnings, not old pain.

She shut off the water, stepped out onto the cool tiles, and began to rub scented lotion into her skin. It was Cameron's favorite vanilla scent, the one he used to say made him want to run his tongue all over her body. Her sex gave a quick, involuntary squeeze, surprising her.

Drawing her pale green silk summer robe around her

shoulders, she went to pull her purchases out of the bag. The bra was black and lacy, with demi-cups that barely covered her breasts. The matching thong was a whisper of lace. It made her feel sexy, she had to admit, admiring her reflection in the big full-length mirror in her walk-in closet. Despite her breasts and thighs, which weren't as firm at the age of thirty-three as they'd been when she and Cam had met eight years ago.

No, don't think about that now.

She pulled her long honey blond hair up with her hands, considering, then decided to leave it down. Cam liked it better that way.

When she drew the first black lace stocking over one leg, she began to get a real sense of ritual, of formal preparation. For some reason she didn't understand it sent a small thrill through her, raising gooseflesh on the back of her neck. And when she slid her feet into the impossibly high black pumps Cam had insisted she buy, the feeling was complete. She understood suddenly that she was doing this for him, but that it also fulfilled some need in her. To please in order to feel whole.

This was a new concept for her. She'd been inside her own head for so long, immersed in her grief, that she'd forgotten to look outside. To look at her husband.

When Cam had first suggested they try to find their way back to each other through sex, she'd balked. In fact, that was putting it lightly. She'd flat out refused, thought he was being selfish and ridiculous. But then he'd reminded her that sex was intimacy, and that bondage was the purest form of mutual trust. It took her a while to absorb that, but she eventually came to realize he had a valid point. And they needed to try something, anything, before the gap between them grew any wider. Tonight was to be a true test.

She drew the stockings up her legs, her hand brushing the honey-colored curls at the apex of her thighs. Blood rushed to the area so fast, she had to cup her mound with her hand and press there. Strange! Why was she so hypersensitive, when she'd been completely shut down for almost a year?

The loud rumbling of her husband's prized Harley pulling into the driveway brought her head and her hand up fast. Cam!

She took one last, desperate look in the mirror, added a little lip gloss with a shaking hand. She was ready for him.

She thought she was. She shivered in fear and anticipation as his steps drew nearer. The door opened with a graceful swing, and there he was. Her husband. He looked so damn good standing there, she had to smile.

He smiled back. "Almost like the old Jillian. I love it when you smile like that. Like you mean it."

"I do." She dropped her head, suddenly shy.

He crossed the room, slid his hands around her waist, ran them up her sides, traced the curve of her breasts. "God, you're beautiful."

His words warmed her, but it was still hard for her to look at him. He tipped her chin up with his fingers. She thought he'd want to talk more, but he just leaned in and kissed her. That lush, kissable mouth of his covered hers, and when he parted his lips she could taste mint, and underneath it the faint sweetness of Scotch. So he'd been nervous, too. She suddenly wanted to cry. This was why she'd been avoiding him, why she hadn't been able to sleep in the bed next to his big, warm body.

He pulled away and said simply, "Are you ready?"

Her stomach grabbed again, but she nodded. "Yes. But what are you . . . I mean, how is this all going to happen?"

"We talked about it, remember? If this is going to work, you have to trust me enough to turn yourself over to me. That's what tonight is all about. We have to learn to trust each other again. Do you remember your safe words?"

"Yes. Yellow for slow down, red for stop."

"Good."

He stepped back and his eyes roamed over her. She knew she looked better than usual in this outfit, so she didn't mind. And she could see his eyes glittering as he looked at her, his pupils widening with lust. He placed his hands on his hips, licked his lips. He gestured toward the bed with his chin.

"Sit down."

She just looked at him for a moment. She wasn't used to this simple, commanding tone from him. He didn't sound mean, but it was clear she shouldn't try to argue with him. A chill of pleasure ran up her spine.

"Now."

Another command; this time his tone was low and demanding. Her sex exploded with heat. She sat.

Cam paced the room slowly, looking at her from all angles, before he said, "Get rid of the bra."

She unhooked it immediately, her full breasts springing from the lacy confines. They felt plump and tender and wanted to be touched, something she hadn't felt in a long time. The fact that she could have this sort of reaction to nothing more than a certain tone of voice was almost shocking. She was trying hard not to analyze it.

Cam walked up to her and touched her breasts with his fingertips, just lazily brushed them over the curved underside, traced them around the edge of the areolas. Her nipples sprang up, hard and ready. But he didn't touch them.

When she looked up at his face he was smiling, just one corner of his mouth quirked up. Rakish, sexy.

He stepped back again and unbuttoned his shirt. She had always loved him without a shirt. He had one of those long, lean, cut torsos, with just the right amount of silky black hair in a line down the center of his well-defined abs. He was built like a pro basketball player: well over six feet tall, with broad shoulders and those lanky, beautifully defined muscles. His black work slacks hung low on his narrow hips and she could see that he was hard already, the outline of his large erection shadowed against the fine wool.

She squirmed on the edge of the bed, her lace thong growing damp.

"I'm going to ask you to do things for me tonight you've never done before. Are you ready to do that, Jillian?"

She swallowed, hard. Was she? Her natural mental response was to fight against the whole idea. She was normally someone who was strong, in control. But her body was rebelling already. Still, how could it be this simple? She knew that Cam's angle had been that bondage was all about trust, that there had to be complete trust in order to make it work. He saw it as a way to get back to each other. It made a sort of weird sense, but she still had her doubts.

Cam repeated, "Are you ready?"

His voice seemed so different tonight; his whole persona was different. Confident. Commanding. But it was still Cam. She could do this. She would do it for him. For them. And, judging from the unexpected way her body was responding already, for herself.

"Yes. I'm ready."

He turned then and moved to the tall dresser, pulled a CD from the top drawer and popped it into the CD player. She recognized the trancelike tones of Enigma immediately. She watched him as he lit a pair of tall pillar candles. The scent of amber wafted into the air, and the warm candlelight was soft and sultry, aided by the glow of sunset outside the windows.

He bent and opened a bottom drawer and took out a long coiled length of black rope. She hadn't known it was in there, didn't know where he'd found it. She didn't really care right now. All she could think of was that he was going to use it on her. Nerves and pleasure washed through her in an exciting, confusing tide.

Cam came to stand before her while the music played, and he rested his hands on her shoulders. After a moment, he swept them up her neck in gentle strokes, then back down, over her arms to her wrists. Gently, he gathered them into one of his big hands and pulled her arms up over her head. She shivered again, feeling unsure, vulnerable.

"Cam?"

"It's okay."

His soft voice was reassuring, but he didn't release her wrists. With his free hand he began to stroke her breasts again, and despite her hammering pulse her body responded to his touch. Her breasts filled, her nipples aching as he teased her skin with the lightest touch. When he finally brushed one hard nipple with his fingertip her whole body arched toward him.

"Patience, Jillian." He sounded amused.

She moaned softly. He rewarded her by tweaking one nipple, rather hard, but she liked it. Somehow it was just what she needed. Her sex began to pound and she squeezed her legs together.

"Lie back on the bed," Cam said.

"Why? What are you going to—"

"Shh. No questions. You're mine tonight. Turn yourself over to me, Jillian."

Yes. She wanted this. And not just because she was following the plan. Now that they'd started she knew she was going to like it, even if it scared her a little. Or maybe the fear was part of what drew her?

She lay down on the bed.

When Cam came to stand over her with the ropes in his hands, her body gave a convulsive shudder. Of need. Of lust. She had never felt anything like it. Gazing up at his tall silhouette in the dim light, she suddenly knew she'd never wanted anything so much in her life. To give herself over. To let herself go. This was exactly what she needed. Yet at the same time, she struggled with the notion. How could this be what she needed? Wasn't it proof of her own weakness?

Cam bent over her and kissed her gently on the lips, then took her lower lip between his strong, white teeth and bit down. It hurt a little.

"You're mine, Jillian. Say it."

The chill that ran through her was part lust, part awe. And she knew that after tonight, she would never be the same again.

"Yes, Cam. I'm yours."

He smiled at her. "Very good. I want you to lie perfectly still now. I'm going to play with you a bit before I tie you up."

Tie you up. Oh, my. He really was going to tie her up. A thrill ran through her, bringing goose bumps to her skin once more, but this time they ran the entire length of her body.

But she didn't have long to think about it. Cam's hands were on her, stroking her stomach, running up her thighs. They seemed to be everywhere at once. She watched him, a look of intense concentration on his face. Finally his hands came back to her breasts, covering both of them, massaging, kneading. Her nipples were hard, hot nubs against his palms.

He looked up at her face, his gray eyes watching her as he took both nipples between his fingers and thumbs and began to roll them. Fire shot from her nipples straight to her already aching sex. She tried hard not to squirm. But when he pinched, hard, she shot up off the bed.

"No, Jillian." He pressed her back down onto the mattress. "Lie still."

She tried. She drew in a deep, shuddering breath, and then he began again, pulling at her nipples, twisting, pinching. They were so hard and engorged she thought they would burst. And her sex was full and throbbing. She wanted his hands there. But she knew she had to wait. To trust him.

Cam kept working her nipples, and she wondered for the first time in her life if it was possible to come just from that. She didn't know how long it went on, an impossibly long period of time in which she was finally able to shut her brain down, to stop thinking, analyzing. Her nipples were sore, but she didn't care. She bit down on her lip to keep from crying out, to keep from moving, but her thighs spread open of their own accord. God, she needed him to touch her there. To use his hands, his mouth. She didn't care. But she didn't want him to stop torturing her breasts.

Finally, he bent his head and flicked his hot, wet tongue at one rigid tip. She groaned. He moved his head and flicked at the other one. Then, using both hands, he pushed the full mounds of her breasts together and moved his head back and forth, his tongue a damp spike of heat as it flickered over her stiffened nipples. His hands felt so good on her, so firm on her flesh, and his tongue was driving her crazy. She almost begged him to take her into his mouth. And then, as if reading her mind, he did.

He drew one nipple in and sucked. He was almost too gentle. She could hardly stand it. She gathered and bunched the bedspread in her hands, trying to hold still, to keep from crying out, from begging him to suck harder. Her sex was absolutely drenched by now. Her whole body quivered.

And suddenly, he pulled back.

"Cam?" Her own voice sounded loud and breathless in her ears.

He straightened up, half turned away from her, and ran a hand through his dark hair.

"Cam, what is it?"

She heard his long, slow exhalation. Waited for him to turn back around, to talk to her. Her thighs clenched around the damp, swollen folds of flesh between them.

"Maybe we need to talk about this some more."

"What?" A startled laugh escaped her lips. "Now? When I'm just beginning to . . ." She couldn't finish the sentence, couldn't say out loud that her body was responding in a way it hadn't for months. Couldn't tell him how desperately she craved his touch. Why couldn't she say it?

When his eyes met hers she saw the confusion there, saw that his breath was coming in short, sharp pants.

"This is . . . already more intense than I expected."

"Yes." It was all she could manage to get out.

He came and sat on the bed next to her. His warm hand fell on her shoulder. "I need to know this is what you want. Not just with your body, but in your head. What is this making you think? Making you feel?"

How could she explain? "Like . . . like maybe I can let go, finally. But it's a little scary at the same time. And physically, it's . . . almost a shock. Do you know what I mean?"

He nodded, his gaze on hers. "It's like you're coming alive under my hands." He reached out and stroked a finger across her hot cheek. "But when you shiver, I don't know if it's because you like it, or because I'm making you afraid."

"Maybe a little of both."

His eyes swept her face. They were filled with concern and burning lust at the same time. "Jillian. Honey. I don't ever want to scare you."

She shook her head, her hair sweeping across her cheek. "It's not you that's scaring me. It's me."

"I'm right here with you. Okay?"

"Yes."

"This is for us. And if it doesn't work, we'll try something else. But I want to do this. And the more I touch you, the more I want this."

"Yes. Me, too. Maybe that's what scares me the most."

Cam leaned in and brushed his lips over hers. Again came that hint of mint and liquor. His hand curled around the back of her head, firm, possessive, as he parted her lips with his hot, wet tongue. Her mouth opened beneath his, letting him in. Her tongue met his, curled and tasted. Her shoulders relaxed as the heat of his mouth flowed through her and came to rest somewhere deep in her belly.

Then he was pushing her down onto the bed, holding her there. She had a quick moment of panic when she realized how firmly he held her, but she was too turned on to let the panic take hold.

Don't think, Jillian.

Again he grasped her wrists and drew her arms over her head, making her feel vulnerable, exposed. Her eyes fluttered open so she could see his face above her. And again she saw that expression of concentrated lust in his gray eyes. He was so focused, so intense. And still his mouth was that lush slash of deep pink that made her want to kiss him.

"Stay right there." His voice was low, a little rough around the edges.

It was hard to hold still all by herself, without him holding her there, while he moved about the room. She tried to concentrate on the music still playing in the background while he knelt beside the bed and wrapped some rope around the bed frame. She could sense what he was doing more than she could see it, but the idea sent a ripple of hot anticipation through her.

Cam moved to the other side of the bed, securing the ropes. If she turned her head a bit, she could see the muscles of his back and shoulders move beneath his golden skin as he worked. He was so beautiful.

He stood, towering over her. When he bent to part her legs with his big hands she tensed. But then he stroked the tender skin on the insides of her thighs, warming her flesh, making her sex fill with a quick rush of lustful heat again, and she opened for him.

He took her right hand in his, stroked her palm open with his fingertips, and leaned in to lay a kiss there, sending a shiver of heat up her arm. Her nipples immediately went hard once more.

Cam moved his mouth over her hand, kissing her fingers, her wrist. It took her a moment to realize that he followed the trail of kisses with a length of soft, darkly colored rope, winding a loop of it around her wrist. Her eyes flew to his face, and a small, reassuring smile played at the corners of his mouth.

"Breathe, Jillian."

Yes. She took in a lungful of the amber-scented air, let it calm her racing pulse. When he pulled the rope so that it had a firm hold, he dropped one last kiss on her hand, then moved to the end of the bed and took hold of her right foot. He massaged it for a moment, stroking with his fingers, then laid a soft kiss on her instep.

She couldn't remember him ever paying much attention to her feet. She couldn't remember ever thinking about it. But somehow that one brief kiss set her body on fire, a trail of flame burning its way up her calf, over her thigh, and straight to her sex, which was hot and needy already. She was soaking wet in an instant.

Cam glanced up, as though he sensed her reaction. He smiled, then kissed her foot once more. Again her sex throbbed with a sudden lance of need. She moaned softly.

"Amazing what we can learn after all this time together." His voice was barely above a whisper.

She couldn't respond. He was already wrapping the rope around her ankle, pulling it tight. Then he moved to her other foot, pulling it to the side, so that her sex was wide open and exposed, except for the scrap of damp lace that still covered it.

He ran his hand up the inside of her leg, brushing the top of her thigh. Her sex clenched in anticipation. But he moved away, back to her foot, stroking the skin of her arch, the undersides of her toes. When he bent his head and began a slow stroking with his lips, she thought she'd go mad with need. Her hips arched up off the bed. He held her ankle more firmly in his hands.

"Hold still, Jillian."

She loved the commanding tone of his voice every bit as much as she loved his mouth on her skin. But in a moment the rope was there again, wrapping firmly around her ankle. She pulled against it once, and found she couldn't move more than a millimeter.

Cam bent over her left side, taking her free hand in his. Once more the blazing trail of kisses, hot on her flesh.

Her whole body was on fire, her sex aching and wet. But when Cam pulled the rope around her wrist, she froze.

"Cam, wait!"

He paused, looked into her face. His was calm, but his eyes sparkled darkly. "Breathe, honey."

She tried, but the air seemed to catch in her throat. Somehow this last rope meant that she would be truly bound, unable to move. Completely under his command. As exciting as it was, it was also frightening on some deep level. She wanted to let go, wanted to trust him, but how could she when she didn't even trust herself?

"Jillian." His tone was low but firm. "I want you to listen very carefully. I am going to bind your wrist and you will not be able to move. You need to give yourself over to me. You need to let it all go. You will be in my hands. *My* hands. I love you, Jillian; you know that. This is your last chance to turn back before we really begin. Tell me yes or no."

She couldn't seem to think. Her body strained against the ropes already binding her feet and her other hand. Was this what she truly wanted? Could she do this?

Her mind was a whirl of chaos edged in panic. She took a deep breath, trying to calm down.

Cam put a hand on her chest, warming her skin. She closed her eyes, let the firm reassurance of his palm absorb the pounding of her heart. Her breasts tingled, her nipples came to peak, and she focused on the scorching heat funneling through her system. Despite her confusion, her body screamed one word at her. And finally she was able to let that word escape her lips.

"Yes!"

CHAPTER TWO

CAM SMILED. HE COULD READ THE YIELDING IN
Jillian's beautiful face as she spoke the word he needed to
hear. The way she was responding to him physically was
amazing. Even in their earliest days together she hadn't
been like this. But he could see the fear and confusion in
her wide brown eyes.

Still, he knew this was the right thing to do, the right
way to do it, to reestablish intimacy between them. The
idea of bondage had been in the back of his mind for a
long time. It was something that had always fascinated
him. Bondage and maybe a little sensation play. BDSM.
He'd had fantasies since he was a teenager about spanking
a woman. The feel of a firm, feminine bottom beneath his
hand, the sound as his palm landed hard on naked flesh.
The idea of doing it to his wife was an incredible turn-on.
He'd had a hard-on pretty much all week just thinking
about tonight, ever since they'd talked about it.

He'd never thought Jillian would go for it. When they'd
reached the point where he was willing to try anything to

tear down the wall that had sat so stubbornly between them for the last year, he was surprised to hear her agree. He was glad she had, because he needed this chance to fix their marriage, to make it right. They'd tried couples counseling early on, but it had been a disaster. The therapist had spent every session blaming him for Jillian's pain. The woman had acted as though he was some insensitive bastard. He'd ended up walking out. Jillian had wanted to try going to someone else, but he'd had enough. Jillian had continued to see another therapist. It had helped some, but there was a level she'd never been able to break through. It wasn't her fault; he knew she'd tried. So it was up to him now. This had to work.

And now, watching her breath catch and her nipples swell, he was pretty sure she was as into it as he was. He was hard already, just from touching her, from tying her up. From thinking about what he was going to do to her.

Her full, rounded breasts rose and fell with her ragged breathing. Her nipples were tight and rosy pink. His groin tightened just looking at her. She was so damn beautiful, spread out on the bed for him, her little pink tongue darting out to moisten her lips.

He could feel her nerves, still, could feel his own heart thunder in his chest. But it was pure lust hammering away at his composure. He took a lungful of air and commanded himself to rein it in, to stay in control. That was his job here. And he needed to be in control now as much as Jillian needed him to be.

He reached out and stroked her smooth skin with his fingertips, ran them over her rib cage, around the edge of her breast, down her side. She shivered, and he felt the urgency of her need as a physical sensation. Suddenly, he couldn't resist. He dipped his hand down into the velvet folds between her thighs and stroked at the edges of her wet cleft. God, she was soaked! His cock filled and jerked against his slacks. He pulled his hand back.

Slow down.

A quick glance at her face and he saw her eyes screwed tightly shut. He smiled to himself at the sense of raw power that suffused him, as it began to dawn on him just how much power he had over this woman he loved. She was his now in a way she'd never been before. He wanted to take her right here, right now. His cock was throbbing, begging for release. But that's not what he was here for.

Instead, he took another deep, steadying breath, and concentrated on Jillian.

He ran a hand over the length of her body, tracing the line of her hip, her thigh, her leg, and back down to her sensitive foot. Her skin was as warm and soft as living silk. He'd never thought of himself as having a foot fetish, but the way she had responded earlier made him rethink the whole idea. As he stroked her toes she trembled and curled them. But there were even more interesting things to do, and her entire body to explore.

Jillian had had a hard time coming in the last year. She didn't seem to feel comfortable enough in her own body anymore, couldn't shut her thoughts down. He intended to change that tonight. He would make her come. Over and over again. He would make her beg. Make her scream. And when he finally took her, when his cock was buried deep inside her body, she would belong to him completely.

His rock-hard cock gave another jerk, but he focused on the sight of his wife spread out on the bed, open and vulnerable. He would fuck her, and fuck her hard, but that would have to wait. For now, she was his to feast on, to please. For now, it was all about Jillian.

Jillian opened her eyes, peering up at Cam. Why was he just standing there, when she needed so badly for him to touch her? God, when he'd shoved his fingers into her she'd almost screamed. And now she was pulsing and so drenching wet it was trickling down onto the silk and linen bedspread beneath her.

Please, touch me again.

But she couldn't say the words out loud. She watched him as his eyes swept over her body, her nipples stiffening even more as though it were his hands on her, rather than his intense gray gaze.

Finally, he bent over her and placed a series of quick, hot kisses over her stomach, then moved to her breasts. His mouth was everywhere and all thought left her head as he kissed and nibbled his way over her skin. When he reached her breasts she arched up to meet him. And when he took one nipple into his hot mouth, she went rigid all over, pleasure sweeping through her in a powerful tide. Her mind stopped entirely when he began to suck.

He drew her nipple into his mouth, pulling on it until it almost hurt. She didn't care. It felt too good. With his free hand, he caressed her other breast. Her nipples felt like they were going to explode, her sex was thrumming with heat, and it was almost as though his mouth were there between her legs.

Yes. Use your mouth there.

But it was too good, his tongue swirling over her hard nipple as he sucked with his mouth, while his other hand tugged and twisted and began to pinch.

Jesus.

She'd never felt anything so good. Her arms wanted to twine around his neck, to pull him closer, but the rope held her tight, heightening the desire burning through her body.

Cam pulled away and she let out a groan.

"Easy, honey. We've got all night. And I intend to make good use of it."

"Wh-what are you going to do?"

"Do you really want to know?" His sexy mouth pulled into a wicked grin she'd never seen on him before, and it made her tremble with anticipation.

"Tell me."

"I'm going to touch you everywhere. With my hands. With my mouth. I'm going to stroke you gently, I'm going to pinch you in all the right places. I'm going to lick every inch of your gorgeous skin. I'm going to play with you in a way I never have before, with my hands and mouth, and maybe a few other things."

He paused and Jillian's sex clenched and tingled. She wished she could press her thighs together to ease the ache there, but she was spread wide open. All she could think of was Cam putting his mouth there as he had said he would. His hot, damp tongue stroking her, his fingers pushing inside her. *Oh, God.*

He continued, his voice low and smoky. "I'm going to make you come, Jillian. I'm going to make you come so hard, with pleasure and maybe a little pain. What do you think of that?"

Think? She could hardly think. All she could do was feel. But Cam was demanding an answer from her.

"I'm waiting, Jillian."

"I . . ." Her voice was nothing more than a raw whisper. "I want that. Yes. Please, Cam."

"Good girl."

The term made her go warm and soft all over. She didn't know why.

He began to stroke her breasts again, tracing the full outline, avoiding her nipples. She shivered.

"And after you've come for me, I'm going to fuck you, Jillian. I'm going to bury my cock inside you and fuck you forever. Tell me you want that."

"I . . ."

He took one nipple between his fingers and pinched, hard. She rose up off the bed, the pain shooting through her and somehow transforming into a deep pleasure that lanced straight to her core.

"I want . . . I want you to fuck me, Cam." Yes, she could hardly think of anything else but his enormous, beautiful cock, golden-skinned as the rest of him was.

"That's my good girl."

Again that warm wash of pleasure at his words.

And then he was on her, with his mouth, with his hands, roaming over her body. He licked her skin, and stopped to kiss and suck here and there. Everywhere he touched her it was like a tiny electric shock, sending bolts of pleasure coursing through her system.

"Does this feel good, baby?"

"Yes . . ." It came out on a soft hiss.

"How about this?" His fingers squeezed her nipples, then were replaced with his mouth. His hands moved over her hips, gripped her thighs for a moment, then his fingers plunged into her dark, waiting heat.

She moaned aloud, the walls of her sex grabbing around his fingers as he moved them inside her. It was almost too much, all this sensation. And when he pressed his thumb over her clit, she thought she'd scream with pleasure.

"Oh, God, oh, God," she murmured, already on the edge of orgasm.

Cam pulled back.

She squirmed on the bed, pulling against the ropes that held her so firmly, that held her spread apart. Cam moved around the room, but she couldn't seem to care what he was doing. The only thing she knew was that he wasn't touching her anymore.

In a moment he returned to the bed, a pair of scissors in his hand. She gasped and tried to sit up. Of course she couldn't.

He smiled down on her, his eyes literally glowing. "I just need a little help getting rid of these pretty panties you wore for me."

With a quick snip they were gone.

His hands were on her again as he knelt on the bed, stroking her thighs, encouraging the muscles there to relax. When he brushed his fingers back and forth across her clit, the fire there roared to a full blaze once more. And then he did something he'd never done before. It began with a gentle tapping of his fingers, but soon moved on to a rhythmic slapping against her mound. She was surprised at how good it felt, teasing her clit into a rock-hard nub. By the time the slapping became a little painful, she was too hot to care. The pain felt good, intensifying the pleasure, until it all melted together and became one sensation.

Her sex throbbed, pounded beneath Cam's hand, until she was right on the edge of coming. And then he reached a hand up and pinched her nipple, hard. And at the same time he pinched her clit between his strong fingers, and the pain and the pleasure shot through her at a hundred miles an hour.

"Come for me, honey." He pinched harder.

Her body ignited, her sex went into a clenching, grabbing spasm and her mind emptied completely. Her orgasm rocketed through her, making her thighs tremble. The trembling turned into a shaking that spread through her body and she called out his name as she gasped for breath.

"Cam!"

As the wave subsided, she ended on a quiet sob. And suddenly her bonds were being released and her husband's strong arms were around her. He kissed her face, whispering her name.

"Jillian, honey, I'm right here."

"Oh, God, Cam . . ."

"Shh. It's alright now. You're fine. You're good."

And for the first time in a long time, she suspected he was right.

Cam held Jillian tight, rocking her as he would a small child. Not that he thought of her as childlike, not at all. She was more a woman to him at this moment than she'd ever been before. But infinitely precious in a way that was new for him.

He could feel the ripples of emotion coursing through her body as he held her, just as earlier he'd felt her waves of response. He had some idea of what she was experiencing. At least, he was trying to understand. It had been such a long time since she'd been able to reach orgasm, and she had never had one like this! Was he really doing anything that different? He was trying harder, but not in the usual goal-oriented way, that much he knew. He'd made a mission of it, of just pleasing her. His own body was still hard and humming with her pleasure as much as his own need. And it gave him a profound sense of accomplishment to have brought her to this point.

He wanted to do it again. And again.

He sensed when Jillian began to calm. The tears stopped, her limbs relaxed, and she lay soft and pliant against him. He still wanted her; his raging erection was a testament to that. But right now it felt good just to hold on to her, to know what he'd given her, and to feel close again.

They sat for a long time before she stirred, tilting her face up to his. He kissed her pink mouth, savoring the familiar sweetness of her mixed with a few salty tears. His heart pounded in his chest. This was what they'd been missing—maybe more than they'd ever had to begin with. He felt his limbs loosen with the realization that he really had a good shot at making it all better. He had to, damn it. He was not going to allow things to fall apart. He couldn't allow it. It was up to him to keep it together. To keep them together. And he would, no matter what it took.

"Cam." Her voice was a husky whisper.

"Right here, baby."

"That was . . ."

"Yeah. How do you feel?"

"I feel . . . good. Lighter. Does that make sense?"

"Yeah, it does." He smiled down at her, pushed her tangle of honeyed hair away from her face. God, he loved her mane of hair. So soft and sexy, especially the way it was now, all tousled around her flushed face.

She smiled back at him. Then, after a quiet moment, "I want more."

"So do I. And I want it now. Are you ready? Because I don't think I can wait one more minute to be inside you."

"Yes, Cam!"

It was all he needed to hear. Picking her up in his arms, he shifted her until she was laid out on the bed again. Quickly, he stripped off his slacks and his boxers. He lay on top of her, careful not to crush her. He needed to feel her silken skin against his. Her plush breasts pushed against his chest. He could feel the hard points of her nipples already. He wanted them in his mouth again, but first, he needed to kiss his wife.

Her lips were plump and warm beneath his. Her

mouth was hot and wet when he opened her lips and drove inside. It made him think about her tight, wet pussy. He knew how good it would feel around his shaft. He lowered his hand between their bodies, between her thighs. Found her slick opening and stroked. She moaned against his mouth. With his fingers, he played with the soft folds, pulling and pinching a little before dipping inside.

She contracted around his finger, hot and tight and wet. He added another finger, then another while she gasped. God, she felt so damn good, he had to be inside her. But not yet.

He pulled his fingers out and stroked her mound, finding her hard little nub and tugging at it, rolling it between his fingers and thumb. Her hips were moving against him, her pelvis rubbing hard against his straining cock, and he thought for a moment he was going to lose it. To come all over her stomach like a high-school kid.

Hang on.

He raised his hips. Using his hand to spread the lips of her sex wide, he carefully guided the head of his cock into her opening. Careful because he knew he was big and he didn't want to hurt her. Not that way, at least. He paused there, meaning to catch his breath, but Jillian wrapped her smooth legs around him, and all he could do was plunge inside. Into that dark, moist heat, into that tight, pulsing tunnel. He pulled out, thrust again, all the way to the hilt. He was buried deep inside her, exactly where he needed to be, and it felt damn good.

"Yes, honey, that's it. You can take it all," he ground out. Jillian met each thrust with her own, driving him on.

He grabbed her firm ass cheeks in his hands, pulled her hips up higher, knowing at that angle he could grind against her clit with each thrust.

She was gasping rhythmically now, bucking beneath him. His cock was heavy with blood and lust, burning with the need to come, but he held back, waiting for her. Her clenching pussy was driving him wild. Each plunge drove him higher, sent shards of pleasure lancing through him. He couldn't hold on much longer.

"I need to fuck you hard, baby."

"Do it, Cam!"

"I need to fuck you, baby . . ."

He thrust into her, into her hot, waiting sheath. She wrapped her legs around his back, pulling him in tighter. Her arms were around his neck, her face buried in his shoulder, biting, sucking. He loved it. His hands dug into the soft flesh of her ass as he sped up, pounding into her like a freight train now. In and out, harder, faster. His cock was ready to explode.

Jillian let out a guttural cry and her velvet pussy convulsed around him, setting him off. He came hard and fast, like a rocket going off in his cock, reverberating through his belly, his whole body. He yelled something, he didn't know what. Didn't matter. Just keep coming. Coming so damn hard he couldn't think of anything else. Just feel. Just feel this ripping-hard orgasm and Jillian shaking beneath him.

He kissed her face all over, couldn't seem to stop kissing her. God, she was fucking beautiful.

"Love you, honey."

"Love you, too."

When was the last time he'd felt this good? When was the last time he'd felt so close to her? This is what they'd needed. This would fix them. Maybe not all at once. But eventually. Meanwhile, even if the practice killed him, what a way to go!

Jillian lay beneath the warmth of her husband's big body. She felt wonderful. Her whole system was still buzzing with the aftershocks of two of the most powerful orgasms of her life. Her husband, the man she loved, was pressed against her still. And for the first time in far too long, she felt a hint of the happiness she'd been missing.

Cam had been right, she thought. This was going to help them. It was going to help her. While she'd been in his arms, while he'd been tormenting her with pleasure, she hadn't thought once about losing the baby.

Damn!

There it was, the memory that had kept her mind tied up in grief for almost a year. She squeezed her eyes shut.

Not now.

But it was too late. She pushed Cam off her, rolled onto her side.

"Honey, what's wrong?"

He sounded truly confused. Well, he was a man. She couldn't expect him to be psychic, especially only moments after sex.

The tears started. She couldn't help it. Maybe it was the powerful orgasms, or just the hour of closeness, but she felt all opened up inside. Cam's hand slid over her shoulder, but she flinched away. Despite the closeness they'd just shared, she couldn't stand his touch. She was too raw. It would send her over the edge, and she might never come back.

"Jillian. Please." He bent over her side, kissing her shoulder, trying to pull her against his body, but she couldn't let him.

She sat up, intending to flee to the bathroom, but he wouldn't allow her to. He held her tight in his arms, pressing her into the warmth of his big, solid body. A sob escaped her.

"I can't do this, Cam."

"Yes, you can. And it's about time. You have to share this part of yourself with me, too. Don't you get it? If you don't, it'll always be there between us."

"It's too hard!"

"You have to do this. It's the only way you'll come back to me."

Was that a note of desperation in his voice? Cam, who was always so strong, who could handle anything? Her heart melted a little at the thought. She was hurting him. She'd known it before, in a distant kind of way. Now she began to understand that losing the baby had been hard on him, too.

"Jillian, talk to me. I can't lose you again, after just beginning to get you back. Come on, honey. We've lost too much already. Too much time, too much of each other."

"I know." She sniffled, and Cam grabbed a tissue from the nightstand and put it into her hand. "I'm trying. And this was . . . wonderful. It was the first time in so long I've felt even vaguely good. Maybe it was too good."

"Too good?" She could hear the hurt in his voice.

"I mean that it's such a contrast to the way I've been feeling for so long, it's a shock. To feel good. To feel close to you again."

The room was almost entirely dark now. The sun had set and the only light came from the candles burning on the dresser. She felt dark inside, too, yet the darkness of the room was welcoming, womblike. She couldn't have faced Cam now, in the stark light of day.

He was stroking her hair, kissing the top of her head, and she allowed herself to relax into his embrace. To feel the safety of him. This was her own fault, she knew. It was her body that hadn't been able to hang on to their baby, and her selfish grief that had driven a wedge between them. It was time to try to make it all right. And she would try. She wasn't as sure of her strength as Cam seemed to be. But she knew she could lean on him, on his strength. He was always there for her. She needed to appreciate that more. She was so damn lucky.

"I love you, Cam. So much!"

He paused, as though he was surprised at her words.

"I love you, too, honey. You know I do. Come on. Lie down with me. Rest. I'll be right here."

She snuggled into his strong arms. She wanted to learn to trust him again, to learn to trust herself. She didn't know how long it would take. She only knew it would be hard. But here she was, with her wonderful husband: a man who loved her in a way she didn't truly deserve. She tried to remember why, but her mind began to drift, and soon, she was fast asleep.

Sometime in the night Jillian awoke. Cam's arms were still wrapped around her as he spooned her from behind. His cock was hard again. His deep, even breathing told her that he slept. She tried to relax back into sleep, too, but she couldn't. Her body was too aware of him. She pressed her buttocks back, pushing and rubbing against his thick erection. She wasn't even sure he was awake when his hand snaked down between her aching thighs and he began to play gently with her. She moved her thighs apart to grant him better access. His hips thrust against her, his big cock seeking entrance. Moving her buttocks higher and her leg up, she arched against his hips until she could guide his cock into her already wet and ready sex. He pushed into her slowly. The pleasure was exquisite, yet it was all softer and sweeter than it had been earlier.

Cam gave her a sleepy kiss on the top of her head as he began to move. His cock was thick and heavy inside her. His fingers glided over her swollen clit, sliding in the damp heat. Her whole body was filled with sensation. Sharp, electric. The dual sensations were incredible, taking her quickly toward the peak. She pushed back into him, onto his hot and throbbing shaft. His hand followed her movement, rubbing, rubbing on her tight, hard nub as he thrust harder into her.

She felt his sharp intake of breath just as the first wave of orgasm hit her. He pounded into her, filling her to bursting, while his fingers pressed hard into her clit, and she came with a blast of fireworks going off in her head. She felt the hot spurt of his seed inside her as she spasmed around him, as they came together in a glorious burst of sensation.

They were both breathing hard. His cock softened inside her, but he didn't pull out. Even soft, Cam was always big. She didn't want to think about anything else right now. He felt too good to her, her big husband with the wonderful cock and magical hands. Why hadn't she remembered this about him? She was going to try very hard never to forget again.

But for now, she was so tired. Once again, she slept.

Eden Bradley has been writing since she could hold a pen in her hand. When not writing, you'll find her wandering museums, cooking, eating, shopping, and reading everything she can get her hands on. Eden lives in Southern California.